FIRST TO FIND

a novel by Mark Gessner

ISBN: 978-0-557-52018-3

"Never mess with a Geocacher
--we know all the best places to hide a body."

-Matt Sargent, aka Prime Suspect

Chapter 1

ON A FLICKERING SCREEN a football field away in the bomb squad van, Sergeant Diethelm adjusted the contrast and brightness dials until he could read the yellow stenciled military markings on the green metal box as clearly as if he were pressing his nose up against it:

30 GRENADE

HAND FRAG

DELAY MC4

In addition to the video feed, the bomb squad robot's chemical sniffers relayed traces of nitrogen, gunpowder, lead, steel, and a few other telltale markers for explosives. X-ray revealed the presence of electronic circuits, a coiled wire, and something that appeared to be lumps of plastic, most likely C4 plastic explosive. Radio-frequency analysis detected the presence of an operating electronic timer. This was the real thing then. His skin tingled. *Shit*. His first real threat in five years. The whole Al Qaeda business had finally hit home. Those motherfuckers wouldn't get away with it this time, not on Diethelm's watch.

The golf-cart sized robot was a new acquisition for the Austin Police Department. It was used, a 1990 model, with a few sensor upgrades, and even at a hundred grand a pop, still better than sending in humans. The robot crawled to the site on tractor treads, steered via commands sent down an optical fiber cable tether that snaked along behind the robot as it negotiated the curved jogging path. It looked more like a miniature battle tank than a robot. Instead of a tank barrel it had a ten-foot horizontal metal boom with a cluster of sensors at the end, any one of which could be rotated into place on command. Better than sending in humans, but there was nothing human-looking about it.

The site had been identified earlier that morning by a passing housewife jogging through the park pushing a doublewide stroller with her two kids inside. She'd stopped to catch her breath on the park bench when she spotted the contrast of bright yellow on olive drab from under a cluster of rocks at the base of a tree near the edge of the crushed gravel trail.

There'd been an influx of middle-eastern neighbors recently, despite her complaints to the neighborhood association. The association couldn't legally do anything to keep them out, nor did they want to. The new residents always paid their assessments in full and on time.

Now her worst fears came true. The foreigners were planting bombs on the jogging trails. Her call to 911 was answered promptly, and the squad had cleared the park and cordoned off a perimeter, deploying their mobile base of operations at the trailhead parking lot, less than a tenth of a mile from the bomb site.

Diethelm made the call to detonate the package in place, rather than risk bringing it out and defusing it. If it was Al Qaeda, they'd likely booby-trapped it anyway. Moving it would be too dangerous.

The robot extended a small telescoping probe from the end of the sensor boom, and stuck a small magnetic disruptor module to the can. The robot backed off a hundred feet, reeling off a line of thin cable as it did so.

Diethelm gave the order to fire.

The disruptor module popped. The tree shook. Rocks, dirt, metal shards, bark, and other debris leapt out dozens of feet in a cloud of smoke and dirt. The explosion wasn't as violent as Diethelm would have expected from an ammo can full of C4 though.

The robot's work was done.

The hazmat team went in first, using handheld detectors to check the air for chemical or biological agents. They found none, and the area was cleared for Diethelm's men.

Diethelm personally led his team in on foot to clear the area, recover, catalog and bag the fragments. They approached the area cautiously.

What they found did not have them calling the Department of Homeland Security. What they found did not require them to catalog, bag, or tag anything. What they found had them scratching their heads. One of the younger men let out a nervous laugh, before Diethelm stared him down.

Over near the bench one of the men found what remained of the electronic timer. It had once been a cheap Chinese-made sports watch. What looked like C4 on X-ray was actually a small package of plastic modeling clay, in neon colors. The coil of wire was the wire spiral of a small notebook in a plastic baggie. The area was littered with broken toys, dolls, die-cast metal cars, plastic superhero action figures, keychains, and coins. The chemical signatures the robot had detected turned out to be trace residues from the ammunition and explosives stored in the can when it had been property of the U.S. Army.

Diethelm crouched, sat on his heels, and leafed through the tattered remains of the notebook. There were dozens of hand-scrawled notes written in there, the first dating back almost two years. A few of the people who had written in the book included miniature Polaroid photos of themselves posing with the ammo can. A folded sheet of paper fell out of the back of the notebook. He picked it up and opened it:

GEOCACHE GAME PIECE

DO NOT DISTURB

You found the cache!

This is a game piece in a Global
Positioning System (GPS) treasure hunting

game called Geocaching. Players use GPS navigation receivers to stash and find little containers like this one all over the globe.

Go ahead, exchange toys and sign the logbook if you like. Be sure to hide the container back just the way you found it. Come visit the website to learn more or to post an online comment about your discovery:

www.cache-finders.com

Toys. It was just a game. Four thousand dollars worth of department funds wasted on blowing up an ammo can full of toys.

Who the fuck hides an ammo can full of toys in the woods?

Chapter 2

THE LAST GOLDEN RAYS of winter sun slipped their grasp from the tops of the pines, and darkness threatened Mount Tamalpais. The wind through the pine needles was a stormy surf overhead, ebbing and flowing, ripping and breaking, deafening, felt more than heard. The wind brought the cold and with the cold came the mist off San Francisco bay. It formed a cold sweat on the faces of hikers hurrying down off the mountain trails. The mist shrouded the windshields and roofs of their SUVs and pickups in the parking lot below. It veiled the treetops in fog and gave steel fingers to the wind. The wind probed these fingers into their light winter clothing and the hikers felt the coldness of that touch, and it wasn't the coldness of winter they felt. It was a deeper coldness, a coldness that reached into their hearts and made them wish to be anywhere else. Anywhere but here.

Had this been the weekend, there might have been a dozen campers in the overflow camping lot. But this was a weeknight, and people had to go to school and to work tomorrow. They couldn't be up here enjoying the wilderness when the important matters of life went unattended. So they hurried down off the mountain, away from that deathly cold and back to life and warmth and home.

The steel fingers clawed at the thin jacket of a dark-haired man huddled on the concrete floor of the women's restroom out in front of the Pan Toll Ranger Station. He wasn't a camper. He wasn't a hiker, either, and he did not afford himself the luxury of getting in a vehicle and leaving the mountain. The plan was forming, beginning. He could feel it. Nothing could get in the way of the plan.

The plan didn't permit him a vehicle. A vehicle could be traced. He'd instead taken Golden Gate Transit route sixty-three, which had dropped him off at the ranger station. The bus fare was only a few dollars. The plan dictated he carry plenty of cash, thousands of dollars in fact, but no way was he paying the ten dollar camping fee.

When the last ranger locked up and left, the man had hiked down the mountainside and slept in the women's restroom. The plan was not specific on where to sleep, but some things were obvious, compelling. It was cold in that room, but the thick concrete block walls and heavy steel door blocked most of the wind. He wadded paper towels under the door and he could sleep. Sleep, that is, when the plan would let him. The plan was everything; it was foolproof. Genius. It animated him. It was his new reason for living.

He ground his teeth in his sleep, and they screamed in protest with each icy breath he dragged in over their worn enamels. He dreamed, and in his dream he was still awake and worrying over the plan. There was no rest until it was done.

The next morning, he woke before sunrise. Hard concrete floor, cold reaching in despite his attempts to block the wind. But he couldn't stay here until light. The park would be open at seven, and a ranger would likely be here before then, getting the station ready for another day. He gathered up and trashed the paper towels, and then he cut the light and cracked the door. He peered out of the women's room. RV parking, main parking lot, trails lit by the dim orange street light above the ranger station. No one stirring. He slipped out and then slowly closed the door. He hiked a few hundred feet up into the forest behind the ranger station.

He leaned up against a small moss-covered cinder block outbuilding on top of the hill, off a spur from the main hiking path. The building was no bigger than an outhouse. It was connected via several PVC pipes to a black cylindrical holding tank, as tall as a man. Some kind of water collection and purification system, most likely. The park was too remote and located at too high an altitude for city water. They must have their own supply. The building blocked the wind, and the tree cover would make him difficult to spot from the station. He leaned up against the cold, green wall. The sun wasn't up yet and it was the kind of damp cold that soaks into your bones and chills you from inside.

It would be great if he could get in, at least until daybreak, but the door was locked.

He found a high window on the side, the kind that hinges at the top and swings out at the bottom. It faced the ranger station. It was open just a crack. He pushed on the pane, but it closed further. He looked around for a stick or something he could use to pry the window back open. Next to an old campsite he found a discarded tent stake. He pried open the window with the stake, removed the screen, pulled himself up, and climbed inside. There were a few lighted gauges and after a few minutes he could make out the outlines of more pipes, running into some type of junction box, which was itself connected to the top of a short metal gas cylinder, about as big as his forearm. The cylinder was strapped to a rack bolted to the wall. There was another unconnected cylinder on the rack. A spare.

There wasn't much room in the cramped building, and what room there was had plenty of cobwebs to keep it busy. The room smelled faintly of chemicals: bleach, maybe something else, ammonia? The junction box hummed, and every once in awhile he heard a clicking noise and the sound of gas hissing through metal tubing, and the rushing of water. This obviously wasn't a building they entered on a daily basis. He'd be safe here for a few hours at least, maybe the rest of the day.

He unstrapped the spare tank and set it on the floor. He wasn't comfortable with this part of the plan. After all, he had enough money to buy a gun. But he'd worked out the plan in advance, each risk mathematically tallied, categorized and computed, and he had to trust it. Couldn't second-guess the plan in the field. That would be suicide. Bring nothing; leave no trace. He worked the plan, and it worked him.

After sunup, he kept watch over the ranger station from his vantage point inside the water building. Rangers came. Rangers went. He kept notes on their routines, he drew diagrams, he figured distances, he calculated probabilities. He engineered everything according to the plan.

Would the bastard even be here today? Was the preliminary research correct? Was there anything out of the ordinary? Had he considered all the risks, did the plan have a mitigation strategy for those risks? Think! He pulled out a carefully folded sheet of paper, unfolded it, smoothed it out on his thigh, and then checked each line again.

At noon he spotted the sonofabitch. Changing of the guard. No one could mistake the stupid grin on that asshole's face as he hopped out of his yellow Jeep Cherokee. Forehead too big, eyes spaced too wide, and the chin off center. His hairstyle hadn't changed since the eighties. Maybe it was a little shorter now. Looked like a fucking boy scout in his ranger uniform. Long way from the country club, aren't we Ricky? Long way from mommy's skirts. The big prick was going to pay.

California State Park Ranger Richard "Ricky" Nelson took a lot of ribbing for his name to be sure, but he had survived by the threat implied in his size (he stood over six two and weighed in at two-thirty), and by simply laughing along with the ribbing. He'd smile and laugh, all the while twisting the knife in your back, or at least planning the twist for some future time when you'd least expect it. With that name, you had to either laugh it off or get pissed. There wasn't any way to just ignore it and he was too proud to change it.

The killer had hell tracking him down on the internet with that famous name and frequent job switching.

He hadn't seen Ricky in eighteen years and fifteen hundred miles or so, but there was no doubting that he was the right guy. From the killer's perch in the outbuilding he could see into the back window of the ranger station. Ricky would work there for the next six hours, checking out after dusk.

Ricky owned a Rottweiler that kept him company in the Pan Toll ranger station, and followed him out into the park on his rounds. Ricky mostly stayed inside the station though. He did fewer rounds than the other rangers. Slacker. Most of his shift he sat glued to the computer terminal in the ranger station. He'd deal with any visitors quickly, then get back to that screen as fast as he could.

Ricky's dog was seventy pounds of muscle and teeth but the killer could tell it was a shitty watchdog. It wasn't even trained for basic obedience. An attacker would be more likely to get off with a good licking and crotch sniffing instead of being ripped to pieces. Still, even a shitty watchdog could be protective if its master were threatened.

That dog had to go.

Near the end of Ricky's shift, after most of the hikers had gone home, he let his dog outside. After sniffing around and peeing on some trees, it laid its head down on its front paws on the sidewalk behind the ranger station, bored. It sniffed at a passing stinkbug, thought about eating it, decided against that, then put its head back on its paws.

Ricky walked back behind the counter to the station's computer terminal, where he was busy in an internet chat room, posing as a sixteen year-old boy, desperately trying to arrange a meeting with an undercover vice cop posing as a fifteen year old girl from Alameda.

Ricky liked them young. When he couldn't actually *get* underage, he'd settle for the *appearance* of underage. But tonight he was going for the real thing, or so he thought.

The killer slipped halfway down the hill toward the station. The dog trotted up to meet him. The dog sniffed, then licked the man's outstretched palm. The man knelt down to pet the dog, setting the spare tank on the ground behind him. "Good doggie, there that's a nice pup," he whispered. He offered a small strip of beef jerky from his jacket pocket, which the dog snatched and chewed. With the other hand, the man slipped the foot-long tent stake inside the dog's webbed nylon collar, just behind the animal's head. The man straddled the dog, grabbed the tent stake with both hands, and twisted hard, turning the collar into a nylon tourniquet. The dog's eyes bugged, its last breath caught in a crushed windpipe. It didn't make a sound. The man pulled up and back for leverage, lifting the dog's front paws off the ground. Within minutes, the dog was dead. The man dropped the carcass and then jammed the tent stake into the ground.

The killer scuttled down the hill to the back window and peered in. Ricky was busy typing on the computer, his back to the window, silhouetted in the glow from the screen, now the only light in the station. He was absorbed. The killer snuck around to the front of the building. Standing in front of the metal door, he looked around. The mercury-vapor lights above the ranger station and parking lot had just switched on. There wasn't a single car in the lot. He heard nothing except the keening wind in the trees overhead.

Kneeling in front of the door, he pulled a few coins out of his pants pocket. Pressing his shoulder up against the door slowly, so as not to make a sound, he wedged first one penny, then another on top of that, then another. This was an old college dormitory prank. The force of a stack of pennies wedged in the tiny space between the door and the jamb prevented the striker from moving when you tried to turn the knob.

Ricky was locked in.

In the internet chat room, Ricky had convinced the girl to meet with him at an East Bay mall later that evening. A few more minutes were all he needed to close up the ranger station and hurry into town.

He didn't have a few more minutes.

The killer scuttled back behind the ranger station and slipped the neck of the tank into a metal vent beneath the window. He sucked in a deep breath, held it, then in six quick flicks of his wrist, twisted the valve on the tank fully open as quickly as possible. He darted off to hide behind Ricky's Jeep, parked next to the station.

Ricky felt a tickling in his nose and throat. Damned allergies. The Claritin wasn't working again. Maybe he should go see a doctor, get something stronger. He finished typing a line into the chat screen, hit the enter key, and then instinctively reached for a tissue to blow his tingling nose. Before he could blow, he heard hissing. He turned to look behind him and saw thin white fumes followed by a greenish-yellow cloud rising from the heater vents. The heater thermostat switched on. His eyes watered and burned as he took a blast of pure chlorine gas up both nostrils. His throat burned. *Something wrong with the heater,* he thought.

He stood up out of his chair, bent down, and tried to switch off the heater, but his eyes were watering from the fumes and he couldn't see. He accidentally punched the HIGH HEAT button instead of OFF.

He gave up on the heater and stumbled around the service counter. In three steps he was upon the door, waving his hands in front of his face. He coughed, gasped for breath. There was no air. A thick ribbon of saliva streamed from his mouth and painted a dark jagged stripe on the sleeve of his ranger uniform and then sprayed across a row of pamphlets on a metal literature stand by the door. He twisted the doorknob while he tried to cover his mouth and nose with the crook of his other arm. The knob would not turn. He jerked violently on the door with both hands, then collapsed to the floor with a deep hacking, rasping cough. A hundred tiny knives clawed and slashed inside his lungs. He vomited, coughed, twitched, and then vomited again. He grasped his throat with both hands as his legs, flailing, kicked the door. He knocked over the literature stand, sending pamphlets crashing to the floor. *See Historic Hearst Castle!* Some of them landed in the vomit and began soaking up the mess. *Visit Scenic Monterrey Bay!*

His bloodshot eyes opened wide and stared blankly at the ceiling. The corneas clouded with a yellowish haze.

He drew a rattling final breath, like a half-snore.

At the mall later that night the undercover cop called off the sting. She wondered why the creep didn't show. These internet sex predators usually didn't get wise to her until she slapped the cuffs on them. Some not even then. Well, no great loss. She'd bag another asshole tomorrow night. There was never a shortage of internet perverts.

Night was filling the voids between the trees, and late-arrival campers might show up at any minute. Full timers, retirees in their homes-on-wheels, free from the day-to-day grind of work, free to go wherever and whenever, might well come to stay in this remote spot on a weekday evening.

A few minutes after the hissing stopped, the killer looked into the ranger station through the back window. When he saw the vomit-splattered body by the front door, he realized that the plan had him now, and it was perfect. Payback's a bitch Ricky.

He looked out toward the road leading into the park and saw no one. There was no one in the overflow camping area. The park was scheduled to close for day-use. He wiped his fingerprints off the door and anything else he thought he might have touched.

The killer next dragged the dead Rottweiler over the mulched path behind the ranger station to the visitor overlook, and threw the carcass over the edge. The dog twisted and tumbled down the rocky hillside in a spray of blood. It came to rest with a sickening snap about forty feet down the side of the hill up against a stand of thick pine trees that were clinging to the side of the mountain. The dog's head was folded under its shoulder at an impossible angle. The body was twisted and broken; the forelegs pointed down, the hind legs pointed up. A marrow-oozing fragment of white vertebra jutted from the dog's back.

The killer retraced his crime scene one more time to make sure that he hadn't left any evidence. He took the rag and stuffed it in his pocket. He threw the tank and the tent stake over the edge. They tumbled all the way through the branches down to the bottom, well past the dog carcass. He walked back to the station to retrieve the pennies from the door. He kicked the door, hard, three times, and pocketed the pennies after they fell out.

The killer froze as brilliant white high-beams broke over the horizon and traced his double-silhouette on the door of the ranger station. An RV rolled past within a dozen yards.

The killer kept his back turned, slipped a payment envelope from the honor box on the front of the station, held it in front of his face and pretended to read it, tried to blend in.

The RV driver downshifted sloppily, then pulled as far as possible down the hill into the overflow lot. The driver, a grey-headed raisin of a man, stepped out, turned to face the side of the RV and began leveling his vehicle for the night.

Shit. He'd need to get out of here fast.

The Jeep. It was parked in a gravel space behind the ranger station, so the old RV guy wouldn't see him getting in.

He found the key for the Cherokee in the ignition. He hopped in and rolled down off the mountain. He'd have to ditch the vehicle, but first he'd need to get someplace where he could catch a Greyhound.

He had an appointment back in Pittsburgh.

Part I
First to Find

Chapter 3

Austin Texas

Monday, February 17

KURT DENZER RUBBED HIS FACE, swung his feet out of bed, fumbled his glasses off the night stand, snatched glasses and boxers off the floor, put them on, and turned his alarm clock to check the time: 6:42 A.M. He walked out to the kitchen. On the way through the door he reached over to pet his cat perched on the arm of the couch.

He shuffled into the kitchen, ignored the dirty dishes festering in the sink for one more day, and loaded the coffee maker. He usually drank his coffee half-caff, but he needed to shake that nightmare, so nothing but a pot of full strength would do this morning. He bent over the counter, rubbed the crusts from his eyes and stared at the pot. "Why are coffee pots calibrated in five ounce cups?" he asked.

His cat Pokey curled up around his ankles and meowed the only answer she knew: "Feed Me."

Kurt was thirty-six. As in his nightmare, he'd been a software program manager at Motorola. And like the nightmare, he had grown to detest both the job and the management. Unlike the nightmare, his layoff wasn't the result of a clerical error and his boss hadn't dragged him screaming back into his cubicle after turning him out.

He was still free.

Broke, but free.

As he punched the start button on the Mr. Coffee, his doorbell rang. He snatched yesterday's jeans off the floor, pulled them on, then opened the door.

Bonnie Heckmann was a short heavy woman in her early fifties, married with two kids who'd finally left the nest. She'd never think twice about popping over to a friend's house uninvited and unannounced before dawn. Kurt had long since gotten used to it.

"Have you seen the new cache listing online?" she asked, tossing her backpack and hiking stick on the couch. She never went hiking without one of her husband's custom-carved hickory hiking sticks.

"Nuh-uh, want some coffee?" he asked, holding up the pot. A year before, a co-worker had introduced Kurt to the game of geocaching, a kind of scavenger hunt using hand-held GPS satellite navigation receivers, and he'd been hooked ever since.

"Well, okay, but we gotta drink up fast sweetie, 'cause someone else is gonna beat us to it," she said.

Kurt towered over Bonnie, his former coworkers, and his family at six foot three. He had shoulder-length dishwater blonde hair worn feathered back in a style leftover from the late seventies that he couldn't seem to leave behind. On his face he wore a three-day growth of reddish stubble.

He divided the coffee pot between two thick ceramic Krispy-Kreme mugs. Bonnie helped herself to his fridge, sniffed the opening of the milk carton, and then dumped a dollop into her mug.

Kurt lived in a cramped two-bedroom ranch house on a hill overlooking Lake Travis, northwest of Austin. From the outside, the house didn't look like much, but back when he had a paycheck, he'd upgraded the interior: granite counters, tile floors, the works. It had an excellent view of the lake.

At the computer in his back bedroom office, Kurt pulled up his web browser and logged on to www.cache-finders.com. Geocache hiders posted descriptions of their hides on that website, including coordinates that finders could punch into their GPS units. Most finders liked to carry a printed copy of the cache listing so they'd have clues and coordinates with them while out on the hunt. Finders could post a comment to the online cache page, indicating whether they found the cache or not, and what they thought about the experience. Sometimes those comments from previous finders contained good clues that could help others find the cache.

"What's the big deal about being the first to find anyway?" he asked, finishing off his coffee.

"Just hurry up and print that thing," she replied, thumbing the keypad on her mobile phone. She had only taken a sip of her coffee and abandoned the rest. "I'll call Maari. She won't want to miss this." She pulled the printout off the printer and checked it to make sure it was all there:

```
www.cache-finders.com Geocache Listing


Kelley's First Cache
by KelleysMom [email this user]
Texas, USA


[click to download geographic coordinates
and hints]


This is our first geocache. Just a small
Tupperware filled with trinkets, hidden in
the woods. We put in some toy cars and some
new golf balls, a bag of state quarters and
a couple keychains. Be sure to sign the
logbook to let us know you were there and
if you liked our cache! Don't forget to
post your comment online here for everyone
else to read too!


Cache Visitor Comments:
```

Kurt and Bonnie arrived at the trailhead parking lot to find Maari already waiting for them there. "Let's go," she said, folding up her copy of the listing printout, after they each had keyed the cache's latitude and longitude coordinates into their GPS receivers.

Maari Hekkonen was in her mid to late thirties and stood just under six feet tall. Sun-bleached hair pulled back in a ponytail, never married, no kids. Bonnie had invited her along for the hunt and she'd of course jumped at the chance to be in on the first find.

They packed up their printouts and backpacks and hiked down the crushed gravel trail, following the directional arrows on their GPS receivers. These devices collected radio signals from a constellation of twenty-four satellites orbiting eleven thousand miles overhead. The receivers decoded these signals to tell the hikers how far they were from their destination, and in which direction to walk.

They walked a third of a mile down the trail, Maari and Bonnie calling out the remaining distance every thirty seconds or so. They all had their own GPS receiver set to display this information, so this calling out was unnecessary. It irritated Kurt but he'd learned that no amount of complaining would change it. Both Bonnie and Maari were strong-willed. Some would say stubborn, but never to their faces.

Maari was Finnish but she had been in the states for so long that her accent had more Hermosa Beach than Helsinki in it. She had a tight physique, and might have even been a bodybuilder at one time. Kurt had always thought it safer not to ask her about it. She had a degree in biomedical engineering from Texas A&M University and had done her time in a top-secret military industrial complex out in California, but she was currently working as a midwife. She had a lot of free time, but she had to be on call twenty four hours a day. This limited the times when she could go drinking and night caching, which was the only real drawback she could find in her new profession. It beat working defense though.

"What's the hint?" asked Kurt.

"'Unnatural Rock Pile,' but I don't see it," Maari replied. In addition to the latitude and longitude, cache hiders usually provided an extra hint, because the accuracy of the GPS system was such that you could still have a fifty or sixty-foot circle to search once the receiver said you were there. Some days the GPS would put you right on top of the cache, other days you'd be scratching your head sixty feet away. Some finders didn't look at the hint until after spending a long time searching, but Maari was one to read the hint even before setting out. She didn't like to waste time.

"Check the coordinates," said Bonnie, lighting a cigarette, taking a break while the other two looked under logs and behind trees. She'd tried to quit before, even went on the gum. She'd gotten addicted to the gum, then had reverted to cigarettes. Cigarettes helped her lose weight, she rationalized. She was also losing weight through geocaching. She had found more than five hundred caches in her first year, and had already lost twenty pounds.

"I don't see any rocks," said Kurt.

"What's that smell?" asked Maari. Something decaying. The smell grew stronger as they approached the cache site.

"I think I see it!" said Bonnie, after they'd walked another fifty feet. "The coordinates are a little off though."

"Newbies," said Kurt. New cachers were likely to complain of bad coordinates until they got used to using their GPS receivers. Still, the veterans welcomed new players. "Now I smell it. It's getting worse."

"I don't smell anything," said Bonnie, who hadn't smelled anything in ten years and frankly didn't miss it.

The cache was only ten feet off the trail, a trinket-filled Tupperware container hidden under a thick overhanging ledge of moss-covered grey honeycomb limestone. A couple of loose pieces of honeycomb were placed in front of the box so that it couldn't be seen from the trail. Bonnie jabbed the rocks away with her hiking stick, then Maari pulled the container out from under the ledge.

"Oh geez, sign it for me would ya? I can't stand this," said Maari, before they'd removed the lid. She scrambled off a dozen feet out toward the trail, waving her hands in front of her wrinkled-up nose. Kurt quickly signed the logbook for all of them, then carefully re-hid the container back under the ledge for the next finder.

"It's up here," said Bonnie, thumbing back over her shoulder. She'd gone further into the woods looking to see if she could spot the source of the smell. "It's a dead dog."

The dog had been buried under a carefully built pile of rocks, at the base of a sheer cliff. Apparently someone's pet had died and the owner had buried it in the woods. Some scavengers, either coyotes or feral hogs, had pushed away the rocks and dragged the carcass halfway out of its grave.

They found two other caches in the park that morning. Their usual plan was to find three caches and then go for breakfast. After finding the dead dog, no one was hungry, so Maari suggested they go grab some coffee instead. She knew a new gourmet coffee shop across the street from the park.

Chapter 4

THE SHOP WAS LOCATED in a small strip at the base of a dizzying hill leading up to the upper middle class Jester neighborhood, just a couple miles from City Park. Jester was developed in the late 1970's, and at the time it had been pretty remote, but now the city had caught up with it and the property values had soared. The rising property values brought in hordes of dot-com yuppies, and almost all of them got their coffee from Java Judi's. In the coffee business, you had to be at the right place at the right time --when the caffeine wore off.

Java Judi's was one of Starbucks' copycats. The success of Starbucks spawned a thousand imitators. Java Judi's claim to fame was that everything on their menu, from the coffee beans right on down to the pure cane sugar, was organically grown, and this was just what the coffee drinking ex-hippies of Austin wanted to hear.

The three explorers got their coffee and settled into a group of overstuffed easy chairs with a small round table at knee-height between them. Their GPS receivers and a few trinkets were scattered on the table among the coffee cups.

Bonnie logged in to the cache-finders website and posted comments for her morning finds on the pages for each cache. The store supplied free wireless internet access and even a few free laptops tethered to selected tables. Usually it was difficult to get one, but the morning rush was over.

The staff were taking it easy behind the counter, blowing off steam. A young woman was clearing one of the taller tables next to the group. She had hauled off a load of empty cups and was wiping the table down with a rag when she paused to greet the group, asking them if everything was okay with their orders. Kurt took one look at her and didn't hear anything after that.

Judi McBride was an attractive thirty-something, petite yet big-boned, with short auburn hair, pale white skin, deep green eyes, and a scattering of freckles. She was in firm physical shape, despite her sworn conviction that her butt was out of proportion to the rest of her body. She was wearing tight faded blue jeans and a tucked-in Java Judi's polo shirt.

Maari and Judi recognized each other and they did one of those quick one-standing, one-sitting girl-hugs. Maari explained to the rest of the group that the two had been in a class together a few months before.

Judi pointed to all the GPS receivers and asked what all the high-tech gadgetry was for.

As a rule Kurt dated only thin women. He wouldn't usually give a heavier woman a second look, but Judi grabbed his attention. She had an inviting smile. Her eyes locked onto his; he couldn't look away. She had a strong, assured, and confident way of carrying herself and an outgoing friendly manner that he found suddenly irresistible. He didn't believe in love at first sight, but there was an instant attraction. Had he known it was mutual, his life over the next few weeks would have been much less stressful.

"We were just out geocaching," said Maari, and Judi's face went blank. Kurt had seen that look before when he and his friends tried to explain geocaching.

"It's like hide and seek for geeks," offered Kurt, handing her his GPS unit.

"Someone hides a box of trinkets, they post the coordinates on the internet, then other players try to find it," recited Bonnie, tapping on the laptop keyboard.

"So do you keep the box?" asked Judi, settling into one of the easy chairs, turning over the tiny GPS unit in her hand.

"No, you open the box, sign the logbook, and trade trinkets if you want," said Kurt.

"Then you write about your experience online here," said Bonnie, tapping on her screen.

Maari apologized and then introduced Bonnie and Kurt to Judi, who reached forward and shook their hands in turn. Judi lingered just a half-second longer on the shake with Kurt, as she bored into his soul with those green eyes. Kurt drew back and wished his grip hadn't been so sweaty.

"Are you on break? We don't want to get you in trouble," said Kurt, looking around nervously.

Maari and Judi laughed. Maari explained that Kurt was speaking to Java Judi herself, the owner of the Java Judi's chain. Kurt asked why she was bussing tables if she was the owner and Judi explained that she was short handed in this store and had to pitch in during rush hour until she could staff up.

Judi's life was extremely hectic right now with her business, and she told herself she really didn't have time for a dating relationship. There was something about Kurt, despite his retro appearance, that gave her butterflies. She made a mental note to ask Maari about him later.

Judi asked Kurt why he wasn't at work on a weekday, and he admitted that he was a laid off software engineering manager out of Motorola. She offered her condolences and he waved her off, explaining that they did him a favor, and that he wasn't worried about it.

"I could last another couple years or so if I stop buying this expensive gourmet coffee," he joked, wiggling his nearly-empty cup.

"Hey!" she said, mocking offense.

"Just kidding. I usually drink store brand," he confessed.

"Ugh. That's gross," she replied.

"We're having a big geocaching picnic next weekend. You want to come?" asked Maari.

Judi said she usually worked weekends, but she might be able to break free. Kurt offered to send her the picnic details and asked for her email address.

In years past, a man interested in a woman might ask for her phone number. Somewhere between the late eighties and mid-nineties that request had changed from the phone number to the email address. If the email contact proved interesting, the phone number might follow. If a woman wouldn't give you her email address, take the hint.

Judi handed a business card to Kurt and then to each of the women. As she handed the card to Maari she rose from her chair and said, "Call me later; let's catch up."

Chapter 5

Hamlet, California

December 17 - 4:42 A.M.

A SMALL WARNING SIGN blocked the trail:

U.S. GOV'T PROPERTY - KEEP OUT

AUTHORIZED PERSONNEL ONLY

The killer bulldozed the Cherokee over the sign, snapping its rotted wooden post. "The U.S. Government can suck my ass," he muttered, flipping off the sign as it fell back and under the Jeep's grill. He cut the headlights and navigated down the gravel path using the parking lights. It was a straight drive a hundred feet down to a row of abandoned oyster farm buildings. Single room wooden shacks on rotted stilts stood half in the water of the bay and half on the land. A dozen of the dilapidated structures kept a lonely vigil over the shore. He wondered what the government intended by protecting these death traps. Probably some historical preservation or some other bullshit waste of good tax money.

He'd driven up U.S. Highway One most of the night, a narrow two-lane coastal highway with more twists and turns than a Michael Connelly novel, and he kept it four miles over the limit to avoid drawing suspicion. Last thing he needed was a routine traffic stop. He'd been having a hell of a time staying awake behind the wheel, so when he saw the abandoned oyster farm on the bay, his first thought had been shelter. His second thought -- ditch the Jeep.

He pulled the Cherokee up between the first two shacks, front tires in the water, transmission in drive. He slid out, planting one foot on the ground while keeping the other foot on the brake. He released the brake and at the same time, punched the RESUME switch on the cruise control. The sport-utility lurched forward in a vain attempt to resume a speed of fifty-nine miles per hour straight into the bay. He damn near went in with it. He had an arm and a leg still inside when it lurched, and only by falling backward was he able to avoid being snagged and dragged in. The Jeep took on water as it rolled further into the bay. It dove, twisted to the left; sunk. The bay still bubbled over the red tail lights of the sunken Jeep as he hiked further north, about a couple hundred feet more.

Coastal grasses covered the trail in places. Between clumps of grass, his boots crunched broken oyster shells. An ancient appliance graveyard loomed into view on the right, followed by a couple more shacks. He eventually found a sturdy old cinder block building. It still had an attached steel door. Judging from the rust, it hadn't been used for a long time. Time and weather had almost removed its foul oyster stink. This looked like the only building in the farm that had once had running water. He stepped in to an employee restroom near the back. A row of porcelain steel sinks, across from a row of urinals, all but one of them busted into little porcelain fragments scattered on the floor. Vandals. A row of toilets, all neatly removed. Salvage, probably cleaned up and resold as antiques to yuppies down in San Jose. Lines of rust marked the yellow tile walls where the stall enclosures had been, long since removed for scrap metal. With the door closed and latched, the wind and the vandals wouldn't bother him here. He could sleep in his coat.

He slept till noon, and then hitched a ride to the Greyhound bus station in Petaluma. There he bought a one-way ticket to El Paso, Texas, cash. He could have gone straight to Pittsburgh for about the same price, but he wanted to make sure his trail wasn't followed, in case the police somehow tracked him into Petaluma. He planned to alternate bus rides with hitchhiking to further obscure his trail and he wanted to be sure to stick to the southern route as much as possible. The *extreme* southern route.

He'd forgotten how much riding the bus sucked. Twelve hundred miles wedged in next to a fat bitch who took up his entire arm rest. Across the aisle, a tall thin man in a stained brown shirt that even Goodwill would refuse was carrying on a lively conversation with himself. He was having a hard time convincing his imaginary friends that bankers were in fact watching everything from tall buildings purposely designed to look like owls. Every once and awhile he'd laugh at the comments of his unseen companions. He chain-smoked imaginary cigarettes, which nonetheless gave him a hacking cough that often produced great gobs of phlegm, which he'd swallow.

Most times the bus heater didn't work and other times it heated the air to the point where he was sure his next breath would choke him. The onboard restroom was too dirty to use.

From El Paso he planned to hitch a ride as far east as he could get. He had to get away from El Paso in case anyone tracked him there from Petaluma.

He stood out by the side of I-10 for two hours in the fucking wind and cold before someone stopped. It was a VW microbus filled with hippies heading to a folk music festival out west of Austin. He'd be going to Austin eventually, but first things first. He had to follow the plan. That's where most killers fucked up. They were stupid and didn't follow the plan. Hell, most didn't even make a plan. Those that did and didn't follow it, well they deserved to get caught, dumb shits. He would not be caught, and he didn't want to be tempted to jump the list and go straight to Austin, so he'd waved the hippies on their way. Besides, dope would fuck your brain, even second hand dope smoke, and the killer had an I.Q. of one sixty-five, at least according to one free I.Q. test on the internet; he wouldn't do anything to ruin that. Takes a shitload of brain cells to make an I.Q. that high. Genius level's what that is. Smoke one joint and you kill off a hundred thousand brain cells or so, that's what he'd always heard. The killer didn't know exactly how many brain cells were in a normal adult brain, but he figured a hundred thousand brain cells would probably amount to half an I.Q. point, maybe more. So he'd waved the hippies on. Even though the inside of the van was warm and he could feel the heat pulling him in, he waved them on.

He only had to wait another thirty minutes before a big gypsum-hauler pulled over. He climbed up and had a seat.

After jockeying the big rig back onto the interstate, the trucker said he was going as far as Van Horn, then he'd be cutting south down U.S. fifty-nine for a big construction project in Lajitas, down by the Mexican border west of the Big Bend. Seems some rich yankee had bought out most of the town of Lajitas, was going to turn it into a resort, put in a golf course, a bunch of condos, a big fancy hotel, that kind of shit, and needed buttloads of concrete to build it. Buttloads of concrete means buttloads of gypsum. So far the yankee had dumped a wad of money into the project, but hadn't gotten anything out of it. "See, Lajitas is so far from everythin' else, the nearest big airport's 'bout a five hour drive," the trucker said. "You want my advice?" the trucker continued, though the killer didn't want his advice. He didn't want anything but to get as far from El Paso as he could, as fast as he could, without having to take the free business advice of any fucking Harvard MBA gypsum truck drivers along the way. "You gonna build y'self a resort, you do it somewhere that folks can fly to."

Fucking genius. It was everywhere.

Chapter 6

December 19 - 3:22 P.M.

Van Horn Texas

PAINTED ON SUN-BLEACHED brick, red and blue stripes above and below, the four-foot-high black letters announcing **DIESEL FRIED CHICKEN** tempted hungry drivers on the interstate, roaring a quarter mile away across the desert. A pile of old tires half as high as the roof baked just below the sign. The interstate had shunted all traffic away from town twenty years ago. A short distance, but long enough to put a bullet into the heart of Van Horn's economy. Now only the most desperate travelers would bother to stop.

Flat, dirt, oil, flat, and more dirt. Fucking miles and miles of nothing but flat and dirt. Permian basin, Texas oil country. Black pumpjacks see-sawing, about one every couple hundred feet, sucking the crude up out of the ground like hideous black metal mosquitoes perched on the back of some monstrous black-blooded creature. With each stroke, they'd draw out their thin proboscides and suck up more of the black ooze. With each stroke the pumpjacks protested their labor with grating metallic squeaks. The killer wondered if they were pumping all this oil, why didn't they have some way to keep themselves lubed? See, a genius would figure out how to design a pumpjack to do that. World was full of morons and dipshits.

He walked up to the window of the DIESEL FRIED CHICKEN station and pressed his face to the glass. The place was empty. A long red Formica counter stood covered in dust. An old backhoe tire decorated the center of the room. A Valvoline-can spittoon and about a thousand cigarette butts lay inside the tire. Outside, only tangled wires and rusted bolts poked up where once the station offered full service gas pumps.

He found a padlock on a rusted hasp on the back door. He rustled around in a dumpster full of old engine parts. He yanked out a massive iron engine mounting bracket, and then whacked the hasp with it a couple times. The hasp and lock fell to the ground, raising a choking cloud of light brown dust. He kicked the lock under the pile of tires. He'd need a place to sleep for a couple days, restock supplies. Maybe shave.

Chapter 7

December 22 - 7:03 P.M.

IT GOT FUCKING COLD in the desert after sundown. He'd been walking for twenty minutes already. Bus station must be somewhere in town. Every one-goat town in America had a Greyhound bus station in it. He'd find it.

There was only one road in Van Horn, that was the old highway, and everything from the Fiesta mart to the **DIESEL FRIED CHICKEN** place was hung off it. If there was a bus station, it'd have to be along the main road.

He picked up another Greyhound in Van Horn, one way ticket to Pittsburgh, cash, no questions asked. He figured if anyone had caught his trail to Petaluma, which was unlikely, they'd have a hell of a time tracking him to El Paso. Then even if they followed him to Texas, which was even more unlikely, they'd lose him right there outside the El Paso bus station. It was simple statistics: multiply the probabilities of these independent and unlikely events, and the combined probabilities approach zero. Mathematical Genius.

The detour along the southern route would cost him several days, but no detective in San Francisco would ever find a direct transportation link to his next victim in Pittsburgh. Besides, riding thumb was untraceable. He wondered why more killers didn't do it.

Chapter 8

THREE DAYS ON THE road without a bath, and the sign in the men's room said, "NO HAIR WASHING IN SINK."

Fuck that.

If there was any doubt before, now he was convinced. Riding the bus sucked. His legs cramped, his hair felt matted, he had that greasy all over feeling, he stunk, and his back was killing him. He had a decent car. He had plenty of money. He could have driven or flown if he wished. But on a killing spree, you had to put comfort aside. You had to leave no trace. You had to follow the plan.

Halfway through his sponge bath, a pimple-faced teen in a Burger king uniform and matching paper crown clattered a yellow plastic mop bucket into the restroom.

"Hey, didn't you see the sign? No bathing allowed in here," said the kid, pointing.

The killer, hunched over the sink, stopped working the rinse water through his hair. His taut muscular shoulders and biceps flexed as he dropped his arms to the sink. His long black hair dripped dirty water into the sink, onto the edge of the sink, and onto the floor. He rotated upward to face the boy. He snapped his right arm out into a clenched fist; flipped his middle finger, bared his teeth in an animal sneer.

The kid turned and ran. The mop and the paper Burger King crown fell to the floor.

Chapter 9

December 24 5:32 P.M.

THE KILLER SLID OFF the bus at the Pittsburgh terminal. He hailed a cab to take him to Murrysville. He paid the driver in cash, and then hitched a ride from Murrysville to the Mini-Mart in Harrison Valley. If you're going to be thumbing a ride, you can't do any better than Christmas Eve or Mother's Day. There's fewer drivers out, but no matter how much you resemble Charles Manson or Wichita's BTK killer, every one really wants to believe your hard luck story about how your car broke down and you're just trying to get home to Mom.

From the Mini-Mart he walked the three miles out the lonely highway to the Club. A blizzard had blown down out of Canada. The snow blew so fast that the highway disappeared under his feet. When he got to the club around midnight, he found the barn exactly where he expected it to be, poking up out of the darkness in a whirlwind of amber security light and snowflakes. Around the back of the barn he found a small window to the basement shop area. It was unlocked, held shut by a flimsy plastic prop-rod.

Chapter 10

www.cache-finders.com Geocache Listing

Ammo Can Exchange - Cacher Picnic
by Bonnie [email this user]
Texas, USA

[click to download geographic coordinates and hints]

Well, we won the government surplus auction! Let's get together to distribute the Ammo cans! They make great cache containers, they're waterproof and easy to paint!

We have almost FIVE HUNDRED CANS to distribute! We got a great deal, these are usually $4-$7 each at the Army surplus stores, but (with our gas costs and trailer rental figured in), we got these for $0.96 each! Whoo-Hoo! Anyway, we're charging an even BUCK FIFTY a can, so that we can use the extra money to buy food and supplies for the PICNIC LUNCH on the Shores of City Park (That's 'Emma Long Municipal Park' for you Outta-Towners!)

So come on by, talk about caching, meet some of your fellow cache hunting addicts.

Post a note here saying how many cans you'll need.

Date&Time: Saturday February 22. 10AM till they throw us out!
Place: City Park, Austin

Cache Visitor Comments:

(0 comments for this picnic - This picnic hasn't been attended yet!)

Did you Find the Cache? Add your own comment! [click here]

"I've never tried it. Is it spicy?" he asked.

"Not really. Go ahead and try some. There's more where that came from," replied Maari.

Kurt worried about eating the homemade venison sausage. Since about the time he turned thirty, his digestive system could take violent offense at the slightest bit of spice, and he couldn't see any restrooms nearby. He tasted some anyway. Mild, not spicy. He helped himself to a bigger chunk. He forked the slippery link up onto his paper plate next to a mound of mustard potato salad, a hunk of German chocolate cake, a stack of nacho chips with cheese (hold the jalapenos), and a charred hamburger on a toasted bun.

Bonnie had ordered up some fine picnic weather. Not a cloud marred the deep azure blue from horizon to horizon. Temperature unseasonably warm, in the sixties going up to the mid-seventies by afternoon, and no wind at all. Emma Long Park didn't disappoint either. The picnickers fanned out over a flat expanse of grass dotted with ancient live oaks at strategic intervals.

Lake Austin, a cold emerald snake that slithered a half dozen miles between downtown and Lake Travis, bounded the park on the south. Except for a few places (Emma Long Park, for example), limestone cliffs covered in lush mountain cedar wall the lake on either side. On a spring day, ski boats, water-skiers, and pontoon party boats usually crowded the lake. Restaurants and bars dotted the south shore closer to town. Secret coves tucked off the main passage swelled with boats at anchor. Their crews sunbathed half-naked on deck, pulling on bottles of ice-cold Shiner Bock, flirting, and blaring an unsteady mix of rock 'n' roll, pop music, and hip-hop.

"Hey stranger, be sure to grab some of that custard-filled a'kern squash too, I made it myself," said a familiar voice from behind.

Kurt turned to face the voice. It was Bonnie. She gave him a more detailed report on who was here and who was slated to arrive than he really needed or wanted. Her excitement ran her words together into a stream of undecipherable babble until he picked out something that he was interested in:

"...and of course Martello is here from New Mexico--"

"No way, not the infamous Martello?" he interrupted, looking around.

"Yes way, he's right over there with the Krager twins," she replied.

Kurt said he'd be sure to meet the legend later, then paid for his allotment of cans by dropping a stack of ones into a decorated ammo can sitting on the table. Bonnie told him to get his cans loaded quickly before they were all gone. He set his plate down on the table and walked up to the trailer to load the cans into his truck.

Kurt walked back up the knoll to the trailer straining under a sheet metal mountain of surplus ammo cans. Olive drab ammo cans formed a huge pile next to the trailer. Another pile behind the trailer partially blocked the gravel road through the park.

He selected ten of the nicest, cleanest cans. Some of the cans had dents and some didn't have lids. He noticed a pile of lids near the rear tire of the trailer. Someone could easily pound out the dented ones and fit them to these spare lids. Nothing would go to waste here. He carried the cans to his truck four at a time, pinching two cans in each hand like a claw. When he was done, he punched the lock button on his key fob and headed back to the picnic.

The park was filling up. People were parking on the grass on the far side of the road, despite the no parking signs. He checked the plates on the cars as he walked back to the picnic area: a couple of Toyotas from Oklahoma, a mud-caked SUV from New Mexico, a beat-to-shit pickup truck from Louisiana. The rest came from Texas. He spotted a few cachers making their way from the lot to the picnic areas, some carrying coolers, some with covered dishes, others with zip-tie baggies full of trinkets. Cache swag. Cachers would be swapping goodies today for sure.

He saw plenty of cachers today but no sign of Judi, the woman he had met the week they found the dead dog. No surprise there. He hoped she'd show up but he knew the odds. Women might show interest, but only until they found out he was out of work. Also he'd noticed that most newcomers introduced to geocaching usually never followed up with future caching, never went caching by themselves or attended any picnics, no matter how excited they seemed while you explained it to them. Come to think of it, Judi hadn't seemed that excited about it either. It didn't help that he'd been sweaty and unshowered the day they met too. Only a core set of cachers ever went to the picnics anyway, even one as large as this.

He walked up to the table by the grill. He couldn't find his plate. He checked the adjacent tables, nothing. Someone had made off with it. Oh well, plenty more where that came from. He grabbed a new plate off the stack, elbowed his way through the crowd at the table and reached for the potato salad spoon.

As he closed his hand around the handle of the serving spoon, a slim hand slipped in from the crowd on the other side and got there first. His hand closed on hers momentarily and he jerked it back. "Oh, excuse me," he said.

The woman looked up, "Beat you to it," she giggled, and began scooping the chunky yellow salad onto her plate. It was just Maari.

He filled his plate again, same contents as before except he added a hot dog to the mix. Loading ammo cans had given him an appetite. He strolled over to the nearest group of cachers. It happened to be a group he knew. Kurt hated mixing at parties; he took his time getting into the socializing aspect of it. He had no problem socializing in college, back when he was a big drinker, because a few beers would loosen him up. He seldom drank anymore; he'd lost interest in drinking the day he turned twenty-one.

The group formed a horseshoe around Martello, the infamous cacher from New Mexico. Martello, a wiry man, stood just shy of six feet tall. A long dirty-blond goatee hung from his chin. His long straggly hair draped over his shoulders. It looked like it hadn't seen *lather, rinse, repeat* since last week. He wore a red bandana head wrap, a black Jack Daniel's tee shirt with holes in the armpits, a faded jeans jacket, and cut-off jean shorts faded white. Martello had over two thousand confirmed finds. He was a legend on the cache-finders web site. He often posted witty comments to the discussion groups online there, including barbs aimed at the management of the site. This drew their ire, but they dared not ban him because he was too popular.

A handful of cachers gathered around Martello, including Maari, her sometime boyfriend Bob, and Bonnie. Kurt balanced his paper plate in his left hand, and began shoveling with his right as he walked up to the group.

"...you're kidding, it was right on top of the cache?" asked one of the men, a pot-bellied guy in a too-short t-shirt, whom Kurt didn't know.

"Would I make this shit up?" asked Martello.

"That's just disgusting," said one of the women.

"So did you call the cops?" asked Bob.

"Believe me, I told the cops right away." said Martello.

"Let him continue," urged Bonnie.

"So there I am standing ten feet away from the carcass, with about forty turkey vultures circling. Some were just perched in the tree above, and others would swoop down every once in awhile to try to scare me away from their kill. But that's not the worst part," said Martello. "When I was hiking back out of the area, I found a jar of urine at an abandoned campsite," he said. (only when he said the word 'urine,' he mouthed it into a whisper, rather than saying it aloud). "That was the one day that I didn't carry trash out on a hike," he laughed.

More waves of cachers came in. Kurt stayed awhile longer, then mingled out of the Martello fan club and over to the shore. Maari had left the fan club earlier to play fetch with her dog in the water. The dog was a huge brown bulldog and didn't seem to mind the cold water, as long as she'd just throw that tennis ball out in it again. Kurt threw the ball a couple times, wondering why the dog always shook off after each fetch, even though it knew it was going back in to get wet again. He asked Maari if she thought Judi was coming. Maari just smiled and said, "you never know," in a way that hinted that well, maybe she did know.

"Hey, Kurt," shouted a voice from off to the right, "Quick! can you give me a hand here?" Ratkus had one foot on the shore, and one foot on his party boat. The boat was drifting away from the shore, and in about thirty seconds Ratkus had to make a choice: either perform a full gymnastic split, get soaked, or both.

Kurt ran over to grab the rope that had come loose from around a thick live oak. He grabbed the rope and pulled it tight, drawing the party boat closer to the shore and grounding it on the shallow mud.

"Thanks man," said Ratkus, "I thought for sure I was a goner there," he said, hopping onto the shore and taking the rope from Kurt. Ratkus was older than Kurt, mid-fifties, maybe more. He had long grey-white hair, drawn back into a ponytail. Australian outback hat. Face of sun-weathered sandpaper, perhaps three days growth of grey stubble. Moderate height, maybe five-ten, muscular, dark tan, but an honest working tan, not from a tube parlor or a bottle, and not from laying out in the sun trying to get a tan. He had a smoker's face, that drawn and dried-out wrinkled look you get after thirty years of firing off two packs a day. Faded blue jeans, long sleeve white denim work shirt. Leather boat shoes, no socks. He looked the part of the crusty old mariner, and loved to play it that way. Ratkus owned no fewer than twelve boats, at least that he'd admit. No one knew his first name, except maybe his wife, and she wasn't telling. He lived in a sprawling limestone block mansion about two miles up the lake towards the Mansfield Dam, perched on a dizzying limestone cliff overlooking the lake. He had installed an electric inclined tram back in the eighties, so that he could get down to his private marina faster than descending the seven-story staircase. He kept all but four of the boats in storage at any given time. He had sailboats and a yacht on Lake Travis, ski boats and a party boat on lake Austin, and a fleet of kayaks on town lake, ready to put in within thirty minutes notice. His passion was boating, but his money came from pure hard work. He'd spent a lifetime growing his landscape supply business. He sold trees, flowers, mulch, rocks, and had a thriving business that serviced most of the highbrow residents along the lake. If you had a million-dollar home in Austin, chances are your hedges, flower beds, and lawn were tended by a guy wearing a Ratkus logo'd golf shirt.

"No problem. You getting ready to put her out to sea?" asked Kurt.

"Little bit later. I was thinking we'd take her up the lake after lunch, maybe pick up a couple of caches on the other side over to Commons Ford park," said Ratkus.

"Commons Ford? Never heard of it," said Kurt.

"Not surprised. It's one of Austin's best-kept secrets. Even the locals don't know it's there," said Ratkus.

"Any decent caches there?" asked Kurt.

"Two or three, one's pretty new, hasn't been found yet. I figure with this group we can drum up some interest," said Ratkus.

Kurt said he'd like to go along, and Ratkus promised he wouldn't leave without him, then hopped onto the party boat and walked back toward the wheel. The party boat had a flat deck, carpeted in indoor-outdoor green, with a light metal railing all around, except for the bow, which was open. A canvas canopy suspended over the stern shaded the cockpit. Two thick grey pontoons supported the deck in the water. A polished wooden skipper's wheel, comically large for such a small craft, dwarfed the wooden podium which housed the engine controls and indicators. Grey wooden boxes mounted to the deck just inside the rail each had a hinged lid. The boxes stored life preservers and of course coolers with plenty of iced beer.

An unwritten law of the lake says you can't put out on a voyage unless you've got plenty of beer in the hold. Next to the speedometer, above the throttle, choke, and battery gage, jutted a metal bottle opener. Next to that hung a wooden holder just perfect for holding one cold bottle of beer. Drinking and boating was a long-time Texas tradition, in spite of any laws to the contrary.

Kurt mingled his way back through the crowd, now finishing their lunches, looking for Judi. He didn't see her. He had to see her again. In the crowd of new faces he could easily have missed her. Then again it was more likely that she wasn't interested.

He made his way back up to the ammo can stash, and helped a half dozen new cachers load up their take. He heard the bell just as he stacked a set of cans in the back of a green pickup. Even from up here on the rise, he could hear Ratkus calling, "all aboard."

He dropped the cans, sprinted down off the rise, hustled his way through the crowd, and climbed on just as the boat filled up. Ten people had climbed on board when Captain Ratkus announced with another ring of the bell that the ship was leaving port. Ratkus sputtered the old gas engine to life, then two barefoot helpers waded in from shore to push the boat off the mud and get her underway.

Kurt took a seat nearest the bow on the port side and searched the now receding crowd on the shore for any sign of Judi. None. The helper on the starboard side jumped in from the knee-deep water. He sat on the deck and slipped on his sneakers over bare wet feet. The boat pulled out into the lake, now about five feet from the shoreline. Too late for Judi to come running up at the last minute.

"Buck up, Kurt, she'll be here..." said Bonnie, who had taken the seat next to Kurt, but more toward the stern. The helper on the port side lifted her foot onto the deck and reached up toward the passengers with her left hand. Kurt, looking past her toward the shore, grabbed her hand and pulled her up onto the deck.

It was Judi.

"You're here!" said Kurt.

"Maari convinced me to show up," said Judi, rolling down the cuffs of her pant legs, "Damn, that water's cold!"

"It's February, silly! Welcome to the party," said Bonnie, lifting a glass of chardonnay in toast.

Judi slipped into her sneakers, which had been sitting on the deck by Kurt's feet. She explained that she had to go clean over to the next picnic area to find a place to park. She walked in along the shore. When the bell rang, she just rolled up her pant legs, kicked off her shoes and started pushing. "I love a good boat ride," she said.

"Well we're glad you could make it," said Kurt.

Judi said she was glad too. "I had a last minute fiasco at my Jester shop, but I got it under control." She had some new employees messing things up, and she felt she just had to supervise. She had three stores and she just couldn't let go, just couldn't let her managers do their jobs.

Judi admitted she didn't have any idea where they were headed, she'd just seen the boat leaving with Kurt on it, and jumped in to help. Kurt explained where they were going and why.

"Oh good, I love an adventure," said Judi.

Chapter 11

A FEW HOURS LATER, the boat chugged back down the lake after the Commons Ford Park caching adventure. Most of the cachers had congregated near the bow of the boat, trading tales of their newest finds over bottles of cold beer.

A reckless ski boat rocketed by within ten feet, sending a huge wave crashing over the bow. The party boat rocked side to side and most of the passengers were soaked to the knees in cold lake water. Ratkus jerked the throttle back to kill the engine. The boat pitched forward violently. Judi slammed into Kurt, and both their drinks splashed onto the deck as their arms pinwheeled for support. Kurt's glasses unhooked from his ears, teetered sideways on his face, paused at his nose for a half-second, bounced off Judi's shoulder, and then hit the deck. Kurt wrapped his left arm tightly around Judi. He pulled her to his chest and simultaneously grabbed the rail with his other arm. Something hard, maybe her pager or cellphone, jabbed into his hip. A cacher standing next to them on the edge of the bow dove sideways and grabbed the rail with both hands, launching his GPS receiver into the lake with a sickening *plop*.

"Move to the rear of the boat!" Ratkus yelled, "All hands astern!" The water soaked the indoor-outdoor carpeting, adding hundreds of pounds of dead weight to the heaving craft. The boat lowered into the water as more waves from the passing boat washed the deck.

Everyone on board shuffled toward the stern as the captain ordered, but one young passenger froze to the spot, panicked, shouting, "We're sinking!" Others joined in the shrieking, and several more passengers grabbed the rails. Dropped beers clattered to the deck and rolled off into the lake, leaving foamy trails on the indoor-outdoor deck carpeting. Ratkus let go of the wheel, cupped his hands into a megaphone around his mouth and shouted, "THIS BOAT CANNOT SINK!" Everyone looked back at Ratkus, eyes wide. The boat was obviously sinking, so why was the captain laughing? He shouted again a reassuring, "THIS BOAT CANNOT SINK!" then laughed some more. The passengers hushed. Not only was the boat sinking, but the captain had gone insane. Ratkus then added in a relaxed tone over the silence, "People, this is a pontoon boat, it simply can't sink! Relax and have a seat. We're going to be slowed down by all the water we took on, but we'll be fine, really. Have another beer on the house and enjoy the ride."

Everyone laughed a nervous laugh of relief, then resumed drinking their beers (those who hadn't dropped them) and playing with their GPS units (those who hadn't dropped them).

Judi turned her head to face Kurt, his arm still wrapped tightly around her. She pushed him away and laughed, "You can let me go now." They settled onto the nearest box, and Kurt picked his glasses up off the deck. The guy who dropped his GPS into the lake was on his hands and knees, hanging over the edge of the bow, searching in vain. Judi and Kurt both tried to help him find it, but the water, so green and murky, prevented anyone from seeing more than a few inches down. Even if they had seen it, no one could reach it on the bottom anyway. After a few minutes they left him crouched in shock, staring down into the green water muttering, "Bummer," over and over, and shaking his head.

Kurt retrieved a couple of new ice cold Cokes, popped the top and handed one to Judi. Judi asked him how the job search was going, and he asked her more about how she got into the coffee business. They spent the rest of the slow trip getting to know each other.

Bonnie and Maari watched them from the rear of the boat. They sipped chardonnay and snickered as they whispered to each other backhand. Judi had called Maari earlier in the week to get the low-down on Kurt. Maari, Bonnie, and Judi knew this, but Kurt didn't, and no one was telling.

Kurt and Judi watched the world pass by from the side of the boat. They laughed and waved to the other boaters passing in both directions. The waterlogged Ratkus party barge chugged on at two knots, practically standing still while the other traffic zipped by at thirty-five or more.

By the time they pulled back onto the shore at Emma Long, Kurt figured he had a good chance to get Judi's home phone number.

They climbed off the boat, surprised to see most of the cachers still hanging out on the shore, munching on cold food, drinking, and telling caching stories. The boaters told everyone about their brush with death, and later someone passed around an ammo can to collect up enough dough for a replacement for the hapless guy who'd dunked his GPS.

Judi headed for the food table and filled a plate with some of the leftover goodies. Someone had continued to cook hot dogs and venison sausage for the last several hours, and she found plenty of drinks. Judi and Kurt had a seat on a cooler, in a group of cachers Kurt knew, including Bonnie's husband Jason. Kurt popped the cap off a Shiner Bock and munched some dry nacho chips; Judi chugged on a Coke and ate a hot dog. Almost drowning at sea (when it comes down to it, just about any near death experience) can give you a powerful thirst and an appetite.

"...so I'm standing there, one A.M., two-way radio on my backpack, GPS in hand, trying to explain to these two heavily armed agents what I was doing unlocking an electrical utility box in the dark," said Jason.

"Wait, they were armed?" said one of the cachers.

"Yes, they came out with weapons drawn," said Jason. "Handguns, Black rifles. They were very curious who I was talking to on the radio."

"Who were you talking to?" asked another cacher, a thin, shy man up from San Antonio.

"No one! I was alone! I just keep the radio on my backpack all the time in case I need it," answered Jason, "It wasn't even turned on. They decided it would be safer for them if I got on face-to-face terms with the ground, fast. Then they had me tell them the combination so they could open the box. You should have seen the looks on their faces when they pulled out the play-doh, the McDonalds beanie baby elephant, and a hot wheels car, along with the cache logbook." said Jason.

"So then they figured you were telling the truth?" asked another cacher, a mountain of a woman wearing a tie-dye t-shirt that was stretched almost to the breaking point.

"You know, the Secret Service never really believes anyone; that's their job. After about a half hour of the third degree, they let me go, but they took my radio and my GPS, and they were going to confiscate my hiking stick too. It took me a couple weeks and a mountain of red tape before I got them back. I had to borrow Bonnie's GPS in the meantime. It seriously slowed me down in terms of my find count. I may never recover," he said.

Kurt turned privately to Judi to fill her in on the details of what had happened. All the old-timers could recite the legend of how Jason got picked up by the Secret Service.

Jason had found a "plain sight" cache in Waterloo park. The cache, disguised as an electrical box attached at chest-height to a telephone pole, had a combination lock securing it. Jason went out for his first try at night caching, but he'd chosen a poor night on which to find this particular cache. It just happened by blind luck that the hospital across the street was treating a visiting adjutant foreign minister for deep vein thrombosis from sitting on a plane for ten hours. The Secret Service had set up surveillance (standard operating procedure for high-ranking foreign officials), and their spotter spied a suspicious individual wearing a backpack, tampering with the electrical system in the park across the street.

"Anyway, to make a long story short, Jason's standing there, flashlight in his teeth, trying to work the combo lock, when a huge black SUV comes crashing through the brush and almost knocks him and the pole over. Two agents hop out with assault rifles, demanding he freeze. Jason about craps his pants. Isn't that right Jason?" Kurt asked, now that Jason had finished telling the story.

"Yeah," chuckled Jason. "I bring a change of shorts every time I go night caching now, just in case."

"Do you guys often run afoul of the law while caching?" asked Judi.

"Not usually. Most of the local cops don't know about caching, but we got a guy on the force who actually geocaches. I've met him; he's pretty cool. He's got a GPS unit that most of us would give our left wingnut for; pardon my French. The park cops are also without a clue, but they mostly leave us alone. I think the Secret Service knows about caching now after that last episode but they probably won't do anything different in the future, 'cause they're a bunch of hard cases and like I said before, it's their job. Best to cache in the daytime if you're worried," advised Jason. He popped the tab on a diet coke, drew off a cold mouthful, and then wiped his mouth on the back of his wrist. "Speakin' of worried, Kurt, did you hear about the dead dog that Martello found on a cache a couple months ago?" He asked.

"I heard he found a dead animal, I didn't know it was a dog though. I just caught the tail end of the story," said Kurt.

"Shoot, I think that would have freaked me out more than the Secret Service did," said Jason. "And finding a jar of pee nearby, that's just freakin weird."

"Agreed." said Kurt, then, jokingly, "Dead dogs all over the place. Gotta be careful out there."

Kurt and Judi spent the rest of the afternoon tossing Frisbee, playing fetch with Maari's dog, wading in the lake, hauling ammo cans for the latecomers, listening to more geocaching legends, eating way too much picnic food, and walking along the shore talking. Discovery. They spoke of their families, work, college, pets, distaste for organized religion, likes and dislikes. Getting-to-know-you and searching for warts. An impelling tension charged the air, each one being careful not to say anything that would offend the other, nothing that would ruin the potential romance they each could feel developing.

Kurt drove home that evening with a painful sunburn on his arms and neck --and Judi's home phone number in his back pocket.

Chapter 12

THE KILLER SLEPT IN the dry warmth, the basement of the barn providing shelter from the biting cold outside. At least that asshole McChasney's dog was out of the picture. From a basement window, he had watched the authorities haul off her mangled carcass. He was hidden well down here and they had no reason to investigate the basement, let alone the crawl space behind the furnace. Must sleep.

Awake. Still dark. His heart pounded and he looked around quickly for escape. He had forgotten where he was, and the darkness closed in on him. He couldn't think clearly, it felt like he was losing control of his thoughts.

He wanted to run.

Instead he took a couple deep breaths and tried to focus, to clear his mind.

Where was he? He could feel the cold concrete floor. He could feel the ancient concrete block walls, blackened with the oily residue of eighty-four years of small engine and hydraulic system repair. The air was thick with the cloying smell of two cycle engine oil mixed with dust and the summery green essence of freshly mown grass, now gone cold, black, and still with the passing of countless seasons. The dead still of mid-winter night. The barn creaked under its own tired weight and the weight of the snowmass on the roof.

He remembered now.

He shuffled over to the ancient wooden workbench, and in the pale orange shaft of light that stabbed down through the basement window from the sodium vapor security lantern outside in the parking lot, he scanned the shelves and racks above the bench looking for what he needed. He was somewhat calmer now, but he knew the panic would return, and when it did it would be fierce and he needed to be ready.

Hand tools, screwdrivers, pliers, adjustable wrenches, ratchets and socket sets, all old but kept clean, each one hung in its designated place on the wall. The maintenance foreman ran a tidy shop and treated his tools well, the mark of a craftsman.

At last he spied a row of old mayonnaise and pickle jars on the shelf. Some were filled with spark plugs, some with cotter pins, assorted washers, split washers, rubber grommets, springs, rolls of electrical and Teflon tape, and the odd collection of nylon and rubber spacers. He selected a mayo jar filled with greasy machine bolts, cannibalized from equipment in the hopes that they could one day fulfill another useful purpose in some other machine part, at some later time. He shook the bolts out onto the bench, and then wiped the jar carefully with one of the rags heaped in a cardboard Quaker State Motor Oil box next to the bench.

He unzipped his jeans and filled the jar. When he was finished, he cradled the warm glass in his hands and raised it to his lips. His nostrils filled with the musky blood-warm ammonia scent of fresh urine. His eyes glazed over, unfocused. Was he in another place, far from here, perhaps another time? Only the killer knew, and then again, looking into those dark green eyes, you got the sense that, well, maybe he didn't.

He pulled a mouthful through pursed lips and choked it down, then wiped his lips with the back of his wrist. In thirty years he never got used to the taste. Like warm sea water tinged with the bitter taste of ammonia. The smell alone was enough to make him gag. He coughed, then clamped his hand to his mouth to suppress the reflex. This ritual would stop the panic, he knew, but only for a short while, as long as the taste remained in his mouth, which would be hours. Long after the taste faded he'd still think he tasted it for a few hours more, and that worked just as well to keep his thoughts calm and focused on the plan.

He found a matching lid, also sitting on the shelf, but filled with small hex nuts that could not have matched the bolts that were in the jar. He dumped out the nuts next to the unmatching bolts, wiped the lid, held it up and rotated it in the light to be sure he'd gotten all the grease and dirt off, then screwed it onto the jar. Satisfied, he set his warm prize on the edge of the bench. He couldn't add this to his collection that he abandoned when he took to the road. Could he come back later to retrieve them all? He thought it unlikely but one never knew, and where there was hope, well, that was something.

As the killer returned to his makeshift bed of frayed (but clean) blue and white Harrison Valley Country Club logo towels behind the furnace and water heater, he caught his reflection in the polished Lexan shield of the old bench grinder. He ran his fingers along the crooked scar on his left cheek. It ran from just to the left of his eye, down through the center of his cheek, where it was punctuated on either side with canine fang marks, and from there it extended through his beard stubble to the left corner of his lip. He had other scars, sure, but this was the biggest and most noticeable. He knew that it made him stand out--easily identified, easily remembered, so he wore a beard most times, then other times tried to stay low, stay hidden, stay dark.

This scar was a battle scar, and he knew every time he saw it or ran his fingers across it that he had won that battle. That bitch had attacked, and that bitch had lost. If he hadn't been carrying his baseball bat home from school that day, he might well be dead now instead. "Fucking dogs," he whispered. Those other two mongrels about shit themselves when they saw how he had taken the alpha bitch down with a home-run swing. They turned tail and ran, the mangy fuckers. Thought they'd gang up on a little kid. He'd shown them all, though the bitch had ripped half his face off and nearly bled him dry before he cracked his bat over her thick skull.

Even in the dark, he could tell that this shop was filled with instruments of death. In addition to being a fine craftsman, the shop foreman was organized. Just like Dalton. He wondered if old Dalton still worked here. He'd have to be decrepit by now. The broken equipment waiting to be repaired was tagged and jailed in a cage along the back wall, and the equipment that had been repaired and was waiting to be returned to service had no tag and was either stacked neatly along the wall next to the bench or hanging from the wall on hooks.

He ran his hands along the line of chain saws, careful not to touch the sharp oiled chains. There were nylon corded weed trimmers, lawn mowers, and electric and manual scissor-style hedge trimmers. Each piece of equipment sported a bright yellow or green paint job, and even in the dim light from the security lamp outside, the colors glowed. Next to the hedge trimmers hung something that looked like a lawn mower engine with a four foot long metal shaft coming out of it and a ten inch steel lawnmower blade on the end. It looked like a weed trimmer, only it was way too big. A weed whacker on steroids. It was hanging from a hook on the wall--no, on closer look it actually took up two hooks, which had to be screwed into a two-by-eight that was then bolted to the wall with five thick masonry lag bolts. It had a wide leather strap on it for keeping it attached to the operator. The engine was painted bright yellow. The shaft was unpainted; it reflected the dull luster of raw steel. The blade was black except for a sharp glint of bright filed carbon steel along the cutting edges. There was no safety guard covering the blade, though he could see a flange where one was supposed to bolt on.

"Ahh, yes it's you. Strange to see you here my old friend."

He lifted the Brush Monster down off the hooks and flipped the leather strap up over his head and under his right arm.

The machine was heavy, but with the strap across his back, it was well balanced. There was a set of handle bars bolted to the pole just above the center. These bars formed a wide, flat "U." The ends of the U had plastic handle grips, and allowed him to get a firm wide grip on the machine. Along one handle grip was a throttle lever, choke, and kill switch, right where he expected to find them.

The killer backed up a step or two away from the wall, and practiced swinging the machine left and right in a wide arc. He then tried an overhead swing, and found the machine to be graceful and easy to maneuver. He smiled, almost laughing in spite of himself as he twirled and danced the machine about the shop in a deadly ballet. The heavy mower engine made a nice counterbalance. It amazed him at how easily it came back to him after such a long time. Like riding a fucking bicycle, he mused.

He pulled the Brush Monster up over his head, and placed the straps back onto the hooks in the wall. He unscrewed the gas cap and waved a hand over the filler hole. The rush of petroleum vapors confirmed there was some gasoline in the tank. He squatted in front of the machine, and ran his fingers along the blade. It gleamed in the dim light of the security lamp, and

"--Shit!"

He accidentally pricked the tip of his index finger. He jerked his hand back, put his finger in his mouth and sucked at the blood. The blade had been freshly sharpened before being placed on the in-service rack.

He pulled his finger out of his mouth and studied it again, rolling it over to expose it to the light. Just a flesh wound. Why the fuck did fingertips bleed so damn much? He wrapped it up tight in a shop rag and shuffled back over behind the furnace to continue his sleep, cradling his warm mayonnaise jar in his uninjured arm.

Chapter 13

"GREAT FOOD - LIVE MUSIC," screamed the corrugated metal sign above the inverted canoe that formed the awning for the Bait & Tackle Grill. The Bait Shop, as the locals called it, had at one time been a lunch trailer parked off the right of way of Ranch Road 620, northwest of Austin.

Over the years the success of the place led to one ad-hoc addition after another until now it sprawled, a complex of oddly-shaped rooms with gravel floors, corrugated metal walls, colorful neon beer signs, vintage boat motors and antique fishing paraphernalia. The Bait Shop had the best fried catfish on any shore of Lake Travis, as well as some of the best chicken-fried steak anywhere in central Texas. The original trailer was still there; it was now the kitchen. Five cooks and order takers did a hurried greasy square dance inside the trailer, while customers ordered through the original trailer window, in the back wall of the main dining room. The Bait Shop recently began to feature live music, and the musicians were set up in the newest part of the structure, which used to be a gravel parking lot. The gravel was still there. It was now the floor.

Judi ordered a catfish basket and an ice-cold I.B.C. Root Beer. The order-taker, who couldn't have been more than eighteen, wore a black push-up bra under an unbuttoned loose-knit top, a dog's choke chain around her neck and a pierced eyebrow under a buzz-cut dyed a fluorescent orange that could never have occurred in nature. "Keep Austin Weird" was the marketing slogan these days. Some took it more personally than others. Kurt ordered a chicken fried steak and a root beer as well. He paid cash for the meal and dropped a couple bucks into the tip jar. He always tipped extra if the waitress or order taker looked hot. Even more if she looked slutty.

They took their drinks to an empty table. A three-piece Cajun band played out in the gravel room, but they wanted to be able to talk, so they grabbed a table for two in the corner of the main dining room. You could still hear the music, but it wasn't so loud to prevent conversation. The main dining room only had about eight tables in it. Each table had a roll of paper towels on a stand in the middle, and a basket full of various hot sauces and spiced vinegars.

"Not a beer drinker?" asked Kurt.

"Sometimes I'll have a beer," replied Judi. "every once in awhile. How about you?"

"Yeah, every once in awhile, I'm not much of a drinker," he replied, then gestured toward the fishing décor, "How about this place, you ever come here?"

"I've driven by a couple times, never stopped in though. How about you?" she asked.

"I come in here pretty much every week. They know me by name. Most times I don't even have to order, they just ask if I want 'the usual.' I even hid a cache here, just outside."

"You're kidding. Did they let you?" she asked, looking around.

"Sure, the manager thought it was cute. She told me last week it brings in a few extra customers a week." he said.

"Where is it, in here?" she asked.

"It's outside. You want to find it or you want me to tell you?" he asked.

Judi didn't want help. Kurt handed her his keys. She went out to his truck, retrieved his GPS from the dash, and began searching around outside the restaurant.

Ten minutes later, the dog-chain girl barked Kurt's name into the microphone. He couldn't remember there being such hot-looking 'girls gone wild' when he was young and on the prowl. Maybe he just hung out with a tamer crowd.

He'd spent most of the last ten minutes watching Judi through the windows. She'd look alternately down at the GPS and then up at the building. She'd crouch down, then reach up on tip-toes to try to see if it was hidden behind the décor on the outside walls. Kurt didn't feel one bit guilty for checking out her body during the whole exercise. Through the tight jeans and polo shirt he could tell she was built.

The receiver had led her from the front of the building, around to the side, then toward the dumpster at the back, and then back up to the front again. Judi didn't know it, but the building and surrounding trees were confusing her GPS signal.

Kurt had hidden the cache inside a painted wooden fish hanging on the fence just outside the side door. There were a dozen similar fish mounted to the walls of the dining room, inside and out, so it really blended in. He'd hollowed out the fish, and it had just enough room inside for a mint tin. A small logbook, a half-pen, and maybe a few coins were all that could fit inside the tin, but still it qualified as a geocache.

"Do you give up yet?" he asked, poking his head out through the side door.

She switched off the GPS receiver and grabbed the door. They both went up to the condiment bar to fill up some tiny paper cups with ketchup, then turned back toward the booth. Bonnie and Jason Heckmann had snuck in and seated themselves in Kurt and Judi's places while the two had their backs turned.

"Mmm-mmm, this looks good!" said Bonnie, who had taken Judi's seat, and was rubbing her hands together in mock anticipation of eating Judi's meal.

"Yeah, tasty. You two picked the best stuff on the menu," said Jason, grasping a plastic fork and knife in each hand, pretending to hijack Kurt's meal, "Bring us some of that ketchup, we're starved."

"Ugh, they'll let anyone eat here, won't they?" said Kurt, to Judi.

"Yes, absolutely no standards. We should go somewhere else, *daahling*" she replied, feigning a snooty attitude, turning her nose up.

Jason and Bonnie offered to let the two join them at a bigger table. They'd just ordered. They explained that they had come for dinner, saw Judi outside looking for the cache, and thought they'd crash their date and give them a hard time.

"Thanks a lot," said Kurt, pulling out a chair for Judi.

"I didn't find it yet, so don't give it away," said Judi, dropping into the chair that Kurt had pulled out for her. Then quietly, looking up at Kurt, "Thanks."

"We wouldn't dream of it," said Bonnie, sliding her own chair out and sitting in it. "You know," she said, waving a plastic knife toward Jason, "that's the difference between dating and married for eighteen years. This schmuck hasn't pulled out a chair for me in I don't know how long."

"Don't let anyone kid you, Red. Chivalry is overrated," said Jason, kissing Bonnie on the cheek. Bonnie had flame-red hair before it turned gray. She lost the color but kept the personality and the nickname.

Bonnie elbowed Jason in the ribs--hard. "Asshole," she said. If you didn't know them well, you'd think she was serious when she said it. It made Kurt nervous the first few times he heard it, but eventually he figured it was just a joke, a very dry sense of humor. Judi picked up on it right away. Kurt could see that she was smiling at the older couple.

The Heckmann's meals came out in another few minutes, and Jason got up to retrieve them. When he came back, he interrupted, "Hey did you hear about what the Kragers found up at St. Edward's park yesterday?"

"Jason, No!" said Bonnie, "let them finish eating first, have a little common decency."

"Yeah, better wait until we're done eating," said Kurt, wiping up some cream gravy with a piece of Texas Toast. "Otherwise I'll retaliate with a cat hairball story that will make you lose your appetite for a week."

When they'd finished their meal, Jason cleared the empty baskets off the table. When he returned he was ready to tell them about how the Kragers found a dead dog while night caching up in St. Edward's park.

"No way," said Kurt.

"Yes way, Ted." Bonnie had been saying "Yes way, Ted," a line from some cornball eighties movie, as an automatic response to "No Way" for the last fourteen years. It was a testament to the strength of their marriage that Jason hadn't once in all that time attempted to strangle her.

Kurt asked if anyone thought there was any connection to that dead dog they found a couple weeks ago.

"Are you guys sure this sport is entirely safe?" asked Judi.

"Oh yeah, it's no problem," said Jason. "There are hundreds of thousands of caches out there; you're bound to run into a dead animal every once in awhile, it's just the law of averages. We found a deer ribcage on a park cleanup once last year. Some newbie thought it was a human skeleton and called the park police. The park cops had a good laugh when they came out and saw what it was," he explained.

"Yeah and then remember the time we found that rotted purse on another cleanup and it turned out to contain I.D. from a lady that had been missing for two years. We never found out if the bag helped them solve the case, but the police were very thankful. The trail had grown cold," added Bonnie.

"Geocaching saves the day," said Judi, poking fun at them.

"It's not like we're trying to be heroes or anything, but we can do some good. Some folks have found needles and other drug stuff, especially in parks near urban caches," added Jason.

"So what was the deal with the dog?" asked Kurt.

Bonnie said the Kragers thought the dog might have been a stray that coyotes killed. There's a neighborhood at the top of the hill. Someone probably let Fifi out for her evening tinkle; she became a snack. The coyotes just happened to leave her carcass by the trail.

"Still it's pretty creepy," said Judi.

"Especially at night," added Kurt.

"Welp, we've got to head out to Wally world to buy some caching supplies for the weekend. You kids have fun. Sorry we crashed your date," said Bonnie.

"Oh no, not at all," said Kurt.

"Never an embarrassing silence with Bonnie at the table," said Jason, which prompted another hard elbow in the ribs. "Oof! See you kids later."

Bonnie and Jason headed out the door with Jason rubbing his sore ribs. They got into their truck and drove off. Kurt and Judi cleared their cups and other debris off the table and threw them in the trash. They walked outside and Kurt helped Judi find the cache, using the low-tech warmer / colder technique. She signed the logbook and replaced the cache. Afterward they huddled in the gravel room to listen to some live Cajun music.

They listened to the music for about fifteen minutes, then walked out. You hear three Cajun tunes, you've heard them all. "You want to catch a movie?" asked Kurt, after they'd climbed back into his truck.

"Sure. What's playing?" said Judi.

"I'm not sure, how about we just drive over to the theater and see what's on?" he offered.

"Sounds good to me," she said.

The tear-jerking romantic comedy starred Meg Ryan and a leading man that neither Kurt nor Judi had ever heard of. Kurt had a crush on Meg Ryan when he was in his twenties, but had outgrown her. Lately he favored the new crop of twenty-something blondes, and it was a constant source of apprehension for him to think that he was growing old and Hollywood kept on stamping out plenty of hot young chicks. What really brought it crashing down for him was during a particularly erotic Pepsi commercial when he realized mid-fantasy that he was old enough to be Britney Spears's father. Pretty soon he'd be a really old fart and none of the young ones would have anything to do with him. It wasn't exactly a midlife crisis, but it wasn't far from it either. On the other hand, looking at the bright side, being thirty six, he could reasonably expect to date anywhere from twenty-something (if he kept in shape) up to fifty-something (if she kept in shape).

They'd shared an armrest in the theater as the date movie spun its sappy, teary magic. As the movie got underway, they held hands over the armrest. Before the movie was half over, they lifted the armrest, and Judi snuggled up against Kurt's side, with her head on his shoulder. He had his arm around her, and every once in awhile she'd look up at him and smile.

Kurt walked her up to her apartment on the third floor. He held her hands in the doorway as they said goodbye. Her hands felt warm, despite the cool night air. He leaned down to kiss her, carefully watching for any signal. He was planning to execute a quick kiss, nothing too technical, more than a peck but less than a World Wrestling Federation tonsil pulling match.

Judi had other ideas.

When they were through, his lips were numb and his whole face tingled. Her body felt warm and soft against his, except for her damned pager, which poked him rudely in the hip again. He found himself unable to speak, and when she looked in his eyes, his brain went blank and his knees threatened to collapse. He grabbed the metal railing on the landing for support. With her electric green eyes, her auburn hair blowing lightly in the cool wind, her well-proportioned body, Judi was the most beautiful woman in Kurt's world. No twenty-something Hollywood brat could ever hope to match the intensity of that first kiss. A kiss like that came only with maturity, confidence, and experience. He found himself hoping she'd invite him in. He knew it was as good as signing the death warrant for any relationship to go further than a kiss on the first date, but he didn't care. It felt so good, so right.

He wanted her now.

"Goodnight Kurt," she whispered, as she turned to unlock the door.

Kurt arrived back at the house to the music of Pokey's yowling. She who must be fed. Pokey could smell the dog on him, could smell the other female, that new female, too. Pokey was not happy to share Kurt's affection with any other creature, and she planned to let him know later by yarking up a juicy hairball on the seat of his expensive ergonomic padded desk chair after he went to bed. He'd discover it only after sitting in it. After he fed the cat, he sat on the couch. His mouth still tingled from that kiss. What was he getting himself into? He had no job, no means of support. Dating was expensive. How could he get involved now?

He didn't care.

He had to have her.

Chapter 14

www.cache-finders.com Geocache Listing

Fore Play - Miniature Sized Cache
by KeystoneCopper [email this user]
Pennsylvania, USA

[click to download geographic coordinates and hints]

You're going to love this one, it's a puzzler! It is not necessary to enter the country club grounds to find this cache! If you do you will be trespassing! Please respect private property. Don't download the hint until you've tried to find it, because the hint's a spoiler. Also don't post any photos of the cache container or the hiding spot! The cache container is tiny. Bring only small items to trade!

Cache Visitor Comments:
(5 comments total)

[click to see previous comments]

[4] December 25 by YaddaYaddaBing [12 caches found]

we decided to do a little caching this
afternoon after ripping opening the
presents, since jimmy got a (surprise!) new
gps receiver. buzzed out to the nearest
cache (this one) and when we got to the
coords, we saw red flashing lights over by
that huge old barn across the road from the
country club. there was golf carts
everywhere, cops, and animal control. we
couldn't get to close, cuz they had the
area taped off. we couldn't find the cache
either but we looked for about 45 minutes.

[email this user]

[5] December 26 by JennysBoy [572 caches
found]

Hey yadda, my cousin's an officer with
Westmoreland County Animal Services. He was
at that deal you guys saw over there. Some
bastard did a hit-and run on the highway by
hole #8 (Gold course) overnight. Turns out
the animal they hit was the greenskeeper's
black lab! Greenskeeper (poor sap) found it
while working in the maintenance barn just
down the hill from the hole. My cousin said
they didn't get nothin' off the scene due
to that big snow we had covered all traces.
Happy frickin' White Xmas, keep yer dogs
inside, and keep on cachin! [BTW, this
cache is an easy find if you just keep
"lookin' up." :-)]

[email this user]

Did you Find the Cache? Add your own
comment! [click here]

Chapter 15

Harrison Valley Pennsylvania
Thursday, December 26

JIM MCCHASNEY WOKE EARLY Thursday morning in the ranch house on the hill overlooking the Gold course, the oldest and prettiest of four nine-hole courses at the club. The sheer white drapes over his bedroom window hovered like luminous ghosts in the grey dawn. A chain of colored Christmas lights bordered the window.

He parted the curtains with the back of his hand. A thick snow buried the courses, his house, the barn, the clubhouse, and everything else for seventy-five miles in any direction. Out on number five Gold, skeletal trees creaking and laboring under a crust of ice poked up out of the snow, threatening to snap a limb if the dawn wind pushed any harder. Toward the back of the Gold, along the banked white forehead of the number eight fairway, the trees receded in a wispy hairline of charcoal grey. Snow clung to the trunks of the trees in splotches, and everywhere you looked it was either white-grey or charcoal grey, with few shades in between.

Jim was usually up well before first light, but this was the day after Christmas and he allowed himself the decadence of an extra half-hour of sleep. The sky was just turning from deep black to light grey, with some lighter grey painting the clouds to the east. Winter in Pittsburgh: leave your Kodachrome in your camera bag. He pulled on his overalls and work boots, and threw on a heavy parka that was hanging on the Queen Anne chair by the door. Jim always dressed professionally, wearing khaki pants, a button-down cotton work shirt, leather work boots, and a matching belt. His duties often brought him in contact with the members out on the course, and he knew appearances mattered.

He kissed Adele lightly on the forehead and she stirred and rolled deeper into their down comforter. Jim stroked her silver hair. They had been married just over forty years, and he loved her as intensely as any twenty-something kid. He hadn't imagined as a young man that romantic love could survive forty years of marriage--but it had. And it had grown into something even deeper that he couldn't have imagined as a young man growing up working the rusted steel mills of Duquesne. Adele had become his best friend.

The winter crew had the day off today, but the work of a head greenskeeper, like proverbial woman's work, was never done.

Jim had planned to take the day off on Christmas, but the commode in the barn had other plans. He fixed the flush valve yesterday afternoon, and he'd have to go in to check on it again to make sure that the replacement valve was holding. A toilet with a leaky valve just trickled, but over a long time a drip a minute could add up to real money. He also had paperwork to deal with, end-of-year reporting and equipment requests that he didn't want to leave until the new year. Best to get it done now so it won't be underfoot come spring.

Jim hopped into the greenskeeper's golf cart. The padded white vinyl seat was brittle and slick in the cold, but Jim didn't feel anything but a whisper of that cold through his insulated overalls. The Club provided a fleet of quiet clean electric carts for its members, but the maintenance crew needed several modified heavy-duty gas engine golf carts so they could run all day and haul loads of crew and equipment. Jim drove the metalflake green cart. Along with the house down the hill from the clubhouse, and free access to play the course when it was closed on Mondays, it was one of the perks of the job. Never mind that aside from color this cart was identical in every way to the other maintenance carts. The day crew during the summer always kept a wary eye out for any glint of metallic green. If they saw that cart coming from far across the course, it was time to quit slacking. "Hey ladies, Jimbo's comin,'" someone'd yell. They'd pick up the pace as long as that cart was in sight.

Jim was a hardened steel rail of a man, standing just over six-foot-six. His slim physique was topped with a neatly combed thicket of black hair that was slicked straight back and kept in place with Brylcreem. "A little dab'll do ya," his wife often teased, but he always used a big dab. Jim had grayed in his twenties; the black came from a bottle. He had a wicked cowlick. His glasses were a throwback to the 1920's, perfectly circular black frames of a type you might have seen worn by a banker, accountant, or railroad telegrapher in brittle sepia-tone photos pulled from a crumbling cardboard box in grandma's attic.

Jim liked things neat and in place. In his hiring, his work, his dress, and in his personal life. Not a hair in his cowlick strayed, nor did any blade of grass in his charge. Not a mower, chainsaw, shovel, or rake was out of service long. "Ship shape" was his motto. He said it about forty times a day, and the crew often gave him a ration of shit about it, behind his back of course.

He backed halfway down the drive, did a tight three-point turn, slid sideways a few feet, then rolled to the edge of the drive. He waited at the highway, leaning forward over the wheel to see if he had a clear shot for the five-hundred-foot dash down the highway to the maintenance barn. A less careful man might not have bothered to check; at this grey hour there was no one on the road.

His drive had already been cleared by one of the crew. It was customary for Dalton, his crew foreman, to have one of his men plow the roads and driveways of the club after a snowfall, even in the pre-dawn hours if necessary, even on a holiday, once the snow had stopped. Dalton didn't have to clear Jim's drive but he did so as a courtesy. This was borne of a respect strengthened from working together daily, sometimes seven days a week, over the last thirty-five years, rather than any petty desire to suck-up to the boss. Jim wouldn't be swayed by any attempt at brown-nosing and Dalton wasn't the kind of man who'd do it.

Ordinarily his black lab Wolfie accompanied him on the passenger seat. Wolfie had been Jim's companion for eleven years. For someone to hit his dog and then not stop or even try to render aid was beyond his comprehension. One officer said that the dog had been killed by what he called "blunt force trauma," most likely a glancing impact, a hit and run. But they couldn't be sure. No one saw anything, and the area had been covered in a heavy snow that had eradicated any trace of the incident.

The cart crunched over the icy gravel to the side of the barn. Jim cut the ignition, then fumbled his keys out to unlock the door to the office. A chill morning wind whipped along the edge of the barn, poking a bony finger of cold into a gap between his parka and neck. He shivered and stepped into the office.

The barn was old, probably at least a hundred years or more; no one seemed to know for sure. It was an unremarkable western Pennsylvania dairy barn, three stories tall, wooden slats painted dark green, faded and now starting to peel, with a brown shingled roof. Three oversized green garage doors spanned the driveway side of the barn. One normal size garage door fitted into the concrete block wall on the lower level, the basement shop. The club installed these doors ages ago, back in the twenties, when this fertile farmland shucked off its agrarian husk revealing a grassy playground for the rich.

The office had its own entrance next to the garage doors, so Jim could enter without exposing all the equipment inside to the elements.

Once inside he switched on the office's overhead fluorescents and portable electric heater, and then shed his parka. Jim felt good to be at work. Despite the cold, he felt comfortable. He belonged here, and part of him didn't want to retire. A man is defined by what he does. To make a man stop doing what he does best because of his age, was--what? Inefficient? Unfair? No, worse than that. It was cruel. He'd miss this place, creaky timbers, leaky toilet and all.

The office crouched in a corner of the cavernous barn, a hundred square feet of dingy but uncluttered space. A long antique metal desk divided the room. World War Two era green metal file cabinets lined the wall to the left, and corkboard covered every open square inch of wall. An antique chalkboard was bolted to the wall just outside the door. On the board someone had scrawled the crew roster and duty schedule. One of the more artistic crewmen had erased a swath out of the middle and drawn a Santa head caricature with a cartoon cloud coming out of his mouth saying "Merry Xmas, Ladies." A rectangular porthole was cut in the wall over the desk, fitted with wire-mesh safety glass. The glass was so old that it was wrinkled near the bottom, and had a perpetual coating of green-yellow grime. The grime was textured such that you couldn't tell if it was on the inside or out. The wire in-basket contained a few papers he had yet to work on. He saved the paperwork for later and walked out into the barn.

The first order of the day was to check on the flush valve he fixed yesterday. He walked into the darkened barn, past the huge brown fourteen-inch square timbers that were holding up the center framework. Parked back within the dim recesses of the barn were five Toro Triplex greens mowers, two red Ford tractor mowers that had entered service a few years before Jim was born, and two Toro Sand Pro trap raking machines. Jim stopped at Sand Pro number two and ran his palm over one of its three circus-sized knobby balloon tires.

"Remember when that kid tried to float it?" called out a silhouette framed by the office door. It was Billy "Dalton" Whorter, crew foreman.

"Hey Dalton, shouldn't you be at home, enjoying Christmas cheer or something?" Jim asked, looking up.

"Humbug!" Dalton chuffed as he walked over to the Sand Pro. He ran a leathery left hand along the instrument panel, while extending his right to Jim. The only instrument on the panel was a mechanical hour meter. The Sand Pro, like most golf course equipment and like all golf course employees, measured service in hours, not miles. Accumulate too many hours; you're scrap.

"Took two weeks in the shop, and two G's worth of new parts from Toro," said Jim, extending his right hand to clasp Dalton's.

"An'at was two weeks I didn't have t'spare," said Dalton, as they shook hands. Dalton's hands were clumsy man-hands with wide flat nails, hairy knuckles, thick stubby fingers, calloused and worn from years of outside work.

"Darn kid," said Jim.

"Good ol' 'Big Keith.' Freakin doper," stated Dalton. Dalton didn't have a problem with profanity, but wouldn't utter it in front of the boss. The substitution came out sounding forced and he regretted it immediately. Keith Busman had always insisted that he be called "Big Keith," even though he was the smallest kid on the crew. Keith swore in his defense that with such big balloon tires, he just *knew* the Sand Pro would float.

"I'll never forget the look on his face when he saw me coming. He knew his goose was cooked," Jim smiled.

"And he was tryin' to start it!" recalled Dalton.

"Underwater!" They both laughed. They had said this last word at the same time. Jim looked down, shook his head, and smiled. The story was an old one, oft repeated over the last seventeen years by generations of crews now long since moved on. Legend. Now, years later, they could laugh. Ever since that day, though, they had screened all new applicants for drugs.

"They just don't build 'em like they used to," said Dalton, rapping his knuckles on the front tire.

"This one's ship shape. It'll probably last another twenty years," said Jim.

Fifty-eight years had passed for Dalton, thirty-five here at HVCC, or simply "The Valley" as the crew called it. He had started as a caddy back in the doo-wop years and had joined the grounds crew long before there were minimum wage or labor laws. He had a leather face to match his leather hands, products of too many summers out in the sun in the years before sunscreen. His cool blue eyes shone out from under a mat of uncombed dark brown hair. He wore a light brown sheepskin coat. Faded Levis extended down his too-short legs to black leather engineer boots.

They sat in silence for a few minutes, the only sound a shrill wind haunting the eaves.

"Next week's the big day, huh?," Dalton said. He was trying hard to avoid mentioning the dog.

"Yeah." Another pause for a few moments, then Jim admitted quietly, "The board's going to put Zupansky in charge."

"I figgered," clucked Dalton, looking down and poking at a Sand Pro tire with his boot.

Dalton, with only an eighth grade education, had been with the crew twice as long as Zupansky and knew more about how to run a golf course than anyone in the whole Monongahela river valley, maybe even the whole state.

"He's got the turf science degree n'at," said Jim.

"College Boy," said Dalton.

"Yeah, but he also knows what he's doing, and he respects you, needs you, you know that?" Jim asked, stressing the point by pressing his index finger into Dalton's thick chest. Any other man touched Dalton like that, he'd draw back a bloody stump, and both Jim and Dalton knew it.

"Okay chief, you say so," said Dalton, letting Jim's hand fall away on its own.

"I know so," said Jim, turning, "and this course needs you too. Darn place would go to pot without you." *Going to pot* was about the worst thing that could ever happen to anything or anyone in Jim's world. It was the polar opposite of *ship shape*.

Jim walked toward the rear of the barn, where the cramped toilet room was located. "Well, this torlit isn't going to repair itself," he called out.

"You need a hand?" offered Dalton.

"No, I've got it, you go on home. Say 'Happy New Year' to Missy and the kids for me."

"Arr-righty Chief. See ya next week," said Dalton.

You couldn't technically (or legally) call it a restroom; it was smaller than a phone booth. There was no sink, no mirror. Employees weren't required to wash hands either by state law or by custom, and if any insisted, there was always the hose out back. The door latched by a rusted metal hook and screw eye.

The door didn't fit in the jamb and wouldn't close completely; there was always a gap, an inch. Considering that the room had no fan or other ventilation, in the eighty plus seasons the club used this barn, including twenty or so in which the crew employed workers of both genders, no one ever objected to the gap.

Parked next to the toilet room was a light green three-wheeled Cushman Turf Truckster. It had been in service since the late sixties. Many a teenage crewman had learned to drive a standard transmission on this baby, and when you jacked her up to overhaul the transmission, you could tell. Still she kept on running. He ran his hands along the crudely painted metal frame, then paused a second at the gage panel to check the battery charge. This one'd need a new Die-Hard before next season. He looked up to see if Dalton had gotten outside yet. He had. Jim could hear Dalton's 'sixty-seven Dodge pickup rumbling out in the drive. He'd have to let Dalton know next week.

Jim checked the toilet bowl for any trace of the blue dye that he had dumped in the tank the day before. There was a hint of blue. Still leaking then. He lifted the porcelain cover off the tank, flushed the tank, adjusted the valve, then flushed again. After three flush cycles, he heard the distinctive *whup-whup-whup-whup* of a mower engine being pull-started downstairs in the shop. What the heck? No one should have been down there. Dalton? *Whup-whup-whup.* The pull-start again, followed by the chugging and whining of a Briggs and Stratton 3.5 horsepower mower engine sputtering to life. Sure Dalton didn't have as much as a high school education but he knew better than to run gas engines indoors without ventilation. The basement overhead door wasn't open, he'd seen that on the way in.

Jim dropped his screwdriver and hurried toward the basement stairs.

Chapter 16

VOICES UPSTAIRS. MCCHASNEY, UNMISTAKABLE, though older now, more frail, a bit of a waver in the voice. Someone else, that gravelly voice, that just had to be Dalton. So he was right, Dalton was still here. Shit, they'd both have to be close to ancient now. He crouched behind the furnace. If Dalton came down, he'd have to kill him quickly and quietly. He'd liked Dalton and didn't want to have to do that.

After a few minutes Dalton left. The killer could hear him start up his truck and crunch out of the drive and onto the highway. A couple of minutes later he heard flushing sounds from the toilet room. Toilet room. That was another thing that pissed him off. When would these rich assholes put in a real employee restroom for the crew? Not like they didn't have the money, tightwad motherfuckers. Twenty years later they still didn't have a proper employee restroom, forcing workers to perform their private functions where anyone could walk by and see and hear. The rich were always sticking it to the working man. Treated them like slaves, then threw them away when the work was done.

He took a deep breath, count of four, held it, then let it out. It was time.

He picked the Brush Monster up off its rack, then set it on the ground. He released the blade clutch, clipped the black wire to the silver-tipped electrode of the spark plug, set the choke, then gave the pull-cord a good quick rip. The Briggs and Stratton gave out a hearty *Whup-whup-whup-whup!* C'mon baby, Jimbo had to have heard that. He pushed the choke in a quarter inch, then pulled the cord again. *Whup-whup-whup*, then the satisfying rumble of the ancient four cycle machine as it sputtered to life. *Good work Dalton my man, only you could keep this old shit running forever.* The basement shop filled with white smoke as the machine burned off a film of engine oil, and he suppressed a cough. McChasney had to have heard the engine starting. He'd be on his way, hoping to tear someone a new asshole, no doubt. He pushed the choke all the way back in, then lifted the bulky machine up and strapped it on. He took several steps backward along and then underneath the creaky wooden staircase. He engaged the blade clutch. The thin metallic whine of the ten-inch blade sliced through the air, forming a ghostly lethal disc, reaching full speed within seconds. With no blade guard, he'd have to be careful not to hurt himself with it.

McChasney--well ol Jimbo was another matter.

Chapter 17

JIM HIT THE STAIRS running. He'd thrown open the basement door out of habit. In the summertime the door was always jammed from the humidity, but here in the dry of winter, it flung open and clattered angrily against the wall of the barn. Contacting the wall, it had sprung back so that it slapped Jim on the back and nearly pitched him hands first down the stairs, but he hung tight to the wooden handrail and bolted down the stairs two steps at a time, a skill which those under six foot three can only marvel at.

When the killer saw that Jim was on the stairs and moving fast, he took three steps out from under and then alongside the staircase, twirling as he did so. In a great underhand swinging motion, he swept the whickering brush monster blade up and hooked it back. The blade shattered the handrail in an explosion of pencil-sized splinters of ancient wood. Many of the splinters would later be found embedded three inches into the ceiling, and a small one pierced the killer's thigh, though he wouldn't notice it until later.

The blade continued in its deadly arc, not even slowed by its contact with the handrail and the boney morsel of human flesh that was once Jim McChasney's hand. It pulverized the hand, sending bone fragments and blood flying out to catch the splinters that it had just ejected. Scaphoid, lunate, triquetrium, pisiform, trapezium, trapezoid, capitate, and hamulus. Eight carpals, metacarpals one through five, and fourteen phalanges (proximal, middle, and distal), all fragmented and embedded in the ceiling for some lucky homicide detective to have cold-sweat nightmares over for the next five years. No piece of that hand larger than a pencil eraser was later found.

A fifth of a second after the rail and hand were shattered, before Jim had even any idea what was happening, let alone time to formulate an escape, the blade completed its arc and sliced deep into his chest. The ping of brass shirt buttons ricocheting off the ceiling and walls rang out over the drone of the engine.

Now the blade slowed briefly as the motor bogged. It wasn't designed to power the blade through sternum, thick slabs of muscle, and organ meat. The engine drone dropped in pitch and the killer instinctively gunned it with a flick of his thumb, pushing the throttle lever further out. At the same time he forced the blade deeper into his victim, flexing his muscles and throwing his weight into it, leveraging the motor block with his shoulder blade, pulling the strap tight against his back, yanking down on the control yoke, and muscling the blade down and deeper into Jim's chest.

Jim McChasney shook violently under the assault and collapsed backward onto the stairs. His feet hooked the stairs and his legs folded under him, powerless to lift, to run, to escape. The entire front of his chest was gone, in its place a tornado of blood, lungs, heart, blade, shirt, and bone. Jim's face and hair and the stairs and wall behind and above him were covered in a fine red spray.

He made no sound. There was no time to make a sound, and even had there been time, he had no lungs with which to expel a breath. He never had any idea what hit him. Even if Jim had gotten a good look at his attacker, and even if he'd had time to recognize him (in all his years with the change of crews he'd supervised about two hundred seasonal workers) he'd never have been able to place the face, now twenty years older, bearded, and consumed with rage. And even if he had time to know the name and remember the details of the last day he saw his attacker, he still could not have understood the rage that consumed this man now twenty years later.

When the blade started kicking up bloody splinters, some of which pierced him on the face, the killer cut the throttle and disengaged the blade clutch. The blade sailed cleanly back up and out of the body, before whickering to a stop. He pressed the kill switch and the engine stilled.

How long had he been forcing the spinning blade down deeper into the chest of the corpse, he didn't know. Forensic examination of the crime scene in the next few days would reveal that the blade had penetrated the stairs to a depth of four inches, and had been moved back and forth, so that the entire middle third of the eleventh step down from the top had been completely chewed up by the blade. He listened in the deafening silence. No sound, no motors approaching. No footsteps. No one had heard. It was still early after all, and most people were still sleeping. The basement was underground, wrapped in ancient cinderblocks, and that had dampened the noise as well.

He set the Brush Monster on the floor next to the staircase. He began to clean up. He still had a long list ahead of him, and he would be damned if he'd be caught on the second one, when there were so many more deserving fuckheads left to take care of.

He was soaked in blood and flecked with bits of meat. He stripped out of his clothes and pulled the handle on the emergency shower. The mechanics down here worked on fertilizer and pesticide sprayers as well as hydraulics and small engines, and OSHA had made the club install a safety shower as protection in case of accidental exposure to the chemicals. The shower had never been used until now.

This was, after all, an emergency.

He carefully pulled the splinters from his thigh and face, working the cold water into the wounds. Must not allow an infection to interfere with the plan. He dried off with some of the shop towels. He pulled on a fresh set of clothes from his backpack and tossed his bloody clothes into the furnace, which eagerly consumed them. He grabbed a five-gallon tin of hydraulic oil from the solvent cabinet at the back of the shop. There were flammable agents in that cabinet. It would be so easy to just torch the place, but that, he knew, was the mark of stupidity. Arson was one of the easiest crimes to solve. Besides, a big fire made a lot of authorities show up very quickly, especially in the winter, and he needed lots of time to slip away quietly.

He carefully checked behind the furnace and gathered his few personal items, stuffing them into his backpack, which he hefted onto his shoulders. He located a two-gallon metal spray canister, the kind used to apply pesticides and fertilizer, which was sitting empty next to the solvent cabinet. He poured a couple of gallons of the hydraulic oil into the sprayer, and tightened the lid. He pumped the handle to pressurize the canister. He knew that he'd spent too much time down here to be able to retrace his steps and get all the fingerprints off everything he'd touched.

He knew that fingerprints form when oils from the skin are left on surfaces. The police use various methods to get the oil pattern to show up. Spray the area with oil, and the police can't tell which oil came from your fingers and which came from your sprayer, or so he hoped. The killer spent about five minutes carefully working his way out of the basement. He started at the solvent cabinet, sprayed the handles, sprayed the doors. He sprayed the floor, and the workbench, and his jar. He couldn't bring the jar with him, it'd weigh him down. He sprayed his entire bed area, after pulling the wadded towels off the concrete behind the furnace. He sprayed the pile of towels, then the furnace exterior. He wiped down then sprayed the Brush Monster carefully. Finally he worked his way to the base of the stairs, where he sprayed what remained of the handrail, and the walls on the way up. He sprayed the body too, and as he ascended each step, he sprayed the one he'd just left. By the time he'd gotten to the top, the basement glistened with hydraulic oil. His shoes had hydraulic oil on the soles, and he left identifiable footprints as he backed out. He sprayed these as well, until the oil had worn off his soles and they became covered in dust from the floor, which only took about ten feet of back-stepping. At that point he withdrew a paper towel from a folded stack of towels in his backpack, and wiped oil over all surfaces of the sprayer. He left the sprayer and the oily paper towel in the middle of the floor.

He walked from the basement entrance at the back of the barn diagonally across to the man-door by the office. He peered out through the dirty glass, saw that no one was parked there. He went into the office, where he found a dirty old army surplus field jacket, probably one of Dalton's that he wore for working around the place. The one he'd worn in hadn't been beefy enough to handle the winter storm. He stuffed the old one in his backpack. He wanted to ditch the extra weight, but he mustn't leave behind any clues.

He hadn't seen the outside world in a day. He noticed, just barely from his vantage point in the office, that the highway had been freshly plowed. He could get away on foot if necessary, without leaving a telltale trail of footprints. He must be careful to cover his tracks in this snow.

It was a long way to Chicago, and it was going to be one cold fucking ride.

Chapter 18

Saturday, March 1

THE CLOCK FLASHED 2:32 AM in red electronic numerals. Kurt had gone to bed more than an hour ago, but sleep was nowhere coming. The date was over hours ago but he still felt Judi's warmth. She wouldn't let him go. He couldn't think of anything else. His mind raced. He kept going back to that kiss, those eyes that demagnetized his brain. Back to that kiss, back to those eyes. He had to have her. *This isn't working. I'll never get to sleep thinking about her.*

He slid out of bed, grabbed his robe, and padded his way barefoot into the second bedroom office. He jiggled the mouse to wake up the screen saver, then logged on to the cache-finders.com website, and began tapping the keyboard. Anything to take his mind off her. Her lips, her kiss, her eyes.

Stop.

He thought about the dog those cachers found on the St. Edward's cache, maybe he'd see if he could read about that.

At the SEARCH PHRASE prompt, he typed "St. Edwards."

The computer came back with a single result:

1) The Original St. Edwards Cache - Austin TX - Last Found - 2 days ago

He clicked up the cache description page and read the comment that the Kragers had posted about finding the dead dog. It was a pretty rare occurrence to find a dead animal near a cache. He was worried that Judi would think there were dead dogs scattered all over the sport. He wanted her to like geocaching, not be afraid of it. He thought about how she'd be fun to go caching with, hiking behind her, watching her ass stretching those tight jeans. Maybe they'd steal a kiss or two out in the forest, maybe go on a camping/caching trip out to Colorado Bend. Maybe make love for hours out under the stars or in the back of his Expedition *--Oh great. Got to concentrate.*

Just for grins, I wonder how many other cachers have found dead dogs out there?

He hit NEW to clear the search page.

SEARCH PHRASE: "dead dog"

Kurt's jaw dropped. He rubbed his eyes. There were almost two dozen hits in the search results. He began working down the list. He eliminated about ten that were just colloquialisms written by finders who were "tired as a dead dog," one semi-literate couple who meant to write "beating a dead horse" but wrote "beating a dead dog" by mistake, that sort of thing. About ten were reports of people who found dead dogs on or near caches. This was interesting. He found the comment that Martello had written out in California, some park called Mt. Tam. Looked like a fun cache (except for the dead dog on it). That one also had Martello's account of finding the jar of urine. Kurt found a comment describing some cachers who found a dead dog in a parking lot in Cheyenne, Wyoming, apparently a stray who had died of starvation. There were cache comments about dead dogs in Pennsylvania, Chicago, and New York, as well as Florida, South Dakota, another two in California, and Maine.

He was as awake now as when he began. He worked down the list, reading each comment. Most were strays or accidents, where the carcass happened to be discovered on or near a cache site. Not surprising, when you consider that in some areas there is a cache every five hundred feet.

He got halfway into the Chicago comment when he saw the phrase "jar of piss." What the hell? A coincidence? He saved off the original search results list, then refined the search, using every synonym he could think of for urine.

This resulted in a shorter list, refined down from the original list. Now his list included the original Mt. Tam post, plus the

Chicago post. When he re-read the Mt. Tam post, he noticed that there was some kind of police action at the nearby ranger station involving crime scene tape. *What the hell is up with that?* he thought. They wouldn't put up crime scene tape for a dead dog. A murder? Robbery? Who the hell'd rob a ranger station? Wouldn't be anything in there valuable enough to make it worth driving all the way out to the sticks. He saved the search results list.

He opened up a new search window, on an internet search engine outside of the cache finders website. This search engine could search cache-finders.com, as well as other websites including the news media. He ran a search for pages containing the words *murder, police, killing, death, body, dead dog.* This returned about two hundred thousand hits, including a fair number of Grateful Dead fan sites. *Don't even want to know about that*, he thought. He was going to be up for awhile.

He paged through the list of hits. There were way too many to read them all, so he just scanned page titles, mostly because it was late and his mind was starting to fade. He came across this item on the third page of results: VALLEY MAN MURDERED WITH BRUSH TRIMMER. Someone was murdered with a weed whacker? Holy shit. Sounds like a tabloid, gotta check that out. He clicked on the link and was immediately asked to register online with the Pittsburgh Post Gazette before they'd show him the article, which was in their archives from last December. He backed up to the search list. He wondered why he had to register (even if it was free) just to read the paper. They'd probably sell his email address to a spam marketer. No thanks.

He added the synonyms for urine to the search phrase, and this cut the number of hits down to only forty thousand. He added the term *cache* and cut the number down to just under three thousand. Still, he was going to be here for a while. The tingling in his lips had subsided. He was on to something here, and it had completely wiped Judi from his mind for the time being. Was someone killing dogs and leaving bottles of urine behind? Was this dog killer also killing people, as the Mt. Tam comment seemed to hint?

He found a page describing a murder in Schaumburg Illinois, on a Motorola corporate newsletter website. He compared this against the comment for the cache from Illinois and found that they were for the same day, the same place. A dead dog, a murder, a bottle of urine, near (or on) a geocache.

What the hell was going on?

Part II
Second to Find

Chapter 19

www.cache-finders.com Geocache Listing

Back to Nature! - Normal Sized Cache
by MotorHed [email this user]
Illinois, USA

[click to download geographic coordinates and hints]

A fine little hike in the Spring Valley Nature Preserve in Schaumburg. An oasis of nature in the middle of the big city. Cache is a clear Tupperware container with a blue lid. Initial contents: a whole bunch of cheap trinkets i bought at the mall next door, and some Motorola pens & badge retractors.

Cache Visitor Comments:
(78 comments total)

[click to see previous comments]

[77] January 17 by RebelJamesDeen [218 caches found]
Jesus Christ there are some SICK individuals in this world. I brought my

family to this place expecting a nice wholesome walk in the park. My kid literally puked when we left the trail and got within 400 feet of the cache. I don't know what the f*** is going on, but there was a dead dog, and blood everywhere! Needless to say, we didn't find the cache, because after Taylor barfed all over his new boots we turned tail and got the hell out of there. We stopped at the rest room on the way out to clean Taylor up a bit. The restrooms were locked but the lock was broken off one, and inside we found signs that the homeless were living there, including (we didn't get close enough to verify this) a jar of piss! It almost makes me retch to write this. I called 911 on my cell. They said they'd send someone out to investigate. Yeah right like I believe that's gonna freaking happen. Probably should unlist this cache until someone cleans up that god-awful mess. I think poor Taylor's probably searched for his last cache, and I know it will be some time before I go out in the woods again.

[email this user]

[78] January 18 by IL_Admin [1048 caches found]

THIS CACHE HAS BEEN TAKEN OFFLINE UNTIL FURTHER NOTICE. Can the cache owner please go out there and check on this in a few weeks to make sure it's been cleaned up by the authorities? Then just email IL_Admin and I'll re-list the cache. Geez, be careful out there folks!

[email this user]

Did you Find the Cache? Add your own
comment! [click here]

Chapter 20

Spring Valley Nature Preserve - Schaumburg, Illinois
Wednesday, January 15

THE TRIP FROM PITTSBURGH had taken far too long. The biggest problem with hopping a freight was that you never really knew where you were going to end up. Sure the train might look like it was headed west, but you could end up north, south, or east without realizing it. And that's just what had happened. He'd been sleeping for a couple hours when he realized the train had taken him north toward Erie instead of west toward Chicago. He'd hopped off the slow moving train near Sharon, Pennsylvania. Damn near busted his knee in the fall. He'd hiked through that town toward Youngstown, Ohio, then boarded what he hoped was a westbound train there. He suffered through two or three more detours, including a lengthy stop somewhere in the middle of rural Ohio for several days, during which he was certain he was either going to freeze to death or get thrown off the train. He'd finally made it to Chicago. Considering that it took him nearly a week to travel what should have been a twelve-hour drive, it might have been faster to walk.

He'd spent the last week completing his research on his next victim. He was beginning to relish each murder. He had expected to feel some satisfaction at dealing a long-deserved vengeance to these pricks, but he hadn't expected to *enjoy* it so much. Maybe he'd missed his life's calling. He'd never before considered making a career of crime. Perhaps a genius *can* make a living at this. Evade the police indefinitely; kill at will. He'd have to consider expanding his list. But for now, there was the plan; there was Zinny. Mister Corporate Human Resources Executive Kiss-Ass Zinny Chorzempa. The killer had plenty of time on the ride over to complete his plan. Plenty of time to relive the injustice, to dwell on it, to pick the scab, let it fester, let it ooze until his rage was unbearable.

Zinny was too easy to find. He had a set routine every weekday. Each day after work, he'd take his dog for a walk in the Spring Valley Nature Center. The route varied slightly, but always started and ended at the same trailhead.

The killer would have to get the dog first. That was the easy part. He'd picked up some rat poison from one of those industrial size plastic outdoor rodent baits they had deployed behind the switch house in Youngstown. He'd spent ten minutes carefully extracting the poison from the inside of the trap.

It was a cake like a urinal cake. The label on the bottom of the bait said it was composed of a fast-acting neurotoxin mixed with Warfarin, a powerful blood thinning agent. The neurotoxin paralyzed the rat, then the Warfarin killed by simultaneously thinning the blood and eating a hole in the stomach. Like an ulcer from hell. The animal would nibble a bit of the flavored bait, then it would drop. Wherever it fell, it would bleed to death internally. Eat a little; bleed a little. Eat a lot; bleed a lot.

He'd picked up a refrigerated shrink-wrap microwave hamburger at the local Circle-K. It couldn't have been very good, because it'd cost him only a buck eighty-nine, but he was pretty sure the dog wouldn't give a shit. He hoped that the biology of a dog was similar enough to that of a rodent for the poison to work. He was an engineer, not a biologist, but he was pretty sure that it would work. A human could eat warfarin in small doses. It was used as medicine for people with blood clots or stroke. But it had to be carefully monitored. Even relatively minor accidents could bleed you out faster than a sleepy teenager in a Freddy Kruger movie.

Most of the poison cake fit into the center of the burger. The rest he kept in a baggie in his pocket. Who could say? He might need it later.

He sheltered in the women's room at the preserve. It was a concrete structure, shut down for the season, with doors padlocked. It sat on an out-of-the-way parking area that had been gated off for the season, so there weren't even any hikers around. The city shut the water off months ago, but that was not a problem. In Chicago in January, Mother Nature provided all the water you needed. He'd been drinking melted snow. He'd even shaved in it. Piled it in the stainless steel sink, then let it melt, then trimmed up the beard, so that he didn't have that homeless look. The padlock had been easy. The lock was rusted and a couple whacks with a rock had busted it clean off. People were stupid sometimes. Well most of the time. They'd spend the bucks to bolt the best burglarproof hasp onto a thick steel door, but then hang on a flimsy old two-dollar lock.

As he was scouting the area around the shelter, an empty plastic drink bottle at the bottom of the trashcan outside the restroom caught his eye. He had to pry it up off the frost at the bottom of the can. From its mouth jutted a pad of blue ice. He'd stopped worrying about cleaning the bottles. There wasn't time anymore.

Glancing side-to-side to see if there were any witnesses, he tucked the bottle in his coat and slipped inside. He latched the door. He quickly unzipped. He emptied his bladder, filling the steaming bottle halfway. He wanted to run, run anywhere. He had to get out. He felt dizzy. The room lurched. He felt trapped. Confined. His hands shook. He dropped the bottle. He scrambled to his knees to snatch it up before it emptied. Bracing himself with a firm grip on the sink, he knew had to suppress the urge to run or it would make him do something stupid. That thought itself, of the panic, of it causing him to do something dumb, frightened him even more, which in turn amplified the panic. He whimpered; tears clouded his vision. His breath thickened. His heart pounded. Cold sweat broke out on his forehead and the room began to twist and swirl and warp, like a funhouse mirror. Nothing made sense. He couldn't think. The walls closed in. Squeezed him. He pawed at the door latch with one hand. His chest hurt. He had to get out.

Get out!

He squeezed the bottle and jammed it to his lips.

The killer was drinking his own urine as often as twice a day now. Each time, the calming effect didn't last as long as it did the time before. Each time, the far-away look, the catatonic state lasted longer. Afterward he cradled the warm bottle longer. Leaving the bottle behind was hard. He was compelled to store them, collect them, treasure them, keep them safe. He didn't understand or even try. He only knew that it must be so.

Chapter 21

5:37 P.M.

ZINNY OPENED THE DOOR of his minivan and let the dog out. The day had been a tough one, but as usual, he'd gotten kicked out of the office by five.

Barkley took off running, also as usual. The city had a leash ordinance, but neither Zinny nor Barkley paid it any mind. Barkley was a friendly dog, but spent most of his time running through the forest. For every mile Zinny walked, Barkley probably covered ten. Zinny pushed the clicker on the van, and the double-chirp and flash confirmed that it was locked and armed. Schaumburg was generally a safe place but Zinny didn't take any chances. He walked, heading for the path into the woods. It was paved in concrete for the first few hundred yards, and then degraded to gravel. There had been enough foot traffic today to mush the snow down pretty well in most places, and the footing was good. The sun had just set, but the sky was clear and a deep azure arced overhead. Zinny liked this time of day best. Twilight.

Zinny was forty-seven, going on forty-eight. His doctor had prescribed a daily regimen of drugs after his heart attack last year. He hadn't been a candidate for bypass surgery. Instead the doctor had decided to go with an arterial stent. Zinny was still taking the medicine, probably would have to take it for the rest of his life. It helped keep the blockages from forming in his other arteries. But the best prescription the doctor could have made was the daily exercise regimen. At least one hour a day of walking or cycling. Zinny wasn't a cyclist, just couldn't see himself wearing those tight black lycra shorts and fluorescent jerseys, so he walked. And so far, in a year, he'd seen a noticeable improvement in his health. He had more energy, he felt alive for the first time in how long? He couldn't remember. At least since his twenties.

The doctor had also prescribed stress reduction. That meant no more working late or weekends. That had been the hardest to give up, but his boss the Vice President had been understanding, having gone through his own heart troubles a few years before. He mandated that Zinny knock off no later than five P.M. each day, then sicced Zinny's secretary on him to enforce the ruling.

After about ten minutes of walking, Zinny noticed that Barkley was gone. "Barkley, here boy," called Zinny, his breath billowing clouds that wafted in front of his face. He whistled, but the dog didn't respond. He heard the faint roar of traffic along the boulevard north of the mall, filtered through the trees and snow. He heard the rushing of the creek a few hundred feet off to the left. He heard his own breathing, and he could feel his heart beat under his heavy wool coat. Only the tell-tale crashing of Barkley through the ice-crusted brush was missing. He retraced his steps, trying to see where Barkley had gotten off the path.

The dog followed the trail of burger-bun crumbs just as the killer had planned. The dog ran right up to him, and when he saw the treat held for him, he tried to jump up on the killer to get it. The mark of a poorly trained dog. The killer jerked his knee up hard into the dog's ribs, sending him sprawling backward into the snow and mud. The dog got back up though, and cautiously approached this time, head held sideways, eyes averted, hoping to get some of the treat.

"There, there big fella, how would you like this tasty morsel?" the killer said, and then he tossed the sandwich toward the dog. The dog snatched it out of mid-air and the cheap burger was gone in two or three gulps, beef patty, stale pickles, bun, neurotoxin, warfarin and all.

He watched the dog for a few minutes. It didn't take long. After sniffing around for more burger, the dog ran off to sniff a tree, marked it, sniffed a few more trees, marked them, came back to sniff the killer's hands, see if he had more treats, circled three times in the snow, whimpered, and then lay down on its side, convulsing and panting heavily. It slavered yellow foam. The foam turned a deep reddish-orange as the dog bled out through its mouth.

After about five minutes, the killer gave the dog a swift kick in the belly. The dog twitched, blurted out a long rattling fart, but didn't even look up. His eyes were open but no one was home. Barkley had chased his last rabbit.

The killer walked a few paces back into the woods. He ducked down behind a snow-covered deadfall and waited.

He heard whistling off toward the path. Zinny had tracked poor Barkley back to the point where the dog had left the trail. He'd be here in a couple minutes.

The killer could wait.

Chapter 22

Motorola Schaumburg Division Newsletter,
January 20, Page 7

In Memoriam: Dziennik Martyn "Zinny" Chorzempa.

Dziennik M. Chorzempa, work/life balance manager at corporate HR, will be remembered as a man of humor, a loving father and devoted company man of 24 years service. "Zinny," as he was affectionately known to his co-workers, started his career at Motorola in the Arlington Heights office in the late 70's, where he was instrumental in molding the company culture and implementing new corporate diversity programs. The changes he made during his 24 years have spread throughout the company. Though his legacy continues, he will be missed.

Chorzempa was brutally murdered Wednesday while walking his dog in the Spring Valley Nature Center. Police are still investigating the murder, and at the time of this writing had no leads. Motorola Corporate has offered a $5,000 reward for information leading to the arrest and conviction of the murderer.

"Motorola is deeply saddened by the death of Mr. Chorzempa," said Dick Mathers,

General Manager of the Schaumburg facility in a statement. "The employees of Motorola were always Zinny's number one priority, and in this time of mourning, we encourage them to seek solace and counseling. Zinny's family, friends and coworkers, both here at the Schaumburg facility, and worldwide, will be in our thoughts."

"Anytime we lose a member of the Motorola family, it is upsetting, and it pulls us together, makes us a stronger family," said Lynn Huffman, assistant vice president of human resources. Huffman also said counselors will be available in the cafeteria Monday for employees who needed to talk.

Employees are reminded that mischarging is illegal. Time must be charged against sick/personal time codes for all hours spent in counseling sessions.

Chorzempa is survived by his widow Millie and their three children, all of Arlington Heights.

Chapter 23

"ALTURUS INDUSTRIES INCORPORATED, HOW may I direct your call?" droned the receptionist, a fat bald man with a terminal case of comb-over. Company policy required a pronunciation of Al'-too-rus, but he slurred it to something like "Al'-trush." He was a security guard dammit, not a receptionist, yet receptionist is what he did, wearing a security guard uniform. He had a badge, but no gun. He'd have to find some time to look for another gig. In this economy, at his age, you took whatever job you could get, and that nagging bitch called pride, you slapped her around, showed her who was boss, shoved her in a corner, and never let her get in the way. Not if you wanted to eat. Pride couldn't cook.

Kurt tried to get out of the house once a week for what he wrote off on his 1040 Form Schedule A as business networking and job search expense, but which was really just lunch with his buddies. Who knew, maybe someday it might lead to a job. Besides, as Kurt's dad always said, if you've never been audited by the IRS, you're paying too much.

Today it was just Kurt and Jason, but sometimes there'd be a couple other guys from the office tagging along. They'd usually pick up a cache nearby if there were any. Today there hadn't been any within five miles, so they had gone straight to lunch.

They'd eaten at a little Korean-owned sandwich shop in the strip mall out by the interstate. You stood in line and watched them build your sandwich while you waited. The cook, actually the owner's wife, weighed out the exact quantity of lunchmeat on a scale before slapping the sandwich together. Real low budget operation; they didn't even have any music playing to help with the ambiance, but the food wasn't bad, and it had the location that brought in hungry software engineers from all the software mills within three miles.

Kurt told Jason about his date with Judi. He mentioned that he couldn't sleep after the date so he kicked off a search for the Krager dog online, and then later found the other dead dogs and urine bottles scattered all over the country. Jason was intrigued, and he volunteered to help Kurt continue the search back at his office after lunch.

Kurt followed Jason around the guard's desk. They walked past a block of empty glass-walled conference rooms into a cubicle farm of biblical proportions. The building used to be an industrial warehouse. The corporation had leased it and outfitted it as an office building for as little outlay as they could get away with. The ceilings were still the original corrugated metal, three stories high. Metal lattice and exposed galvanized ductwork crisscrossed the open space above, while high-intensity discharge lamps blared a harsh light down on the workers below. The tiny cubicles were cheap pressed metal and grey cloth, badly in need of refurbishing. Metal grid tracks hanging overhead carried bundles of black networking cable and power to and from distribution points.

Jason settled into his cubicle near the back of the farm, and tapped the keyboard. From the adjacent cubicle, and from cubicles somewhat further off, they could hear explosions, gunfire, laughter, and the occasional shriek, over constant frenetic keyboard tapping.

"Another LAN party?" asked Kurt.

"Yep," said Jason. "When the cat's away..."

Kurt wondered how this company stayed in business. He'd been here a dozen times. Each time he ran a mental tally. At least seventy-five percent of the employees were goofing off at any given time. Gaming, internet surfing, socializing, you name it, these guys had slacking down to an art. Someone could write a book about all the techniques these guys used to avoid work.

"Yeah, those guys have a network party just about every day," explained Jason. "Some of them play eight, ten hours a day, if the game's hot. You want to try the search or should I?"

"You go ahead, it's your machine," said Kurt.

"OK let's call up what you did the other night and start from there," he said, with a burst of key tapping.

Jason pulled up Kurt's previous search. He clicked through on the Post-Gazette article. He registered under a bogus name, and then displayed the full article in a new window:

Pittsburgh Post-Gazette, December 27 - Page B3

VALLEY MAN MURDERED WITH BRUSH TRIMMER

HARRISON VALLEY (AP) - In a scene uncharacteristically grisly and violent for this small community, a local man was murdered Thursday morning at the Harrison Valley Country Club. Police report that the victim, James Albert McChasney, 65, of Harrison Valley was attacked by an unknown assailant with a brush trimmer. McChasney was the head greenskeeper at the country club.

Sources close to the investigation say that McChasney was working in the maintenance barn the morning after Christmas, finishing up some work on a plumbing leak. His badly mutilated body was found in the basement stairway of the maintenance barn, a shop area where mowers and engines are repaired.

Police have no leads in the case. Anyone with information about the murder is requested to please contact the Harrison Valley Police Department. The Harrison

Valley Country Club has posted a $75,000 reward for information leading to the arrest and/or conviction of the murderer.

According to the assistant greenskeeper, a Mr. Terry Zupansky, 43, of Murrysville, the brush trimmer that was used in the attack was a "Brush Monster" brand, an industrial strength variety not available to the general public. The Brush Monster is so bulky that the operator has to strap it on using a thick leather strap.

The trimmer used in the attack had had the protective blade guard removed. Zupansky said that this was commonly done to allow a tool to do its job better. Zupansky said that the "Monster" requires a strong operator, someone who works out. "We only got three guys on the crew what can even lift it," he said. Police stressed that Zupansky, in line to succeed McChasney as head greenskeeper upon McChasney's retirement, was at his grandmother's house in Murrysville during the time of the attack and is not considered a suspect in the investigation.

Billy D. "Dalton" Whorter, foreman of the day crew, stated that McChasney was "a very well liked man, a very fair man. He was the best greenskeeper we ever had."

The Post-Gazette has discovered that the day before the murder, police responded to the maintenance barn at McChasney's request, in a matter involving his dog "Wolfie," which was found dead on the road running through the golf course. Police have stated that the two events are unrelated.

McChasney, who was slated to retire January 4th, is survived by his spouse Adele, 63, three adult children, and nine grandchildren.

"Jeez that's messed up," said Jason.

"Holy shit, a fucking weed whacker?" said Kurt.

"You see that seventy-five K reward? Man those rich country club dudes must be really hacked off," said Jason.

"Shit, what I could do with seventy-five K right about now," said Kurt.

"There's still a lot of information in these other searches. Let's see what we have," Jason said, "Okay I think --let's try to clean this up a bit." Jason applied various filters to the search results, then after some more tapping had distilled it down to a handful of entries. He rose, turned to his markerboard, erased a big swath out of the middle of some software design diagrams with the heel of his hand, wiped the hand on his pants and then quickly drew a table. "Okay so here's what we have so far, based on your search." In a clumsy block print, he wrote the following:

DATE	PLACE	PEE	DOG	BODY
12-15	MT. TAMALPAIS	Y	Y	?
12-26	HARRISON VALLEY	N	Y	Y
01-15	SCHAUMBURG	Y	Y	Y
02-27	AUSTIN / ST EDS PARK	N	Y	N
02-17	AUSTIN / CITY PARK	N	Y	N

"That look about right?" asked Jason.

"Yeah, that's good. I like the chart. Lets you see what's missing." said Kurt.

"So it looks like we have two confirmed dead bodies, possibly a third. I haven't heard of any murders in Austin recently, have you?" said Jason.

"No," said Kurt.

"--and the Kragers said that the dog was just buried by its owners, so no foul play there. So then we also have four dead dogs and two bottles of urine. Let's see if we can find any bodies with that Mt. Tam cache," said Jason. He keyed in a new search, looking for any news reports concerning a murder at Mt. Tam. Nothing. It could have been too long, or maybe it hadn't been newsworthy, or maybe the local paper in the area wasn't publishing its stories online. Or maybe there was no murder. "How 'bout we call Martello," Jason said.

"You got his number?" asked Kurt.

"I'll check his profile on the caching website," said Jason, opening a new window and tapping some more. "There's his cell number, grab my desk phone there and punch it up."

Kurt punched up the number. He heard three shrill ascending tones and a female voice saying, *We're sorry, you must first dial a one, then the area code and number. Please check the number and try your call again.* Kurt sighed, punched the switchhook, and then redialed the number, prefacing it with a one this time.

Holding a hand over the mouthpiece while the call clicked through, he said, "How long have phone networks been digital? You'd think if they had enough intelligence in their system to bring up a recording to tell me I need to dial a one first, that they'd have the capability to just insert a one in front of what I dialed, then patch it through without pissing me off by making me dial the whole freakin number aga--."

"Yo," interrupted the voice on the phone.

"Hello, Martello?" said Kurt.

"Yeah. Who's this?" asked Martello.

"It's Kurt Denzer and I've uh, got Jason Heckmann here too, a couple cachers you met in Austin last month," said Kurt.

"Sure, what can I do for you two?" said Martello.

"We're calling about that dog you found up on Mt. Tam last winter," said Kurt.

"Well, it's still winter here, but what about it?" laughed Martello.

"Sorry about that, it's spring here already," said Kurt, "We're curious about the police tape around the ranger station. Did you ever hear anything more about what was up with that?"

"No, I haven't, but I can call the folks I was staying with, they go up there all the time, maybe they know something more. Why?" said Martello.

"Just curious, we found some strange goings on with some caches, and we're just gathering data, looking for a pattern" said Kurt.

"Tell him we're looking for a body," whispered Jason.

"Jason says to tell you we're looking for a body," said Kurt.

"No shit? Okay, let me see what I can find out. I'll call you when I hear anything," said Martello.

"Thanks man," said Kurt. He put the receiver back on its cradle and pushed the phone back into the corner of the desk. Jason kept his desk neater than most engineers. You could actually see most of the surface.

"Okay, so there's no bottle of urine in the Pennsylvania murder, but we have a dead dog. Looks like the dog may be an accident though," said Jason.

"Seems kind of fishy, like too coincidental, you think?" said Kurt.

"Maybe. We can do a search on that and see what we find," Jason said, opening up a new search page. After paring it down a bit more, the search returned no hits. Dead end. Still the lure of the seventy-five thousand dollar reward kept that murder on the top of Kurt's list.

"Hey Jason, get in here, the Swedes just came online and we're getting our asses kicked," said one of the slackers, popping his head up over the cube wall.

"Duty calls," said Jason, shrugging.

"Catch you later," said Kurt, "Have fun." *What a bunch of slackers,* he thought.

Chapter 24

Alamogordo, New Mexico
February 10

THE KILLER CROSSED THREE NAMES off his list, Ricky Nelson, Jimbo McChasney, and that polock Zinny Chorzempa. There were more names, but he'd needed a break, needed to get some clean clothes, take a real bath. He'd also needed to do more research on a few of the other names on his list. With the break, his anxiety, his panic attacks had subsided.

The freight out from Chicago had brought him straight to Alamogordo without incident, and in record time. The trains out west were more organized and easier to follow than that fucked up rat's nest they had back east.

Breaking with his previous pattern, he rented a hotel room out on the edge of town. He spent most of his time at the library. He knew all internet access was traceable. He'd been doing some very detailed research on his next victims, and public internet was critical to avoid a trace. He would only research one victim at any given internet access point. He could get free anonymous access at the library.

New Mexico. Snow capped mountains. Great gypsum deserts. Beautiful scenery, nice friendly people, and they even had their own special brand of Mexican food, except who the hell wanted a fried egg on top of their enchiladas?

It was a great place to add to your list.

Chapter 25

National Solar Observatory - Sunspot, New Mexico
February 14

RAMONA HAD SPENT THE evening in her quarters in the cramped Quonset hut down the hill from the Vacuum Tower Telescope. She'd been examining the images from the day's viewing and the atmospheric distortion was still as strong as ever, perhaps even more so than before she'd applied her newest algorithm. She'd gone over and over her code, checked each line against the design, and then checked the equations against her derivations. Second order partial differential equations, vector calculus, and lots of plain ordinary high school algebra. Ramona loved math. Math was her life. The computer stuff was unavoidable if you wanted to actually do anything useful with the math. She wasn't a computer geek, hated computer geeks in fact, but that was how she had to make her living.

Her quarters were spartan. A single bed, a single bulb in the ceiling fixture, cold yellowed linoleum floor, a small upholstered chair in the corner on which she had piled her parka and leggings, and a dorm-sized refrigerator filled with a variety of organic vegetable drinks in single-serve plastic bottles. Next to the doorway to the left, a small desk and chair. Through the doorway, a cramped bathroom and shower. No tub. She'd dispensed with the luxury of hot baths for a shot at developing some breakthrough mathematics that would leave her mark on the world of space science.

The work she did for Locklin was so secret, buried under the cloak of the black project, that she'd never gain any fame from it. Still, she had the satisfaction of knowing that any time there was a war, which was pretty much all the time, her work in computer adaptive optics was used daily to help missiles and other projectile weapons identify, track and destroy enemy combatants. And the bastards deserved it, if the images she saw on the TV were true. Dirty foreigners, yellow or brown skinned bastards, groveling in jungles or hiding between sand dunes, never bathing, never knowing personal hygiene, shitting and rutting outdoors like animals, not even having the decency to speak English. Unable to organize themselves into stable Christian democratic societies, they deserved their fate; they deserved to die. She was glad she could help the U.S. Government eradicate every goddamn last one of them.

Defense was her career, but Astronomy had always been her passion. It's what had led her to mathematics and finally to adaptive optics. The same technology that helped missiles and shells find their targets in Iraq, Syria, Korea, and a half-dozen other declared and undeclared wars, helped clean up the atmospheric distortion in telescope images. The atmosphere was the enemy of good astronomy. No matter how great a telescope you built, if you operated it from the surface of the earth, you had to look through sixty-odd miles of atmosphere, which was constantly in a state of flux, wrinkling and distorting your image. It's why stars twinkled, and why NASA had spent billions developing and servicing the Hubble Space Telescope, to get it out beyond our atmosphere so it could see clearly.

Now her algorithms would allow earth based telescopes to achieve more clarity than Hubble, by sensing and then filtering out the atmospheric distortion mathematically. This was her chance to shine. She'd be published. She'd be famous in the world of astronomy. Maybe they'd name a crater or an alien mountain range after her someday.

She'd taken the sabbatical after working at Locklin for fifteen years. Her supervisor was glad to give her the year off just to keep her from leaving for good. It was hard to find good optics experts in the defense industry lately. The pay wasn't so good as the commercial world, and many employees these days had moral issues around developing tools that would be used to kill lots of people, some of them innocent. Not Ramona.

The code checked out line for line against the design. *Shit.* She was hoping for a simple coding error. It was easy enough to do in that goddamned C language. Stupid language was designed by Unix geeks back in the sixties, designed to be so arcane and twisted that only Unix geeks could figure it out. Job security. Even after fifteen years, she wasn't a C expert. She kept a well-worn pocket sized C language reference book handy at all times. By two A.M. she had checked the design line-for-line against the base algorithms. That too checked out. Still, those distorted images stared at her up from her laptop screen, mocking her. It had to be something wrong with the laser sensor board she'd installed in the telescope. She was too tired to continue debugging the problem tonight, and besides, she'd need to view the sensor in the daytime to debug it.

The killer hid in the line of trees across the service road from Ramona's Quonset hut. She had her curtains pulled, but there was a crack. It was late. Most of the scientists here were asleep. Not Ramona. The killer crept up to the street, and carefully snuck across the powdery snow to the window. He put an eyeball up to the glass and peered in through the crack. Her lights were on. He could see her working at the computer. Her back was turned to him, and it was dark outside. She couldn't see him. He thought about busting in through the door and taking her now, but it would be too messy. There were a line of Quonset huts, and someone next door would hear the noise. No way to guarantee that she wouldn't scream.

She was the homeliest bitch he'd ever had the misfortune of working for. Face wrinkled from decades of cigarette smoking, long hooked nose, flyaway dishwater blonde hair that looked like it rarely met with comb or brush. A hairstyle unknown to fashion. Seeing her from behind, so vulnerable in her t-shirt and panties barely covering her wide ass, he couldn't wait.

She scooted back her chair and folded the lid of her computer shut. She was getting up from the desk. He twisted and scuttled back into the forest. He watched her silhouette move back and forth through her quarters, then switch off the light. He'd have to wait until tomorrow.

Chapter 26

THE DUNN SOLAR VACUUM Tower Telescope stood over a hundred thirty feet high. Its concrete cone stabbed straight up into space from the summit of Sacramento Peak like the nose cone of a mammoth nuclear missile. At the tip of the brilliant white cone, a narrow service walkway surrounded the central protrusion of the scope's bulbous window turret. The entrance window, a thirty-inch diameter quartz glass, covered two mirrors that could be swiveled remotely to track the sun as it moved across the sky. The huge cone itself didn't move; it was fixed to the ground, and indeed extended a couple hundred feet more underground. Light from the sun passed through a long vacuum chamber, further limiting the ability of the air to distort the image. At ground level inside the concrete structure lay a forty-foot circular control room packed with instruments, spectrographs, sensors, optical benches, observing tables, and enough networked computer firepower to keep an army of computer geeks safely out of the gene pool for years.

But this morning, there was no one in the control room. It was too early. Most of the scientists were still either finishing up with brunch in the mess hall, or attending an all-day seminar down at the nearby Apache observatory on the other side of the mountain. Not Ramona.

Ramona's laser sensor array was installed in the instrumentation chamber, in the dead center of the control room. The instrumentation chamber was about the size of a hotel elevator, but cylindrical and only half as tall. Its inner walls were mirrored with pure silver. It had a rack fitted near the top for placing sensors and filters directly into the path of the sunlight before the light continued on its way through the vacuum chamber two hundred twenty-one feet to the primary mirror below. The sunlight in the instrumentation chamber was the most intense of anywhere in the entire light path. The chamber had three separate latches on its heavy metal door, which was also silvered inside.

The entire vacuum chamber, all three hundred plus vertical feet of it, floated suspended in a pool containing ten tons of mercury. A technician could rotate the two hundred ton chamber with ease by hand if necessary.

She was the first one here, so she'd have to go through the whole telescope power-up procedure by herself. She pressed the main power button, and then listened for the filter wheels to stop grating as they rotated into position. The main telescope computers started their boot-up procedure. She could see across the room as the Unix terminals stepped through their startup scripts, dumping the results to their consoles in shades of amber and green on black. She opened the turret using the handbox controller, then patched in the correct azimuth and elevation coordinates for the sun. The sun wasn't up yet so the sun tracker pointed at the horizon, patiently waiting for the sun to rise. When the sun rose, the tracker would automatically lock onto the sun's image and center it. She re-checked the calibration, and then checked the level indicator to make sure there was enough coolant.

The coolant checked out okay, so she pulled a fresh mag tape out of the box next to the main processor, threaded it into the drive, pressed LOAD, and closed the drive cover as the tape reels spun out and back automatically to feed a few feet onto the take-up reel.

The power-on sequence completed, Ramona could now concentrate on her own work. She boarded the tiny elevator platform, and punched the UP switch. The elevator hoist gave a growl of protest, then pulled the platform upward toward the top of the cone. The rickety metal platform was open to the air, with only a waist-high metal railing between the passenger (only one person could ride the elevator at a time) and a spectacular fall to the control room floor below. The elevator was fixed to a track on the inside of the cone, and so as she rose, Ramona inched both upward and diagonally toward the top center of the cone.

She opened the hatch to the outside platform, stepped off the elevator, and carefully fixed a tiny reflective laser target to the center of the quartz window. She'd need this to calibrate the sensor below. The sun still hadn't risen but outside the sky was turning from dark blue to light blue. The weather had been mild the last few days, and they'd even watched much of the snow melt, but the pre-dawn air was still cold. There was no wind, which was fortunate since she hadn't expected to be up here long and she wasn't wearing a coat. She had to be careful not to frost the glass with her breath.

After she had fixed the target, she leaned out over the railing and watched the sky to the east. The dawn of her day. It was beautiful. She'd debug this little sensor glitch, then the world would know her name. Well, at least the world of astronomy.

Chapter 27

THE KILLER WOKE TO the beeping of his watch alarm. He'd been spending nights in the restroom at the observatory visitor center. It was actually heated at night, though he was prepared to bundle up in his parka if needed. That was a nice break. Getting access to the visitor center after hours had not been easy. He'd been prepared to break in, but he really wanted to avoid attracting attention. So he signed up for a tour on his first day on the mountain, cased the place without being obvious. He'd toured the compound, visited all the telescope and lab buildings, and watched all the geeks in their lab coats and parkas running around taking pictures of the sun. He couldn't imagine a more boring job. How many pictures of the sun did they need? The place was so remote that they just left everything unlocked most of the time. Except for the visitor center. There wasn't much to steal in the compound anyway, just a bunch of test equipment and lab stuff. Not much market for that. There were laptop computers everywhere, but a thief would have an easier time down in Alamogordo ripping off a liquor store or something. Sunspot was just too remote to bother with.

After about forty-five minutes, the tour guide had taken them into the Dunn Solar Telescope control room. There were about twenty-five people in the group, including a group of college kids from Utah State, visiting scientists from Estonia, and a huge clan vacationing from Iowa with a passel of small kids. Halfway through a stimulating presentation on the history of the Echelle Spectrograph, one squirming two-year old decided he'd had enough of science. He pitched a temper tantrum and ran screaming toward the perimeter of the control room. He slapped random buttons on one of the electronics racks, then wet himself.

The tour guide ran over to grab the kid before he ruined a week's worth of observations or a million dollars worth of equipment, and the kid's parents weren't far behind, yelling for their kid to settle down and behave. In the fracas, the tour guide left his key fob and note cards on the spectrometer console. The killer saw his chance and he took it. The tour guide, the college kids, the scientists, and the parents all drifted toward the shrieking toddler to pry him off the electronics rack. The killer dropped back toward the console, then slipped out the door and into the snow, keys in pocket. He was never missed. His plan was to follow Ramona the next day, and see where he might have an opportunity to take her out.

Ramona spent most of the morning alternately in front of the computer terminal and then the optical bench, running diagnostics on the laser sensor array. These checked out, but still the image quality remained fuzzy. The only thing left that could be at fault was the sensor element itself. Since she'd checked her code and software design the night before, it had to be a hardware problem. Most likely static electricity in this cold dry weather had zapped the electronics. She'd have to pull the sensor out of the light path and replace with a spare unit. That would have to fix it. She switched the laser off, and the sparkling red calibration test pattern on the optical bench blinked out, leaving only a fuzzy image of the sun. She was so close to success now, she could taste it. She glanced at the warning sign plastered on the hatch:

[DANGER]

CONFINED SPACE – BURN HAZARD

AUTHORIZED ENTRY ONLY

WARNING

BEFORE OPENING INSTRUMENTATION CHAMBER:

- DROP CHAMBER VACUUM

- DEPLOY AND LOCK UPPER QUARTZ WINDOW SHUTTER

- CLOSE MAIN MIRROR COVER

- POWER OFF TELESCOPE
- ENGAGE TURRET BRAKE
- CHECK RESCUE EQUIPMENT

She opened the vacuum release valve. Air hissed into the chamber. Ignoring the rest of the safety procedures, which she was certain were just mandated by the lawyers to protect the observatory's ass, she unfastened the three latches on the hatch, pulled her dark red safety goggles down over her eyes, and then swung open the heavy door.

Chapter 28

THE LIGHT WAS BLINDING. Intense. Painful. Even from twenty feet back, in the main doorway to the control room.

He'd been watching her for days, learning her patterns, waiting for some opportunity. His first plan was to push her from the upper platform, but he couldn't figure out how to get up there before she did. The old hoist was noisy and there wasn't any other way up. He'd be spotted up there before he could get his chance. Then he saw her open the chamber.

Why had she ignored the DANGER sign and opened the chamber? Was she stupid? Or just arrogant? On second thought, he didn't give a shit. This was opportunity. He pulled on his leather gloves, threw up a forearm to shield his eyes, and then rushed up behind her silhouette and kicked her hard in her mushy wide ass. She didn't even have a chance to grab the hatch door on the way in, not that it would have done much good. Her knees buckled and her forehead hit the sensor array, tearing her goggles off. She sprawled forward into the instrumentation chamber with a surprised chirp, landing hard on the polished quartz glass floor.

Her hair, cotton blouse, and blue jeans flashed into flames. Her goggles clattered to the floor of the chamber and melted into a bright red sticky pool. Her skin reddened, crackling like crispy fried pork rinds. She rolled over and held up one arm defensively toward the ceiling, to block the light, but it was as futile as holding up a hand to stop a shotgun blast. Her goggles gone, eyes focusing three hundred times the power of the sun onto her retinas, blinded. She moaned a low ululation, and flailed her arms around in a desperate attempt to grab something to pull herself from this oven. Her flesh bubbled, popped, and boiled in a steamy hissing that would continue until the discovery of her blackened corpse. The stench was immediate, vile and unbearable, like burning hair, only a hundred times stronger.

Smoke boiled out from the top of the chamber and drifted to the top of the control room.

He stifled a retch as he slammed the hatch. Fingers of amplified sunlight reached out from around the edges of the door, tracing their path through the smoke, grabbing and scraping at the hatch for their next victim. The moan rose to a steady high-pitched note, then abruptly stopped.

He slipped out of the control room and peered out the heavy whitewashed wooden door of the telescope building. Three tall blonde scientists were shuffling up the hill from the mess hall, smoking cigarettes, jabbering in a foreign language, and laughing. Despite the biting cold, they wore only hoodless sweatshirts and jeans, no hats. They were dressed for a spring picnic in the middle of winter. They just had to be Swedish. They could be headed to this telescope, beyond it to the Evans facility, or to the hilltop dome, maybe even to the scenic overlook. If they were coming to use the Vacuum Telescope, they'd be here in less than a minute, in which case he was fucked. There wasn't time to waste, and there wasn't anywhere else in the telescope to hide if they were going to be working here. If they didn't notice the smell, which was possible since they were smokers, they'd find Ramona's charred remains in about two seconds when they saw the smoke leaking out from around the edges of the hatch door. There wasn't any way to sneak out without being spotted. In a panic, he jumped onto the elevator platform and hit the UP button.

Two of the Swedes bid a hearty good day to their comrade, who continued on to the Evans facility and another day of exciting coronagraph studies.

The killer was just stepping off the elevator platform and outside onto the service walkway at the top of the cone as the two scientists entered the building far below. He crouched down onto the platform and watched as the third scientist strolled toward the Evans building, whistling a classical tune as he did so. He thought it might be Sibelius, but he couldn't be sure, maybe Debussy.

Through the trap door, he could hear their excited shouts: *"Perkele! Vittu!"* Even though he didn't speak a word of Swedish, he knew they'd found Ramona. He was trapped. He looked down the side of the cone. There were no ladder rungs or other service access. The trees were too far away to jump into, and one mistake at this height would be his last. He was trapped. Down the hill and behind the administration building, he saw the cherry-top of the Sunspot Fire Department's emergency medical truck flashing red and white and the siren pierced the frigid morning air. In about two minutes this whole place would be thick with firemen, and another twenty minutes after that, the sheriff would arrive from Cloudcroft. He felt the world close in tight around him. He grabbed the railing and gasped for air.

Chapter 29

"I'M FUCKING BORED," SAID Kyle.

"Me too. Let's go shoot some cans," said Parker. The two boys lay on their backs on the living room floor, each tossing a golf ball up into the air, trying to see how close they could come to the crystal ceiling fixture without actually shattering it.

"Nah, can't. Dad caught me shootin' at the lighthouse from the deck last week. He took my twenty-two and I'm out of CO_2 cylinders for the BB pistol," said Kyle. The lighthouse was actually a cylindrical water tower that the neighborhood association considered an eyesore, so they'd had it painted up to look like a lighthouse. The illusion was very good if you were more than a half mile away, but any closer it looked like a cartoon. Still, it was apparently enough to fool the very wealthy who purchased homes in this neighborhood.

"Mmm. Onslaught Deathmatch?"

"Nah, I already beat all the levels on the 'Godlike' setting"

"What about a net game then?" asked Parker.

"Nah, those dicks are all a bunch of team killers and pussies," said Kyle.

"Surf some TnA?" offered Parker, his ball hitting the ceiling and knocking loose some of the texturing material in a shower of gypsum.

"Nah, Mom locked down the proxy so I can't get the good porn sites anymore," said Kyle, brushing the gypsum dust from his hair.

"We could maybe try to hack it?" suggested Parker.

"It's hopeless, she had my cousin patch it through some kind of router or firewall, and it's locked behind the network panel in her closet. I tried," said Kyle.

"Let's go tease your little sister then," said Parker. He'd had a crush on Kyle's little sister ever since she'd started wearing a training bra.

"Can't. She's away at band camp," said Kyle. Kyle, the older and taller of the two boys, was sixteen. He was muscular with wavy blond hair. He'd just gotten his driver's license and a brand new Lexus SUV for his birthday. They lived in a seven thousand square-foot house on top of a hill overlooking Lake Travis, just down the street from the faux lighthouse. The house had cost Kyle's father a million and a half dollars. He worked eighty-five hour weeks as a Dell operations executive to keep up the payments on this monstrosity. He had ground his lower teeth down to stubs, and his blood pressure was so high that he'd recently begun pissing blood, but he put off seeing the doctor, because in his position taking sick time was frowned upon.

The house had a billiard parlor, a theater complete with about a thousand popular movie titles, two kitchens (one on the main level and one downstairs just inside from the pool), a fully equipped game room including the latest top-end video game console and hundreds of games, a sauna, and a swimming pool overlooking the lake. There was also a small Astroturf putting green out next to the pool, complete with a real sand trap. In the garage there were two tandem sea kayaks and enough camping and hiking gear to outfit an Everest expedition.

Still the boys were bored.

"Hey I know," said Parker, "My uncle's doing this game called Geocaching. Wanna try it?" Parker was small for his age, thin, olive complexioned with short dark hair. He lived in another million-dollar home three doors down. Though he didn't have the guts to get in trouble on his own, coupled with a bolder companion, he could come up with some very creative ways for making mischief. Building the fireplace out on the top of the cliff in the J Canyon preserve had been his idea. They'd spent a weekend cutting trees and making log seats and arranging rocks around the fire pit. They'd had plenty of wild nights camping out there around the fire, drinking Sam Adams beer and passing the occasional joint whenever Kyle could bum some off his older brother Chase. Chase was in finance. Those guys could afford to drink themselves stupid all the way through college, and then when they got out, they were grinding their teeth, pissing blood and making payments on million dollar homes.

"Geo-what? What the hell's that?" asked Kyle.

"Some geek hides a box of junk in the woods and other geeks come out to find it using GPS," explained Parker, his Titleist gracing the chandelier with a glassy *ting*.

"That sounds gay," said Kyle. "What's in the box?"

"Toys and shit. Mostly junk. Sometimes there's a buck or two. One time my uncle found a hundred thirty bucks," said Parker, sitting up.

"A hundred thirty? No way. How do you know where to look for the box?" asked Kyle. His credit limit was more than a hundred times that amount, still, like Chase was fond of saying, one could never have enough money.

"It's on the net, there's a whole website and shit," said Parker, getting up and heading for the computer room.

"Let me see, what's the address?" asked Kyle, as they scrambled into the computer den and woke the machine.

"Here, let me type it in," offered Parker.

"No fuckhead, I'll type it in," said Kyle, slapping the smaller boy on the back of the head. They pulled up the website, typed in Kyle's zip code, and waited a second as the list of nearest caches filled the screen. They clicked on the nearest cache. It was just outside the security gate to their neighborhood.

"Holy shit, that one's close. What if we went out and raided a few of the boxes, took the good shit and trashed the rest?" said Parker.

"Cool, like pirates," said Kyle.

"Yeah, like fuckin Captain Ahab," said Parker, "Fuck with the geeks a little bit, watch them scurry like ants to see who's pissing in their gay little game."

"Ahab was not a pirate, you dumbfuck," said Kyle.

"Whatever," said Parker, "You know what I'm talking about."

"Maybe we could fill some of them with dog shit or maybe piss in them or something." suggested Kyle.

"Cool," said Parker, "I know where I can find a dead cat too. "

"Fuckin-A, Let's go," said Kyle.

Chapter 30

THE KILLER TOOK SEVERAL deep breaths and wrestled the panic back down. No time for that now. He had no jar ready. He decided he would rather die in an escape attempt rather than be captured. He'd come too far to be captured, and by firemen and scientists. He figured that he could slide down the side of the cone, using friction to slow his descent. The cone was steep though; it was a longshot. The impact would be less than falling one hundred thirty-six feet, but how much less he couldn't say. It depended on the coefficient of friction between his jeans and the concrete surface, his initial velocity, the cosine of the angle that the cone made with the ground, the thickness of the snow bank at the bottom, and a number of other lower-order factors he just didn't have time to compute right now. To maximize the friction, he'd have to spread his arms and legs and hug the cone on the way down. He estimated his landing velocity would be equivalent to jumping a quarter of the height of the cone straight to the ground. Thirty-five feet, give or take. He might break a leg, but at least he had a chance to escape.

He swung a foot out over the service railing on the back side of the cone. He straddled the railing and then swung his other foot and crouched on the outside of the railing. He switched his grip to the lower rung of the railing, lowered himself off the edge, and hung suspended from the railing, feet dangling down the side of the cone.

He let go.

He dropped.

His stomach lurched up into his chest, and he tensed. Free fall. Much too fast. He'd miscalculated.

Suddenly his feet hit something, snagged the toes of his shoes briefly; he continued falling. Whatever it was, it scraped its way up his legs and chest. He caught only a glimpse of it as it slid by his face and up his arms. Instinctively, he grabbed just as it passed his wrists. His left hand missed, but he had it firmly in his right. He bounced and dangled by his right arm, the force ripping and burning at his shoulder. He quickly threw up his left arm and held fast. He had snagged a heavy steel cable. What the hell? He hadn't seen that from up top; the cable was painted white to match the cone. From here he could see what it was. It ran from the twin lightning rods on either side of the top of the cone, down the sides of the cone a dozen feet. The two cables then curved inward to meet at a T-junction, then looking down between his legs, he could see a single cable continued all the way down the back side of the cone to the ground.

He grabbed the vertical part of the cable in gloved hands and half-slid, half-rappelled his way down the back side of the cone. When he reached the ground, he backed twenty feet into the forest, checking to be sure that no one saw his descent. The paramedics had entered the building and the forest canopy and trunks were flashing red with the light from their truck. He continued to back up until he noticed he was on a mulched trail. A trail marker indicated that it was National Forest Trail T234. He wasn't sure where this trail went, but one thing was certain. It went *down,* away from the observatory. Right now anywhere else was better than up on this mountain.

He hiked five miles through the slush, all downhill. It took two miles of hiking just to clear the smell of burning bitch out of his nostrils. The trail ended up in a remote desert state park in the foothills above Alamogordo. From there it was an easy hike to the state highway and freedom.

Chapter 31

NO MATTER WHERE YOUR murder spree took you, it was always good to be back in Texas. The mountains of New Mexico were just too fucking cold. That and the air. Something was wrong with the air there. He couldn't put his finger on it but it gave him an uneasy feeling, a feeling of dread. It made his chest tight, like a constant squeezing. The feeling of dread had played hell with his sense of panic. While in the mountains, he'd had to drink from the urine bottle as much as three times a day.

It wasn't the murder of that Willard bitch, that had been easy-- too easy--and he'd gotten away clean, no broken bones. But now he was back south where the temperature might get cold, but never too cold or too long. Most of the time it was fine, except in the summer when it was too fucking hot and you'd better not be going around homeless because the homeless don't have air conditioning.

The only problem he had now was the rain. It rained all fucking night. Once he'd hopped off the southbound freight on MoPac, he'd headed straight for shelter. When you're homeless in Austin, or just posing as homeless, your options for shelter are limited. He'd had to hole up under a bridge. Kicked some fat homeless bag out of the crawl space under the bridge on 360 and 183, cardboard sign and all. *How do you get to be fat when you're homeless?* he wondered, as he watched her roll down the hill toward the freeway. *Never mind.* He needed to be alone, needed time to dry off. The rain was blowing sideways, so he'd crawled up into a narrow gap under the bridge to get some extra cover. The gap was just big enough to fit a man, and there was a ledge where he could lay out flat, between the beams and the concrete abutment, safely out of the wind and the rain.

And he slept.

Chapter 32

THE KILLER FELT THE squeezing again, the tightness in his chest, and for a moment he thought he was back in the mountains with that thin mountain air leaching the life out of his lungs. The light peeled his eyes open. He blinked back the brightness of the day, even here under the bridge, and he realized that he was pinned at the chest. What the fuck? The gap had been big enough to let him in earlier this morning, now what the hell was going on? He wiggled and twisted, exhaled deeply to flatten his chest, and then slipped out. Barely. He shimmied out and climbed down off the ledge. What the fuck? Had the bridge deck moved?

He scratched his head and grabbed his backpack, pulled it off the ledge in the gap. As he ate his breakfast, which this morning consisted of a single-serving can of mixed peas and carrots, a handful of beef jerky and a cranberry apple breakfast bar, he looked up at the gap. The roar of the traffic below on Mo-Pac expressway was deafening, but through the din he could almost hear the voice of Professor Rodchenko droning on.

Rodchenko had been his professor in mechanical engineering 1051, an introductory course in statics and dynamics. The killer had elected to take this course even though his major was computer engineering. He thought it would be an easy elective. How difficult could it be? The course kicked his ass and he'd had to drop it once he got his first exam scores back. But he never forgot old Doctor Sergei Rodchenko. Romanian maybe, definitely Soviet bloc. Big tall goober, stood around seven feet tall, short black hair slicked straight back with Vaseline. Looked, walked, and sounded like fucking count Dracula, except instead of wanting to suck your blood, he wanted to inject your brain with trusses, members, frames, and free body diagrams. Especially free body diagrams. Only when he said it, it was with that thick eastern European rolling R sound, and you couldn't help but picture a real body, a pale human corpse, with two tiny red fang marks on the neck, put there, most likely, by old Count Rodchenko himself. Rodchenko had this really annoying habit of walking up behind you while you were working on something, a quiz or whatever, then saying, "Vell, I tell you..." and then he would wait half a minute, like he was pondering over what he was going to tell you, and you'd really be wanting to hear it, but then he'd just shake his head and walk away, so you never knew what the fuck he was going to tell you. *Vell*.

What little he did pick up in that course came back to him now, and he shuddered. Another ten minutes in that expansion gap and he would never have been able to slip himself out. You heard about it from time to time, some homeless trash found dead under a bridge, asphyxiated or maybe some bones broken, no sign of foul play. No one paid those stories much mind. What's one more dead homeless motherfucker? That's one less bullshit hard luck story scrawled on cardboard trying to bum whiskey money off you at the traffic light. The police just bagged 'em, tagged 'em, and hauled 'em off. End of investigation. But it wasn't foul play, it was the goddamn expansion joints. Count Rodchenko had taught that concrete, like most other solids, expands when heated and contracts when cooled. Same reason why sidewalks are broken up into square slabs instead of poured as a continuous ribbon. Step on a crack, break your mother's back. Gaps have to be designed in to handle the expansion. In a sidewalk it's a small gap, maybe an inch or so. They stuff the gap with some compressible black fiberboard shit to keep rocks and other debris from clogging the gap. Under a bridge though, the gap is huge, sometimes big enough to stuff a fat homeless bitch in--by night. By the heat of the day though, maybe only a skinny kid could fit in the gap, maybe only a cat, depends on the gap. There's no need for filler material because it's under the bridge where shit can't fall into the gap, (unless you consider a fat smelly homeless bitch to be shit, which he did, he most definitely fucking did) so they just leave the gap open. And it had almost crushed him.

Gotta be more careful, that's all.

Need to find a better hideout. This place was too fucking noisy, and there were homeless people shuffling around all hours of the day and night, talking to themselves, talking to the birds, talking to the street signs, trying to talk to him, trying to *touch* him, for Christ's sake. Sure they all looked crazy, and statistically he knew that more than half of them were legally and medically insane, but one of them might be able to identify him later and he couldn't have that. Now that it was morning and the rain had stopped, he shouldered his backpack and began scouting for a better hideout. The research he had done at the library in Alamogordo told him all he needed about which way to go. Southwest, toward the Pennybacker bridge. He climbed up from under the overpass and began walking. It was prime rush hour, so another homeless guy shuffling along the highway with his pack would fade into the background. He walked. He walked down the northbound breakdown lane of highway 360. He walked south; he walked facing traffic. He didn't look up, instead he carried that pitiful dejected look that the homeless were so good at projecting when they were trying to hard luck you out of a dollar on the street corner. About a mile down the hill, just past the light at Spicewood Springs road, he noticed a little beige concrete building just down from the road. It was a restroom facility for a small park. One side men's, the other side women's. Perfect. He wasn't homeless, just posing as one, and right now nothing would feel better than a good hot bath. Failing that, he'd take a good hot sponge bath in a sink. When you were living out on the road, you took what came your way and you made do. And in this case, the city of Austin parks department was welcoming him to their fair city with hot and cold running water, and a locked private room in which to luxuriate in it.

He stepped into the men's side (the door was propped open with a small rock, to keep the place aired out), carefully slid out of his clothes and set them on top of his backpack. He got the hot water running and splashed warm handfuls on his face. He looked at his face in the mirror. He was pretty rough looking. He'd been a month on the road in homeless guise since his trip to Alamogordo. He fished in his pack for a disposable razor and soaped up his beard. He didn't shave his face clean, because he still needed to cover the scars, but he was able to trim back the beard, shave his neck, make it look like a respectable hairstyle instead of a nest. The beard mostly covered the scar. He'd be able to walk among civilized people again. He washed the soap off his face with the hot water, then proceeded to wash his hair. He lathered up his whole body and rinsed off, using an empty Gatorade bottle from his pack to gather the rinse water. The building was concrete, circular metal overflow drain in the middle of the floor, heavy steel door with a sliding latch bolt. He wasn't going to be bothered in here. Stainless steel sink, stainless steel toilet. All the comforts of home. It was still just a little chilly from the overnight rain, but the hot water felt good as he poured it over himself and let the dirt of a month on the road wash away and down the drain.

He dried off using handfuls of paper towels from the dispenser under the polished stainless steel mirror. He jammed a sock into the drain to plug it, then threw his clothes into the sink. He filled the sink with hot water and a handful of liquid pink soap from the pump dispenser bolted to the wall. He hand-washed his black T-shirt, jeans and boxers. He rinsed them, wrung out as much of the water as he could, then put them back on. It was going to be a sunny day, and it would be warming up. He'd walk them dry by the time he got to the Pennybacker. If he was going to be homeless, at least he'd be as clean as he could. Besides, he had some shopping to do before he dispatched the next asshole on the list. The Wal-Mart greeter was likely to raise an eyebrow at a homeless man walking in the front door, maybe even throw him out. He had to go in looking and feeling clean. This one had to be done just right. No fuckups.

By tracing the curvature of highway 360 on his map, he decided that he could take a shortcut through the park he was in, a long narrow park called Bull Creek District Park. There was a trail running from just outside the restroom building toward the direction of the Pennybacker. If the trail went straight through, which he suspected it did, then he could cut some distance off his trip, and at the same time stay out of the sight of any law enforcement officers who happened to be driving along 360 and want to question a long haired man wearing sopping wet clothes on a sunny spring morning. That would be just what he needed right now, to draw attention.

He started off down the path. It followed the park road for a few hundred yards, then passed over some huge boulders and then onto a gravel path along Bull Creek. To his right up the hill ran highway 360. To his left and below ran Bull Creek, which raged with the excess runoff from last night's rainfall. The creek cut its way through layers of rock, at times spreading perhaps twenty or thirty feet wide, and at times narrowing down to a dozen feet. Each time it narrowed, the rush of the water was deafening. When it widened out, the only sound was the muffled sound of traffic from the highway at the top of the hill. The trees were starting to bud and come into bloom. Spring in Texas is the best time to visit. He loved it here. This was his place. Not Austin in particular, he didn't care for Austin, but Texas. Goddamned hot in the summer, but it was nice most of the other three seasons, and depending on where you lived, you might not have too much of a problem with bugs.

About a half mile down the path he got a piece of trail bark stuck in his boot, between his ankle and the boot leather. It was so thick it forced him to hobble and slowed him down. He sat down on a flat rock and pulled off the boot. With the wet socks, it was wedged on tight. He gave it a sharp yank, and it flipped up and over his head and landed in the weeds behind him. *Fuck.* He stood up, then stumbled over into the weeds. He got only a few hops before he lost his balance and fell face first. He picked himself up and beat the bushes looking for the wayward boot. He saw the boot at the edge of the creek through a stand of trees. He hopped back toward the creek, half hopping and half walking on tiptoe with his stocking foot. He grabbed the boot, and as he was trying to put it on while hopping on the other good boot, he noticed a brown shape across the creek.

It was an abandoned Studebaker or some other prehistoric vehicle, wedged between some boulders and some trees that had grown up around it, sealing it off from the world. It had obviously been here and undisturbed for a very long time.

He shimmied across a fallen tree to the other side of the creek. There were no paths over here, no sign of humans other than this ancient machine. There were no markings on the car. The paint had completely gone over to dark brown rust. It had at least fifty bullet holes in the rear fenders, large caliber. It sat at the base of a steep rock cliff. He couldn't tell if the car had come from up on the cliff or from upstream during a flood. The interior was a cavern. Holy shit they built cars big back then. There was no upholstery left, and vandals had taken most of the instruments. A family of bark scorpions had taken up residence under the engine block. The hood was up, exposing the engine. The number 1312815-3 stamped in the heavy steel valve cover testified to a time long ago when someone actually gave a shit about being able to procure a replacement part for this old crate, but that time was ancient history. What he could see here was a good place to hide out. It was dry, near the Pennybacker, and had good access to the highway, yet no one knew it was here.

Chapter 33

"YOU KNOW, YOU'RE SITTING on one," Kurt said.

"You guys put these damn things everywhere. Is nowhere safe?" Judi laughed, looking around her seat as if a mouse were loose nearby, "Where is it exactly?"

"It's under the seat, to the right there. Look for a mint tin stuck to the frame with a magnet," said Kurt. The young couple had spent the afternoon pedaling pedal boats on Town Lake, eating cotton candy, touring the botanical gardens, visiting the Umlauf Sculpture Museum, flying a pair of huge parafoil kites, and exploring the wilderness of Zilker Park.

The Zilker Zephyr, a narrow gauge kiddie train ride, was also popular as a ride for courting couples. Kurt's knees pressed up against the seat in front, but Judi had no problem fitting in. The train wasn't very wide, so they spent the whole ride pressed side-to-side. At the end of the ride, the train passed through a short tunnel, the closest thing Austin had to a tunnel of love. A savvy gentleman would wait until the date was nearly over before offering to purchase a ticket on the Zephyr. And an even more savvy gentleman would be sure that he and his date occupied the last seat on the train, because that seat would linger in darkness the longest as the train crawled through the tunnel when it pulled into the station.

As she signed the tiny logbook in the magnetic mint tin, Judi asked how Kurt's job search was going.

"It's starting to pick up a bit," he said.

"That's good, maybe we will finally get you off the streets during the workday," she said.

"Yeah, I'm a real menace to society," he laughed, "stumbling around in the bushes looking for trinkets. Speaking of which, did I tell you I stumbled onto a sort of a mystery?"

"A mystery?" she asked, "What kind of mystery?"

He filled her in on the search that he and Jason had done the other day.

"Shouldn't you call the police?" she asked.

"I don't really have enough information to do that now," he said, "I don't know who is doing it, and I don't even know if it's a real pattern of murders or just a coincidence. There's a seventy-five thousand dollar reward for one of the murders though. I'm going to try to piece just together enough to cinch that prize, then I'll go to the cops. If it is a murderer, he's in remote places like San Francisco, Chicago, and Pennsylvania. He's not even in Texas so I'm not worried."

"Pennsylvania?" she asked.

"Yeah, place called Harrison Valley," he said.

"Never heard of it," she said.

"It's up by Pittsburgh somewhere, out in the country," he said.

The train pulled their car out of the tunnel and into the station. It was the last ride of the day. The sun was setting and most park visitors headed to their cars.

Kurt and Judi ordered Italian food in one of those chain restaurants that tries hard not to look like a chain. The service was inattentive and slow. They sat on the same side of the booth. The conversation became more personal. After forty-five minutes of waiting for their food, they were suddenly in a hurry to leave the place. They paid the waiter for their cokes, cancelled their orders, and left hungry. They drove to Judi's place in Kurt's truck.

They sat in the parking lot, kissing. After ten minutes, Judi invited Kurt upstairs for coffee.

Judi lived in one of the nicer apartments out on the northwest side of town. Just off loop 360 and Spicewood, tucked away in a little corner of the hill country. Limestone walls, nice kidney-shaped pool with hot tub, it was a quiet upscale place, but not too snooty. It also had good access to the Bull Creek Park across the highway.

Her apartment was at the top of the stairs, on the end of the building, so that there was no neighbor on one side. Judi didn't like noisy neighbors so she specifically requested an end unit. She had her own single-car garage downstairs. The apartments had built-in security alarms and a metal security gate.

There was a small color TV hanging under one of the cabinets in the kitchen, and a token fireplace in the living area. The bedroom was in the back; it had a great view of the limestone hillside across a small creek. She had a small home office in the front bedroom, with one of the brand new Apple Macintosh computers. She also had a dog, a geriatric Brittany mix named Nipper, who slept at the foot of her bed. He was a good watchdog despite a touch of arthritis. He had a sweet disposition and a tendency to lick the backs of people's knees, whether they wanted it or not.

Judi's taste ran slightly to the frilly side, with sheer curtains and lacy things and a few knick-knacks. She had a plush green couch in the living room, a large picture of some Gay Nineties coffee drinkers framed in thick rustic walnut hanging above the couch.

From the corner of the frame hung Judi's polo shirt. Kurt's shirt was draped over the large panel TV on the facing wall. Their socks and shoes were scattered next to the couch. Kurt and Judi filled the couch, arms entangled, each ripping at the fasteners on the other's remaining clothing, when suddenly Judi stopped.

"Kurt, I'm sorry, it's too soon. I can't, I'm not ready," she said, pushing him away.

"Huh?" he said.

"I think we'd better stop," she said, breathing heavily.

"But..." he said. "What happened? We were getting along so well."

"Yeah, too well. It's too fast. I'm dizzy. Here's your shirt. I'm very sorry," she said, "It's late. I think maybe you'd better go now before I change my mind."

"Will I see you again?" he asked.

"Yes. I mean--I want to see you again. I just think we're moving too fast." she said, slipping her shirt back on.

Chapter 34

THE KILLER SLIPPED OFF his backpack, set it on the rock, and unzipped it. He checked his equipment carefully. He'd hitched a ride up state highway 183 to the new Wal-Mart out on Ranch Road 620, and there he'd found everything he needed. One stop shopping. Two hundred feet of nylon rope, several solid rubber stretch cords (Amazing! Stretches to over 3 Feet!), a small roll of heavy duty picture hanging wire (10 gage, solid), a six-inch folding serrated hunting knife, an LED keychain light, a seven ounce can of Startz brand Extra Strength Engine Starting Fluid, a butane lighter, a spray can of black automotive primer, a couple bottles of Gatorade and water, some sports energy bars, a pack of beef jerky, and a roll of high-strength black duct tape. He'd paid cash. His scarred face would stand out, but after midnight at Wal-Mart, he wouldn't be the weirdest looking dude in the store. His image would appear on the security cameras, but it was a risk he had to take. They wouldn't be looking for him anyway.

He climbed up on the rock ledge, sat down and tried to catch his breath. The walk from his Bull Creek hideout in the old rusted car had taken him a half-hour and he needed a chance to rest before he executed his latest plan.

The building was a cheap four-story glass office building of the type that scarred central Texas like a real-estate melanoma. By day it was impossible to see in through the heavily tinted glass, but at night, from outside with the offices lit up, it was easy to see what was going on in an entire side of the building all at once. From his vantage point in the adjacent juniper forest, The killer could see everything in the fourth floor on his side, all the way down to the ground level.

The killer waited at the back door. Smokers had to go out the back loading dock door to smoke; it wasn't permitted up at the front of the building or inside. Even at this late hour, well past nine-thirty P.M., a couple of engineers were out at the employee picnic table smoking. The table was two hundred fifty feet away from the door, putting them just outside the two hundred feet legal smoking limit. They'd propped the normally-locked door open with a small rock, in violation of both common sense and company security policy.

The air conditioning plant and other equipment near the loading dock made a hell of a racket, even late at night. One of the units had a compressor that was about a month past due on maintenance. When running, it sounded like one of those cheap Japanese dirt bikes with a hole in the muffler.

The smokers were bitching about their jobs, having to work late, and fantasizing about winning the lottery. Of course neither of them actually played the lottery, so they really hadn't paid for that particular fantasy. He sneaked up to the propped door from behind the dumpster. He glanced back toward the smokers to be sure they were not looking his way, and then slipped in the door. He slipped in from the side to avoid the stare of the security camera.

He ducked into a fire stair on the ground floor. This was the risky part. He mustn't be caught here. But it was late, there were only a few die-hards left and those that weren't smoking were in their cubicles or lab facilities, busy working and trying to get home by a decent hour (defined as before midnight). He had already made the preliminary phone calls to the receptionist to find out which office the victim was in.

He knew from previous experience that the victim, an incurable workaholic, would be working alone late. He ducked into the fire stair, hid behind the landing and listened. The smokers would be returning and he didn't know where they would go. He heard the back door open and the smokers return, laughing and coughing. They passed right by the fire stair door and punched up the elevators.

Chapter 35

STALNAKER REACHED INTO THE cabinet behind his desk and pulled out his bottle of Springbank. The label looked like a cartoon, as if some bored high-school kid had printed it off on his color ink-jet printer and glued it to the bottle with Elmer's Glue. The packaging was amateurish, but the juice was good, there was no question about it. At a hundred forty bucks a bottle, it had better be. Springbank was the finest single malt Scotch whisky money could buy. Stalnaker reached into the file cabinet, pulled out a tall glass, and then poured himself a double. The light aroma of coconut filled his nostrils. He licked his lips in anticipation.

The amber liquid warmed his tongue and throat. When he had swallowed and exhaled through pursed lips, the scotch hinted bitter chocolate. Ah, the finish. Long and pleasant. *That was what you bought an expensive single malt for*, he thought, though Stalnaker hadn't actually purchased this bottle. He'd swindled it off his company's assistant controller, a deliciously sexy thirty-something blonde named Jennifer. Jennifer's husband worked in field sales, and unlike most salesmen, he wasn't a drinker. Never touched the stuff. A customer had presented him with the bottle as a thank-you gift for arranging a deal with particularly favorable terms. Stalnaker had been down in finance rapping Jennifer up, trying to finagle a particularly challenging piece of inter-office ass, when he spied the bottle in a shopping bag under her desk. Her husband had given it to her to get rid of. Jennifer knew at least two people in the office who would appreciate a free bottle of scotch, though she'd been deceived by the cheesy label and thought it was some cheap brand. Stalnaker had offered her sexual favors in exchange for it, which she flatly declined, but gave him the bottle anyway, happy to be rid of the lecherous bully and the bottle alike.

His chest and head warmed by the scotch, and with his crotch still tingling from his marketing assistant Darlene's expert servicing, he clicked his mouse and brought up last quarter's marketing report.

Stalnaker was a vindictive sonofabitch. Many in the company would say sociopathic, though no one would dare say it out loud, even off premise. He had bullied his way to the position of CEO in a short five years, serving for three years as Director of Marketing before he blackmailed a board member into demanding the previous CEO step down. The old bastard didn't even know what hit him.

At last the bitch had gone home. Darlene was a great fuck, a real desktop bucking bronco, but lousy company. She had a shrill voice and though she had been beautiful (actually stunning) years ago, her face was now leathery. Ten years beyond her prime.

Stalnaker's rule on inter-company sexual relations was simple. Fuck him when he wanted you to, then leave quietly, and you might keep your job. He'd tease you with a token promotion (but you'd never see it). Refuse any advance, no matter how perverted, and you were history. You'd never see the knife coming. In short, he maintained prison rules. It didn't matter if you were good looking or not, and it didn't even matter if you weren't female. He wasn't gay, he just used any means possible to dominate, to intimidate. Everyone in the company knew about his sexual harassment, but it was never called that. In a big corporation it would have been difficult (but not impossible) to operate this way, but in a small company a sociopath like Stalnaker could rape and pillage with impunity. In a better economy, he might have had some difficulty retaining people, but in this economy, it was either take some harassment from the top dog every once in awhile, or lose your gig.

Darlene was no fool. She knew that Stalnaker was just using her, but she'd been secretly working a trap to blackmail him, which would take another few months to pull off. Another few months of sucking his smelly little pecker under the desk, another few months of letting him grab her ass. A small price to pay to become Director of Marketing within a year. The position would more than triple her salary. She'd finally live in six-figure territory, with stock options, a corner office, and all this without an MBA. She hated Stalnaker. Despised him. Detested him. Wanted to kill him. It was all she could do to keep from biting his crooked pencil-dick off each time he shoved it in her mouth. Watch him bleed to death right there in his overstuffed executive leather chair. But in the end it would be more satisfying to have him promote her, then later force him to resign in disgrace. He'd be ruined. She'd want him to be around to experience that, knowing that she (a mere woman, one of his many corporate fuck-toys) had stuck the knife in his back and twisted it hard.

Darlene might have been lousy company but Stalnaker had to hand it to her, she was a damn good marketer. She had an aggressive take-no-prisoners guerrilla edge. Her forecasts were always right on the money. He couldn't find fault, and he tried. Her strategy was top-notch, and she could work a trade show floor like a cheap hooker outside a plumbing convention. She'd get out on the floor, outside the booth, smiling and greeting customers like they were her best friends. She wouldn't sit on her hands and chitchat like the other marketing managers. She was sharp on the technology too, and the customers couldn't stump her, though many tried. As a result, she brought in the leads, and good qualified leads, not the usual tire kicker shit his other marketing fuckups brought in.

Still, he'd consistently seen to it that her employee performance reviews were never more than satisfactory. Rate your people too high, and you'd lose them. You had to keep them working harder. One way to do that was to bully them, and a really good way to bully them was to give them merely satisfactory reviews. Give a top-performing employee a bad review and she'll look for work elsewhere. Give her a satisfactory review, and she'll work twice as hard next quarter to try to ratchet the review up a notch. Which of course never happened. If you ever let the mule actually eat the carrot, he'll stop pulling the cart.

Chapter 36

AFTER A FEW MINUTES of quiet, the killer ascended the stairs to the next landing. Still quiet. His initial recon of the building indicated that there was no one on the first and second floors in this end of the building. The third floor had two offices lit up on this side and you never knew who would take the stairs instead of the elevator down to take a smoke. People were crazy about their health sometimes. He knew some assholes who would go to McDonald's and order a Big Mac, fries and a *Diet* Coke, thinking that they were eating light. Some of the smokers might have the same idea, keep smoking like a fiend, but then take the stairs and you won't die. Stupid shits. You always gotta watch out for stupid shits. The killer kept himself in good physical condition, and except for an occasional swig of Old Granddad and a recently developed taste for murder, he had no vices.

He stopped at the landing to the fourth floor. Digital Fabrication Systems Inc. What a crock of shit. He knew that Stalnaker would be in the fifth office down, and that the other offices on this end of the hall were dark. He'd assume they were empty. This was the hard part. He did not know where his victim was. It had been twenty minutes since he'd seen him through the window in his office. Now he took the chance. He pushed open the fire door.

The killer knew from long experience that most people before leaving work for home will hit the can, just to reset their pee-clock for the road. He knew that Stalnaker lived way out in Lakeway, a good twenty mile drive, and that he'd want to stop off to drain the main vein before bailing. He also knew from having worked with the guy before that Stalnaker would probably knock off no later than eleven P.M. So that gave him some time to set up. He pushed into the hallway, and then crept a few feet past the first darkened office. The door was open, and no one was in there. He noticed the lights on in the office down the hall to the

147

left. That was Stalnaker's office. He could hear clicking and some light country music coming from the office. It was so late that even the cleaning crew had gone home for the night. He pushed past the janitor's closet and into the door marked MEN.

The lights were off in the men's room, a lame attempt at corporate cost savings, even though anyone with a high school education knew that it cost more to switch a fluorescent light on than it consumed all day if just left running. He left the lights off so as not to draw attention, and slipped into the handicap stall. He clutched his LED key light in his left hand, and slung his backpack over the right shoulder. By the ghostly circle of LED light, he could see that the bathroom had been meticulously cleaned, but that some shithead had used the stall and hadn't flushed. Probably that bully Stalnaker, asserting his dominance over the place, marking his territory. His victim's office was only two doors away; he dared not chance a flush. He'd have to deal with the smell, and the loss of a prime place to sit. He hung his backpack on the hook, then sat on the floor furthest from the commode, pulled out the bottle of Startz engine starter and one of the tube socks, loosened the cap from the bottle, and waited.

In the total darkness he waited, ether at the ready. He checked his watch, and the little glowing face said 10:37. Wouldn't be long now. He went over the plan in his head, step by step. There were only a few places where it would be tricky, but he felt he had a good grip on what needed to be done. The motherfucker would pay, that was for sure. And this one would be done right. The killer would enjoy every agonizing minute of it, and Stalnaker would suffer a long, long time.

Fifteen minutes later, the door opened and startled him. A pie-wedge of yellow light from the hall expanded into the room. The overheads blinked on with a click and a buzz, and he heard the slick shuffle and click of fine shoe leather on industrial bathroom tile. He was fortunate that the victim wasn't expecting a murderer to be hiding in the bathroom. He was fortunate that the handicap stall was the furthest from the door, and the furthest from the urinals.

The footsteps stopped at the urinal, and his victim unzipped, tooted out a small fart, and cut loose a stream.

The killer stood up slowly. He shouldered his way out of the stall, simultaneously dumping some of the Startz into the balled-up sock. He swept up to the unsuspecting Stalnaker at the urinal, and with his right arm, nutcrackered him into a tight hold. He pressed the ether-laden sock firmly up against Stalnaker's nostrils and mouth. Urine splattered onto the floor, soaking the victim's pants as he let go of his penis to pull the sudden arm from his throat.

After a couple minutes of struggle, the victim fell limp, and the stream pouring onto the floor subsided to a trickle. The killer jumped up to lock the door, then duct-taped the sock onto his victim's face. Mustn't use too much ether, wouldn't want to kill the bastard by accident. This one needed to be hurt bad first.

He used a paper towel to wipe his fingerprints off each surface he'd touched. He balled up wads of paper towels into the commodes and flushed each one to overflowing. He did the same for the sinks, opening the taps and letting the water flow. This began to coat the floors with water to wipe all traces of his footprints in the urine.

He was calm. Time was on his side now.

He lifted the limp Trent Stalnaker onto his shoulders, over the top of his own backpack. He poked his head out into the hall, and lumbered toward the fire stairs.

Everyone would be gone from the building, if the pattern of the previous few days held. Out the back door, and into the woods. No one in the parking lot. The security camera would just miss him if he took a sharp left along the building.

He headed down the path to the ledge under the Pennybacker bridge. It was a steep, torturous path, even when not carrying a man on your shoulders, and the killer twice nearly slipped off the edge into the water a hundred-fifty feet below. Halfway down the path he just dropped the man and dragged him the rest of the way by his feet.

A few minutes before midnight they arrived at the ledge under the Pennybacker. The ledge was difficult to get to, and most homeless people wouldn't bother, though there was good cover under here. You couldn't just walk up to this ledge, like you could on most other highway bridges in Texas, because the Pennybacker was a suspension bridge that spanned Lake Austin from the lakeshore on the south up to a hundred-foot cliff on the north.

They were under the northernmost edge, out of the sight of any witness, not that there would be any witnesses at this time of night, not on the muddy lake below.

He had been checking the papers. The Lower Colorado River Authority (LCRA) had drained Lake Austin to rid it of Hydrilla, an imported aquarium plant that occasionally choked the waterway. Draining the water from the lake killed off most of the plants. The water level was too low for boating, but the LCRA was scheduled to raise the water level in a few days. No one would be boating underneath while he tortured and killed Stalnaker.

The victim stirred, and the killer placed the ether-soaked sock back over his nose and mouth. He'd set Stalnaker down on the ledge, and was now preparing him for his demise.

He bound Stalnaker's hands and feet tightly with a length of the rope. Now came the hard part. He had to get Stalnaker twenty feet out and up three vertical feet into the expansion joint. This was not going to be easy. He gagged Stalnaker with a strip of the black duct tape.

He dragged Stalnaker out along a support beam fixed into the cliff. The beam went about twenty feet toward the point where one of the huge arches met the span. The beam was just wide enough for a man to rest on it, but unfortunately the space above the beam was only tall enough for a crawl. He inched backward along the beam, dragging his unconscious victim behind him. When his feet hit the arch, he crawled back over the top of his victim and pushed. When the victim's feet touched the arch, the killer crawled back over him and onto a crossbeam that was at right angles to the reddish steel arch. He took one of the ropes that was tied to the victim's feet, and tied it off to the crossbeam. He had gotten this far and did not want his victim to end up falling to his doom while unconscious. That would not satisfy the plan.

With a clumsy pulling and huffing, he transferred the drugged man to the crossbeam. This beam was narrower than the beam that had gotten them out here, but there were two beams side-by-side for strength, with only an inch gap between. Now he had Stalnaker perpendicular to the direction of travel of the road, and parallel to the expansion joint, just three feet overhead. Now came the really hard part. He had to lift the man directly up and over the water, and jam him up into the expansion joint.

It had taken him an hour to get this far, but there was no need to hurry. His measurements had shown that this gap would reach its maximum opening at five A.M. He'd have to wait here a few more hours. He leaned up against the arch and rested.

Chapter 37

March 5th - 3:45 A.M.

JUDI SLID OUT OF bed, unable to sleep --again. Kurt was miles away but still he was all over her. She grabbed her robe. Anything to take her mind off him. His lips, his kiss, his eyes, his hair, his intoxicating scent, his strong arms holding her, squeezing her. How could she have pushed him away?

--Stop.

She knew damn well why. Kurt was special, there was something about him; she had seen it right away. No, she didn't believe in love at first sight but when she first saw him she wanted to know more about him. *You sleep with them too early; they dump you. Fast.* Got to make them work for it, make them beg, play a little hard to get, make them know (not just think) you're the one who hung the moon. Otherwise they fuck and run, slam bam and no thank you ma'am. Even the good ones. They couldn't help it; they were just men. She wouldn't repeat that mistake again. Had come damn close to it though. Sex would wait. First he had to be made to worship the ground she walked on.

She thought about the mystery Kurt had uncovered, all those murders with the gross bottles of urine nearby. Maybe she'd see if she could also find what he had found, see if there was any danger. She didn't think Kurt was very savvy when it came to sensing danger. He seemed to be walking around in condition white all the time. He was kind of a dreamer.

She logged in to the cache-finders website, then brought up the search page.

At the SEARCH PHRASE prompt, she typed: `bottle, urine`

The computer came back with a single result:

1) Mt Tamalpais Romp - Mill Valley CA

She clicked on the link, which brought up this page:

Mt Tamalpais Romp - Normal Sized Cache
by Winkie378 [email this user]
California, USA

[click to download geographic coordinates and hints]

A fun cache hidden in a CA state park up on Mt Tam. Large Tupperware Container, the usual trinkets hidden inside. Bring fresh batteries for your GPS; it's a long hike in and out. Cache should be easy to find.

Cache Visitor Comments:

(14 comments total)

[click to see previous comments]

[13] December 17 by JellyRollJudie [32 caches found]

OH * MY * GOD!!! DO _NOT_ GO OUT THERE! A DEAD DOG is covering it, I mean a really freaking huge dog and it's STARTING TO DECOMPOSE! I WILL NEVER GO CACHING AGAIN!!!! I REPEAT DO NOT GO THERE AND NEVER GO IN THE WOODS ALONE!

[email this user]

[14] December 18 by Martello [901 caches found]

Enjoying a long vacation in the Bay area this week. Hiked up to the cache on Mt Tam today and had to chase off about a dozen huge vultures that had begun to feast on the carcass. I climbed down, then carefully retrieved the cache box with a long stick. What's scarier than the dead dog is that I found a sealed mayonnaise jar full of what appeared to be *urine* in an abandoned campsite uphill from the ranger station. Ran into a couple state cops in the overflow camping lot on the hike back out. Security was crawling all over the place for some reason. The Ranger station was closed and the station and its little parking lot were both taped off with yellow "POLICE LINE DO NOT CROSS" tape. The cops kinda blew me off; they said it was probably just coyotes that got ahold of some camper's dog. They didn't even take a report. Seemed pretty busy with the Ranger station thing. I'm requesting the admins of this site to please unlist this cache so no one else goes out there and has to deal with this mess. I've lost my appetite for at least a week, that's for dang sure. Sorry JellyRollJudie, I hope you'll continue to play the game. We'd hate to lose you over something like this. Plenty of other caches out there...

-Martello (visiting from Alamogordo NM)

[email this user]

Did you Find the Cache? Add your own comment! [click here]

That must have been what that freaky longhair dude was talking about at the cacher picnic back at Emma Long. But Kurt had found others. She thought about it for a minute, then tried as many synonyms for bottle and urine as she could think of.

The computer came back with the following results:

1) Mt Tamalpais Romp - Mill Valley CA
2) Back to Nature! - Schaumburg IL
3) Photosphere - Sunspot NM

She didn't see any Pennsylvania murder. That was odd. But Kurt hadn't mentioned anything about New Mexico. She called up the New Mexico listing:

Photosphere - Normal Sized Cache
by SunWatcher [email this user]
New Mexico, USA

[click to download geographic coordinates and hints]

This cache, like its name, is a spherical object, camouflaged to blend in with its surroundings better. In addition to the usual cache goodies, the cache contains a small camera in a baggie. You are to take a photo (a sphere with a camera, get it? Photo + Sphere = "Photosphere." Also Photosphere is a part of the sun) of yourself with the Sunspot solar observatory in the background. Please include the frame number so I can put your name on the photo when I post them online later after the roll is finished. The cache was placed with permission on the Sunspot observatory grounds, since I actually work here as a solar astronomer. Have fun & Happy Hunting! Be sure to stop in at the nearby visitor center when you get here and take a guided tour of the observatory.

Cache Visitor Comments:

(78 comments total)

[click to see previous comments]

[78] February 19 by ClimbingFool [1723 caches found]

Nice cache. Love the high altitude vistas on the hike back out. You flat-landers better bring some oxygen, 'cause the mountain air is thin! Pack in plenty of water too. Speaking of which, if you have to take a whiz, it's probably a good idea to just use the restroom at the visitor's center. Who pees in a glass jar, then leaves the jar in the woods behind the visitor center? I found it at the cache site, but that couldn't have been a geocacher who did that, could it?

[email this user]

Did you Find the Cache? Add your own comment! [click here]

So some cacher had found a jar of urine out in the mountains of Alamogordo. Well stranger things had happened; leaving a jar of urine in the woods wasn't a crime. Weird, but not criminal. She brought up a popular internet search engine, keyed in a search for any news of a killing in Alamogordo. *Shit*. There were almost two thousand hits. Too much information. She added "Sunspot" to the search, and that cut the list down to two hundred. She noticed a mention of a "solar observatory" in the original cache post, so she added that to the search as well. Bingo:

Alamogordo Daily News, Feb 17 - Section C, Page 5

SOLAR SCIENTIST KILLED IN FREAK ACCIDENT

SUNSPOT (AP) - A visiting scientist was killed last Saturday afternoon in a freak accident at the Sunspot National Solar Observatory. Sunspot Sheriff's deputies report that Ramona Willard Lexton, 38, of Fort Worth Texas, a visiting expert in digital adaptive optics, was burned to death when she fell into a solar telescope instrumentation chamber during a test.

Sources at the Sunspot observatory say that Lexton was working alone in the Vacuum Tower Telescope Saturday morning when the accident occurred. Her charred remains set off the observatory's fire alarm systems. Sunspot's volunteer firefighters responded to the scene within minutes, but it was too late to save Lexton.

According to a spokesperson for the observatory, Ms Kelly Raliman of Alamogordo, Lexton was an experienced, world-renowned expert in adaptive optics.

"She should simply have known better than to work on this equipment alone. And to work on this particular piece of equipment in the daytime is just inexcusable, I can't imagine what possessed her. We'll never know."

Raliman went on to say that the particular telescope involved in the accident is the only one in its power class in North America. Raliman said that Lexton had been perfecting a new digital technique for improving the stability of photosphere images through the use of a new computer image-processing algorithm to remove atmospheric distortions. Raliman stressed that the observatory had clearly posted safety procedures on the instrumentation chamber, and that the NSO was investigating why those procedures were ignored.

Lexton, who was in Sunspot on a yearlong sabbatical from Locklin Defense Aerospace in Fort Worth Texas, is survived by her parents and nine siblings, all of Fort Worth Texas.

4:30 A.M.

Judi's head was getting heavy. She couldn't think straight anymore. She found that she had spent the last few minutes trying to read and re-read the last paragraph, and it was mixing in with a half-dream of pulling espresso shots for nine little dwarfs. Time for bed. She emailed the links for the New Mexico death and cache comments to Kurt. She was pretty sure he hadn't said anything about New Mexico. He'd welcome the new information.

She hoped she hadn't scared him off by stopping short earlier. Nothing frustrated a guy more than slamming on the brakes once his motor got revved.

Part III
Third to Find

Chapter 38

STALNAKER'S MUMBLED PROTESTS WOKE the killer. He applied more of the engine starting fluid to the sock and covered Stalnaker's nostrils with it. The victim fell limp again. The killer massaged a cramp out of his shoulder. Sleeping on a two-foot wide beam a hundred feet up in the air wasn't easy or restful. He'd have to get some good sleep tonight, back at the abandoned car. He was going to stick around after this murder. He wanted to read about it in the papers, see it on the news. He was starting to enjoy the publicity. No one had put the string of murders together, and they probably never would. Too bad. Part of him wanted to let them all know of his genius.

He checked his watch. Close enough. The gap would expand to its maximum width in fifteen minutes. He checked Stalnaker's bindings and found them tight. He threw two short sections of rope up and over a pipe that ran across the bridge just on the other side of the expansion gap. He tied the other end of one rope to the bindings on Stalnaker's hands and the other rope to his feet, then reached out and grabbed the free ends of each rope. He tied these off to the beam on which he was sitting. He'd need to get off this beam soon or a cramp would do him in. He brushed off a wave of claustrophobia, an urge to stand up and stretch so strong that he had to steady himself on the beam to prevent it from happening automatically. As he grabbed the beam, an old abandoned hornet's nest broke loose under his white-knuckled fingers and tumbled down to the mud below.

With Stalnaker tied to the pipe next to the expansion joint, the killer was ready to begin stuffing him into the crack. He carefully pulled on each rope, first the hands, then the feet. Stalnaker rose up off the beam, bent in half at the waist, swung out over the lake, and inched up toward the expansion joint. With each move, the killer tied the rope off. It was slow work. Soon Stalnaker was hanging six inches below the expansion joint. The killer tied a length of rope around his own waist and onto the beam on which he was sitting, and as he did so his left thigh went into a terrific spasm. He swung the cramping leg up onto the beam to straighten it out and work out the cramp, but as he did so he slipped off the beam on the other side.

As he fell, he instinctively reached out and caught the beam under his armpit. For what seemed like an eternity he hung there, dangling over the muck far below. The rope tied to his waist offered little consolation now; it didn't even come into play. One arm was wrapped around the beam up to his armpit and the other flailed wildly for balance. There wasn't time to think. The leg cramp was gone now, overpowered by a sharp pain in the upper arm where the beam had caught his weight. Adrenaline surged through his veins and he swung his free arm toward the beam so that he was now gripping it with both arms up to the armpits, and his chin perched over the top. He kicked wildly and shimmied himself up onto the beam and hung there, head over one side and feet dangling over the other. Crabbing sideways with a twist, he was fully on top of the beam again. He lay there face down for some time, eyes closed, gripping the beam with arms and legs, catching his breath, glad to be alive.

After he regained his composure, he performed the most dangerous maneuver of the whole night. Stalnaker's body was a foot away, hanging six inches below the deck, out over a hundred feet of air and about four feet of thick, reeking muck below that. He couldn't just reach out and lift the victim up into the crack; the leverage wasn't right. So he flipped over onto his back, knees bent, heels hooked under the beam. His torso hung out over the water, and with his hands he reached up and shoved the unconscious man up as hard as he could. When he was finished, Stalnaker was wedged sideways into the gap between two huge slabs of concrete, his left shoulder facing the water, his right pressed up against the deck of the bridge. He had to bungee Stalnaker's feet fast to the pipe to keep them from flopping out and pulling the man free. Chest and pelvis, both were wedged in tight. Trent Stalnaker wasn't going anywhere ever again.

He scissored back onto the beam and took a few more minutes' rest.

Once he was sure that Stalnaker was securely wedged into the expansion joint, he reached up and pulled the duct tape off the drugged man's face, taking a furball of mustache with it.

An hour later the ether had finally begun to wear off. Traffic had started to flow across the bridge, mostly from the north to south. With each passing car and truck the expansion joint pinched closed a fraction of an inch, then released. The killer stayed up on the beam near his victim for another hour, to make sure that the traffic flexing the bridge didn't release Stalnaker from his prison.

Seven A.M. Traffic was in full swing now. Stalnaker's body filled the tightening joint. He groaned with each passing car. His ribs and pelvis ached. His arms were bound tight; he couldn't move them. Legs bound, unable to kick free. The ether wore off. It left him with a throbbing headache. He tried to scream, but he couldn't draw in a whole breath, he was wedged that tight. The screams came out in short bursts punctuated with gasps.

Stalnaker soon calculated that no one could hear him over the roar of the traffic overhead. He'd been an engineer himself long ago before he evolved into a sociopathic corporate executive. He figured out where he was and what was going to happen as the sun heated up the bridge.

The killer crawled back to the ledge under the bridge, and from there scrabbled down the side of the cliff to the base of the arch, where the arch met a diagonal cross-beam halfway to the water. From there he could see Stalnaker, and Stalnaker could see him, about fifty feet away. Stalnaker struggled to get free.

"I wouldn't try to move too much if I were you," said the killer.

"You sonofa... bitch... Get me... down... from here!" demanded Stalnaker.

"Why would I do that, when I went to so much trouble to get you up there?" he shouted back. He was enjoying this part. "And I wouldn't advise kicking free either, I've got your pathetic little cock tied off to the beam and if you fall you'll only get about twenty feet down before your balls are ripped clean off." He lied about the cock-tying part. He'd actually bought the materials to do it, was planning to do it, but reconsidered when he saw Stalnaker's crusty little pecker poking out back in the men's room.

Stalnaker hushed for a few minutes as if to consider his predicament. He couldn't see his genitals, and by now his pelvis was becoming numb under the crushing pressure of the expansion gap. He couldn't feel the wire, but that didn't mean there wasn't one. "Why are you... doing this...?"

Chapter 39

March 6.

"MAN, SOMETIMES THESE MOVIES really hack me off, can't they count?" asked Kurt, leaning back into the couch after taking a sip of his soda. Nipper lay on his side at the base of the couch, twitching as he chased dream squirrels.

"What do you mean?" asked Judi.

"That bad guy fired off way more than six shots," Kurt explained, pointing the remote control at the gunman on the TV screen.

"Huh? I counted eleven," said Judi.

"Yeah, that's what I mean, anyone knows guns only hold six shots, yet they keep showing guns that just shoot and shoot unbelievable amounts of ammunition without reloading, it's like a video game," said Kurt.

"That looked like a Glock nine millimeter. Those can hold up to fifteen rounds," said Judi.

Kurt stared at her for a second in disbelief. "Get outta here, they do not." Then after a pause, "how do you know that?"

"I know lots of stuff. Someday you might find out just how much, mister," she said, with a nudge.

Kurt nudged her back and said he'd like to find out someday, sooner rather than later. Judi changed the subject, asking Kurt if he'd like a snack. They walked out to the kitchen, where Judi pulled out a bag of carrots and a tub of hummus. She began to fix a snack. Nipper woke up and followed them into the kitchen, where he tentatively licked the back of Kurt's knees.

"You know, something bugs me about this dog murder thing," Kurt said, crossing his arms and leaning up against the counter.

"Yeah what's that?" she asked, arranging the baby carrot pieces on a small plate.

"Well, some of the murders have a dead dog and a bottle of urine, and some have just a dead dog..." he said.

"Yeah?" she said, scooping the hummus out into a small bowl.

"...and some have just a bottle of urine," he added.

"And some don't have a body," she teased.

"Yeah, there's that little problem too," he added, "and then one of the Krager twins finds a dead cat stuffed in a urine-filled cache out in Lakeway."

"Well, some of those might not even have anything to do with each other, like the dead cat. Why all of a sudden is it a cat instead of a dog?"

"Yeah, I thought about that. But I don't think it's all a coincidence. Maybe some of the bottles of urine are ending up in places where cachers don't find them. Like the country club murder. The bottle could have been found at the scene by the cops but maybe they didn't release that info to the media," he said.

"It's a mystery," she said, carrying the plate and bowl out to the living room.

They parked back on the sofa, where the commercial was just wrapping up. Kurt prided himself on being able to hit mute exactly as the commercial ended and the show resumed. He took it as a good sign that Judi had surrendered the remote control so early in their relationship. Judi couldn't tell how he knew when the commercials were over. Must be a guy thing. The show continued, with a rural car chase, a foot pursuit with no less than twenty uniformed cops, and another standoff in an abandoned farmhouse. Fifteen or twenty minutes of this passed, including several commercial breaks. On the last break, Kurt hit mute again, just as the show faded and the first commercial came up.

"How do you do that?" asked Judi, crunching on a hummus-covered carrot stick.

"Do what?" said Kurt, reaching for a veggie snack.

"How do you know exactly when the show is going to end to hit mute?" she asked, holding his remote control hand up and pointing to the mute button. Kurt admitted he didn't know; he just got lucky sometimes.

They sat in silence as the TV drew them in. Despite the mute, the TV worked its strange mental suction. They both stared at the four minutes of commercials filling the gap between stretches of movie, mindlessly munching on carrots and hummus. Finally Kurt broke the silence.

"So were you making up that stuff about the gun?" he asked.

"No. Hold on a sec." Judi climbed up out of the comfy couch, set a half-bitten carrot stick on the coffee table, wiped her mouth on a napkin, and walked into her bedroom. She returned carrying a palm-sized Kahr PM9 nine-millimeter semiautomatic pistol, muzzle down.

"Holy shit! Is that real? Where did you get that?" Kurt asked, sitting up straight, leaning away from Judi and the gun.

"Of course it's real," she said.

"Is it loaded? Can it go off?" he asked.

"Not if handled properly," she said, "and yes, it's always loaded. Doesn't work if it isn't."

Judi dropped the magazine, worked the slide, ejected the round from the chamber, checked it three times both visually and by putting her pinky finger in the chamber, then drilled Kurt on the basic three gun safety rules until he could remember them all in any order.

"Finger off the trigger until ready to fire, Never point the gun at anything you don't intend to destroy, and what's the third?" she asked.

"Treat all guns as if they're always loaded," he recited.

"Good. Keep those in mind, and we won't have any accidents. There will be a quiz later," she said.

She handed the pistol to Kurt, who operated the slide, practiced inserting an empty magazine a few times, then drew a bead on Judi's mantel clock and dry fired it, manually cycling the slide between each 'click.'

"Hey this is pretty wild," he laughed, turning it over in his hands, "I didn't know you were into guns."

"Well, actually I'm not *into* guns. It's not like a hobby for me or anything. But I decided a couple years ago after my roommate got raped, that I would never be a victim."

"No kidding?" he asked.

"Yeah, she was one of these women who just never thought it could happen to her," said Judi.

"Is she still alive?" he asked.

"Yeah, she lives out in L.A. She got the hell out of here after the attack, never came back. Can't blame her... She was at home alone, I was off attending the Java Expo in Vegas..." said Judi.

"...somebody break in?" asked Kurt.

"No, not really. She let the guy in," she said.

"No way! Did she know him?" he asked.

"No, not at all, but think about it, Kurt, when an injured stranger bangs on your door, what do you do?"

"Hmmm... Good point," he said.

"This guy starts banging on the door. It's around two A.M. So my roomie bolts up out of bed. As soon as the door's open, this guy's miraculously recovered from his injuries and he's immediately on her. He's about six-one, two-forty. Maybe mid thirties or so, but he just looks older somehow," said Judi.

"Wow, I can't believe it. When did this happen?" asked Kurt.

"Let's see... couple years ago at least," she said. "Guy got off on an insanity plea, only got like fifteen years in a state hospital. Damn lawyers. So anyway, she's just laying there, finally too beaten down to resist anymore, when a neighbor blows the door down with his shotgun."

"Whoa, no shit?" said Kurt.

"Well he didn't really blow it down, he first kicked it a couple times and it wouldn't open," Judi said. "So he aims his shotgun at the knob. The knob was blown clean out of the door. I found it behind the couch. So the door flies open--"

"--Wait, where did this guy come from?"

"Well, it's like two-thirty now and the neighbor, this eighty year old man--an insomniac--hears the pounding, the door slam, then the muffled screams. He actually calls the cops right away, but they put him on hold."

"What?"

"Yeah, the poor old geezer wasn't sure it was a real emergency or if it might just be a domestic squabble, so he calls 311 instead of 911."

"311?"

"Yeah, the non-emergency number," she explained.

"I didn't even know there was such a thing," he said.

"Most people don't. You have a cat up a tree, a neighbor's party gets too loud after midnight, your car breaks down; you call 311. Takes the non-emergency load off 911," she said.

"Huh! Whaddaya know. --Good idea," he said.

"In theory, yeah, but the reality is, they don't advertise it so I'm not sure it actually does any good. Then even if you do actually call it, the assholes that answer the phone are all like all pissed off that you called because you're bothering them or something, and so they try to give you the run-around like it isn't their problem," she said.

"Fuckin bureaucrats," said Kurt.

"Yep, the world is run by clerks," she said.

"So what happened with your roomie?" he asked.

"Well first the guy he spends about ten minutes messing around with 311, getting the run-around, they tell him to call the sheriff, it's out of our jurisdiction, are you sure you really heard something, could it be a cat, that kind of thing. Then he finally gets fed up with that shit and just hangs up," said Judi. "Turns out the guy's a bird hunter, or was. He grabs his shotgun and a handful of shells, neither of which have been outside his closet since 1968, and shuffles over to Dee-Dee's place as fast as he can, which ain't too fast," she said.

"Okay, so he blows the door open, then what?" Kurt asked.

"The neighbors across the street heard the shotgun blast and called 911. The cops show up in about ten minutes, guns drawn on the old man! They grab the shotgun, throw the old geezer face down on the ground, dislocating his shoulder and breaking his nose. They cuff him, then they take both the old man and the rapist into custody. Ambulance shows up about two minutes later and they take Dee-Dee off to the hospital. Doctor said later she would have been dead in another half hour. It was that close," she said.

The TV continued flickering during the story. The action movie had ended and they were a few minutes into a Hitchcock mystery film. Alfred was doing his cameo appearance, posing as a rich art lover, getting out of an expensive British touring car and viewing some roadside art for sale. The sound was still on mute. Kurt had become so absorbed in Judi's story that he had missed his cue to put the sound back on.

"So anyway, I haven't talked about this in a long time. It gets me worked up. I get so pissed, you know?" said Judi.

"I can imagine. You okay?" he asked, putting a hand on her shoulder.

"Yeah, I'm okay, it's just I keep thinking if I had been there, what could I have done?" she said, turning her back to him, inviting a massage.

"You weren't packin' heat then?" he asked, rubbing her shoulders.

"No, I was scared of guns. I trusted the cops to rescue me," she said, rotating her head downward into the massage.

"You're tense. So what happened to the guy?" asked Kurt, intensifying the massage.

"Oh yeah, wow that feels great. Of course they eventually figured out the old man was the hero, and they apologized and sent him to the hospital. The rapist, that asshole could be out in another eight years on good behavior," she said, "Um, that feels good. Can you dig in with your thumbs more? ...Oh yeah."

They sit in silence awhile, Kurt working her shoulders, both staring at the muted flickering TV.

Chapter 40

"THEY TRASHED 'STUMPIN AT the Switchback,' 'Run to the Lights,' and 'Doomed dot Com,'" said Jason, passing the printout around:

```
www.cache-finders.com Geocache Listing


Cache Visitor Comments:
(25 comments total)


[click to see previous comments]


[25] February 27 by CallMeAhab [5 caches
found]
we b the pirates that pissed in ur gay box
we tried 2 shit in it but neither of us had
2 go so we pissed insted. HA! next time we
will leve a dead cat for u pussys. HA HAH
HA! get it? dead cat - pussys! HA! u fuckin
quears!
[email this user]


Did you Find the Cache? Add your own
comment! [click here]
```

"Maari said that three others have turned up missing as well, and 'Low Water Stash' was found packed full of dog crap. And we think the little juvenile delinquents are responsible for shoving that dead cat in 'It Sneaks Up on You' and peeing in 'It's been on FIRE!' which was a rockin' cache and still pretty new."

"Fucking sociopaths," said Kurt, passing the printout back. "What are we planning to do about it?"

"We thought we'd try to spoof them. We think it's some kids, probably teenagers. There's a pattern. They're all centered on 'It's been on FIRE!' and spread outward from there. So it's like they started with that cache and just used their GPS to find the nearest ones. They're lazy. We called the cops, but they can't help us because plundering geocaches isn't a crime. In fact, they wanted to know more about geocaching because they said it sounded like littering or misdemeanor abandonment of property, which *is* a crime. We've got some serious educating to do with the local police," said Jason.

"So what can I do to help?" asked Kurt.

"Here's a map of their pattern so far," said Jason, spreading out a printout from the cache-finders website on the table. "We think based on the caches they've plundered so far, all ammo boxes, all less than a medium level of difficulty, no multiple-stage caches, no puzzles, that they'll hit one of these five caches next." He circled five caches in orange highlighter. The orange highlighter ink mixed with the ink on the inkjet printout and smudged to a brownish-black. "We're going to try to spoof them. What we want to do is move the containers on the next few likely target caches a couple hundred feet in any convenient direction. Re-hide the container and mark the new coordinates, then email the new coords to the cache owners. We're going to have a bunch of cache owners in Austin edit their cache pages with a note saying that the caches have been moved, that the posted coordinates are bogus, and for finders to email the cache owners to receive the correct coordinates. We won't be moving all the caches in Austin, but the pirates may call our bluff and try these next few, and when they don't find them we're hoping they'll give up and go find some other trouble to get into.

"That sounds pretty clever. Did you think that up yourself?" asked Kurt.

"It was actually Bonnie's idea. She's pretty sharp," said Jason.

"Where do I come in?" asked Kurt.

We'll need some people who can get out there to move these cache boxes and also we want to set out a webcam on this one near the office buildings here. Can your Monday morning unemployed cacher group help out? You guys aren't doing anything all day," said Jason.

"Funny, asshole," said Kurt.

"Just kidding. I know you're busy looking for another gig. But if you can help us catch these little mortar-forkers, it would be great. They're ruining the game," he said.

"What do we do with them once we catch them?" asked Kurt. "Like the cops said, it's not against the law to plunder caches."

"That's entirely up to you. If they're little kids, you could try to scare them. Sometimes little kids will scare just if an adult walks in and catches them doing something they know is wrong. If they're bigger kids, high schoolers or whatever, get a picture of them or write down their license tag, maybe we can tell their parents what they've been doing. Just be careful," said Jason. "Oh, and another thing, don't breathe a word of this on the internet. No postings, no group emails. Keep it strictly via phone. We don't want any word of our spoofing to get out or it won't work. So far it's only you, me, Bonnie, Maari, and the cache owners who know about it, and they've all been sworn to secrecy."

Kurt promised to keep it quiet as he folded the map into his back pocket.

He spent the next day working with some of the other unemployed cachers to set up the wireless webcam on one of the likely targets that happened to be close enough to an office building to yield useful images if someone went after it. Fortunately Austin had park preserves everywhere, including adjacent to some prime office space. Everybody knew somebody, especially in a small city like Austin, and it only took a little networking to find someone with a friend in the building, and then from there to get a colleague to set the webcam on the window ledge in their office, and aim it out at the park. The resolution wouldn't be great, but they might be able to see who was going in to pirate the cache.

One of the caches was in St. Edward's Park, and the other two were in Bull Creek District Park. He planned to start with the Bull Creek caches. As luck would have it, he hadn't yet found either cache. He decided to ask Judi if she wanted to go along to help out. He suspected she would jump at the opportunity to go out with him again.

Chapter 41

"IT'S A CACHE CALLED 'Swept Downstream,' out on Bull Creek," Kurt said, reading the information off his computer screen. "It looks fairly challenging. When can you get free?"

"I'm going to be heading out of here in about two hours to scream at some of my local suppliers. By the time I finish with that, I'm calling it a day," Judi said, "How about four?"

She was looking for any opportunity to get close to Kurt again. She couldn't put him out of her mind.

```
www.cache-finders.com Geocache Listing


Swept Downstream - Normal Sized Cache

by DerbyDude [email this user]

Texas, USA


[click to download geographic coordinates
and hints]


You'll find a very ancient automotive relic
at the coordinates. I don't know how old it
is or how it got here, it looks like maybe
it washed down the creek a very long time
ago. Someone told me maybe it fell off the
cliff, but if that's the case how the heck
did it get up there? The top of the hill is
nothing but weeds and fancy apartments.
Your challenge when you get here, apart
from pondering how this relic came to this
```

place, is just to figure out how to get to the coordinates. Do you swim across the creek, or do you climb down the cliff face? Be careful. Cache container is a 30 cal ammo can, carefully camouflaged.

"Wow, that must be from the 1940's," said Judi.

"Yeah, late thirties or early forties. Ford," said Kurt.

"You're making that up," said Judi. "How do you know that?"

"I'm a big Ford fan," he said. "Besides, I can see the Ford logo on the trunk lid."

"You jerk," she said, slapping him on the shoulder. "Man it's really wedged in there, between the trees and rocks. How do you think it got there?" asked Judi.

"Well there are two theories I heard. Maybe it washed down the creek. This creek could get pretty high when it rains. Then again, maybe it fell from up there," he said, pointing up the sheer rock face.

"But how did it get wedged between the tree and rocks?" she asked.

"I'm pretty sure the rocks were here when it landed, but those trees can't be more than about thirty, forty years old. I'm sure that the trees grew up around it after it got here," said Kurt.

"We may never know," said Judi.

"You're probably right," he said.

"Where do you think the cache would be?" she asked.

"Well, if it was me hiding it, I'd put it underneath or inside the vehicle somewhere. Look inside the dash, there where the radio used to be," he said. "I'll look in the engine compartment. Watch for critters."

They each rooted around the vehicle for a few minutes. The car was completely rusted and full of leaves. A family of bark scorpions had made a home under the engine block. They scuttled for cover when the intruders poked near their house with a stick. Nipper was no help at all. After wading across the creek he marked every tree, plant, and rock until long after he'd run dry.

"There it is," she said.

"Where?" he asked.

"Right there in the dash, where the radio would go, just like you said," she said. "It's covered in leaves. Looks like someone made some serious camouflage for it."

"Okay, that's awesome. The little bastards haven't gotten this one then. Pull it out and let's move it," said Kurt.

"Oh shit," she said, suddenly serious. "Kurt, we gotta leave--now."

"Huh? Why?" said Kurt, craning his neck to see over the hood.

"There's a bottle of urine under here."

Chapter 42

JUDI CALLED UP A local pizza delivery joint while Kurt flipped through the TV channels. It was amazing; you really could have fifty-seven channels on the cable, and not find anything interesting to watch. Just like that old Bruce Springsteen song.

"Do you think that jar is related to the stuff that we've been tracking on the net?" Kurt asked, sitting on the couch petting Nipper's head. Besides licking the backs of knees, Nipper was fond of placing his head on your leg whenever you were seated, whether you wanted a dog's head in your lap or not.

"Either way, it's creepy. I think we should call the cops," she said.

"Yeah but last I checked," he said, "it's not illegal to piss in a jar."

They had approached the cache site carefully and slowly by shimmying over the creek on a fallen tree. On the way out, they had waded straight across the creek as fast as possible. They were soaked to their hips in frigid creek water. They'd sloshed out of the park as fast as they could slosh.

Now Judi was wearing fresh dry clothes, with her holstered PM9 tucked inside her waistband where it could be seen outside her T-shirt. Kurt wrapped himself in Judi's too-small pink terry cloth bathrobe while his clothes tumbled in her washing machine.

Judi continued to nag him, so Kurt called the cops on 311. The fastest way to stop a woman from nagging was just to do what she wanted. Especially if she was armed and you were wearing nothing but her pink bathrobe.

After about ten minutes of bouncing back between "It's not our jurisdiction," and "Please hold," he got someone at Austin PD. The officer took his name, address, phone number, and listened to the story. The cop seemed more concerned about the geocaching, which was new to him. "People are leaving metal Ammunition boxes out in the woods?" he asked. "That's either littering or misdemeanor property abandonment. Anyway it's probably against park rules." Finally the officer told him there was nothing the police could do because it's not a crime to be homeless and urinate in a bottle in an old abandoned car. Nonetheless, the officer asked for a description of the killer. That's when Kurt had to admit to the officer that he couldn't describe the killer because they'd never actually seen him. That was the end of the call.

"So when did you start carrying a gun?" Kurt asked, after the pizza arrived. They ate in front of the TV, from paper plates and pizza cardboard on Judi's coffee table. Nipper showed no interest in the pizza. He'd been taught not to beg.

"Well, I didn't know what to do after Dee-Dee's attack. Our house was a mess. You know I had to clean it up myself? I about puked my guts dry, and at the same time all I could do was cry for my poor roomie. I was scared. Angry. Really angry," she said. On the muted TV, an angry muscle dude with rebel sideburns was yelling at his son who was frantically trying to weld together a custom chopper motorcycle. The choppers they built were cool, but neither Kurt nor Judi could stand all the yelling and insults that were apparently required to put one together.

"Wow I can't believe you had to clean it up," said Kurt.

"This is something they don't ever show in the movies. What happens after the crime. Someone has to clean up the mess," she said.

"Gross," said Kurt, setting his pizza slice back on his paper plate.

"Yeah, anyway, after the cleanup I got to thinking, what could Dee-Dee have done to prevent the attack?" she said.

"So that's when you decided to get a gun?" he asked.

"Not right away. I was scared of guns; remember? First I thought, well, she shouldn't have opened the door. But I asked myself, would I have done the same thing?" she said.

"Shit, I would've," said Kurt.

"Yeah, me too, I think anyone would," she said.

"So what are you supposed to do?" he asked.

"Well, first I bought some pepper spray, but the stuff doesn't work like you see in the movies," she said. On TV, the muscle-boss was throwing tools and parts around, yelling and pointing an accusing finger at one of his employees, who averted his eyes and kept his head low while he twisted and hammered a piece of metal in some kind of heavy vise.

"So I went to this martial arts place in a strip mall down on Lamar, right, I figure I could learn to do karate moves or judo or something," she said.

"Yeah?" Kurt said, picking up his slice of pizza again.

"I learned some defensive moves that have been really helpful, but it takes years to learn martial arts well enough to fight off an attacker bigger than you, and then what if you're faced with a gang of attackers, or someone with a knife?" she said.

"Yeah, kinda like in Indiana Jones where he shoots that fancy sword fighter," he said, taking a bite of pepperoni and cheese.

"Yeah that was pretty funny," she said, wiping the corner of her mouth with a paper towel. She was fresh out of napkins. "So I figured I don't have years to learn a martial art that won't be as effective as what the police use," she said.

Kurt thought about responding, but didn't say anything. He covered his crust-filled mouth with his hand instead. What was it about pizza that made you want to keep eating it until you exploded? "You gonna eat that crust?" he asked.

"You can have it," she said.

"So you went out and bought a gun then?" he asked, grabbing her uneaten crust off her plate.

"Hell no, I didn't know the first thing about guns, Kurt. So I went to a shooting range," she said, lifting another greasy slice off the cardboard and dropping it onto her plate.

"Wow, I wouldn't have thought of that," he said. The robe slipped off one of his knees, and he reached for another paper towel to wipe his hands before he could adjust the robe.

"Uh, you need to tuck that robe back around your knees, mister," she said, pulling the robe back up for him. "Yeah, I pass by there all the time on the way to my Round Rock store, so I knew they were there, just never gave 'em a second thought. Figured all gun people were redneck 'Rambo' assholes and militia, who needs that shit, you know?"

"Yeah," he said. The chopper guys on TV were all standing around a demon-themed bike, trying to get it started. Their shop was full of smoke, and the muscle-boss dude was looking pissed. He went into his office and slammed the door as they cut to a commercial. The TV was still on mute.

"Turns out there were just normal everyday people in there. When I walked in I was literally shaking. I mean every wall was thick with rows and stacks of machine guns, military-style black rifles and shotguns and boxes and crates of ammo and what other stuff I don't know. The place smelled of solvent and burned gunpowder and leather. It was like an arsenal. The gun shop I mean. The range was in the back. I almost turned and bolted, but I thought, if this is what I need to learn, I've got to do it," said Judi.

"Wow, I'm not sure even I would go into one of those places," said Kurt, taking a swig of lemon-lime soda from a Styrofoam cup.

"Well, I wasn't either. But I went in anyway. I kept thinking of that psycho rapist, and all the blood, and that steeled me for whatever I needed to do," she said, "No one's assaulting me."

Chapter 43

THE RED LIGHT ON his desk phone flashed. On, On, Off. On, On, Off. Jason picked up the receiver and punched the MESSAGE button. At the same time, he flipped open his computer screen and gasped as he read the overnight email message count. One hundred twenty-one new messages since yesterday afternoon. The crap must be hitting the fan somewhere. Phone messages had priority though. Anyone who was peeved enough to call got his immediate attention.

The message was just from Martello. He punched the number seven to play the message:

"Jason, Kurt, this is Martello, in Alamogordo? Look I called those friends of mine in California. You guys were right. They had a dead ranger up there. Guy's name was (get this) Ricky Nelson. I shit you not. Heh-heh. Poor schmuck. I hate it when parents do that to their kids. You know I used to work with a database programmer named Ronald Reagan? Shit you fucking not, same spelling and everything. Anyway, that's all they knew, just the name, and that he was found murdered last December, maybe a couple days before I found the dead dog. That's what all the tape was about. Anyway, that's all I got for now. Call me if you need anything else. Cache on, dudes."

Jason punched the FORWARD button and followed that with Kurt's cell number, sending the message to Kurt's voicemail. Kurt had been out of work for a couple months and could use the seventy-five thousand dollar reward for the Harrison Valley murder. Jason hoped this lead would help. He really didn't have time to track it down himself.

He clicked open the first email. It was a spam message for a breast enlargement pump. Great. That's all he needed, even bigger man-tits than he had now. Delete. One down, one hundred twenty to go.

Chapter 44

KURT FUMBLED THE PHONE out of his pants pocket while he tried to steer with his knee. The tiny phone clattered over the console and onto the floor on the passenger side of the Expedition. Why the hell did the phone always ring when he was driving or in the shower or on the shitter? He could be available all day, surfing the web or out geocaching in a park on a trail, yet the minute he was doing something else that required two hands, that's when the phone rang.

The light turned red. He slowed to a stop, slipped the transmission into park, popped the seatbelt, bent over, and reached down for the phone. He snagged it in his right hand and then sat back upright. He flipped the phone open and checked the screen. It was a voicemail message, not a call. He pressed the TALK button and listened to the message from Martello, as the traffic light changed to green.

Before the next intersection he swung the Expedition into a wide U-turn across four lanes of traffic. He needed to get back to the house to follow up on this newest lead.

As he rounded the top of the hill on ranch road 2222, he caught a glimpse of red and blue flashing lights in his rearview. *Shit. What now?*

"License and registration please," said the cop, a roly-poly Travis County Sheriff's deputy. The guy could have been a teddy bear, except that he was bristling with guns and clubs and mace and handcuffs and radios and other serious cop shit. The deputy had to weigh at least three hundred pounds, all stuffed into a crisply starched brown sheriff's uniform. He wore mirrored sunglasses perched above a bulbous nose and a thick blonde caterpillar of a mustache. His head was cropped into a neat military flattop that just didn't go with the mustache.

"What's the problem sheriff?" asked Kurt.

"Sir, I'm citing you for an illegal U-turn, and for failure to use seat restraints," said sheriff teddy-bear, "please wait here in your vehicle."

"Do you have any other questions?" asked the deputy, handing Kurt his license and his copy of the ticket.

"Yeah, actually I do, said Kurt. "As long as I've got you here, I'm tracking a possible interstate serial killer on the internet, and I want to know the best way to get the authorities involved in helping catch the guy, once I figure out who he actually is."

The sheriff reached up and lowered his glasses with one hand. He reached around his bulk and stuffed his citation booklet in his back pocket with the other. Without moving his head, he looked Kurt up and down to see if he was serious. He pushed his Hollywood shades back up onto his face with his thumb. "Sir, the best advice I can give you is to drive carefully, keep your seatbelt fastened and if you see anything suspicious, call 911. Let law enforcement handle the matter. That's our job. Have a nice day." Before he turned to walk back to his cruiser, he handed Kurt his business card.

"Thanks," said Kurt, then immediately regretted having said it.

Chapter 45

JUDI SCRAMBLED UP THE face of the cliff and perched on the top. Nipper beat her to the top, then ran off to explore the new place. Dogs could be such mountain goats sometimes, even creaky old dogs with arthritis.

The land at the top of the cliff was flat and overgrown with weeds. A few hundred feet from the edge of the cliff ran a chain link fence surrounding a ritzy apartment complex. Under the weeds Judi's hiking boots crunched on limestone gravel. Rusted beer cans, the ancient kind made from steel and opened using one of those openers that made a triangular puncture hole, were scattered about the area, their labels long obliterated by decades of weather and rust.

She placed her radio alongside her cheek and pressed the push-to-talk button. "Blue unit in position," she said, "over."

"Roger that, blue unit. Yellow unit in position," said Kurt, into his yellow walkie-talkie, from his hiding spot in the weeds a hundred feet from the rusted car. Many cachers carried walkie-talkies to stay in touch on their cache hunts. Perfect for staking out the suspected hideout of an interstate serial murderer too.

"Kurt, can we just cut all that 'blue unit,' 'yellow unit' shit?" asked Judi, "Over--Sorry, can I say 'shit' on here? Over."

"Yeah, you can just talk normally," said Kurt, disappointed. He actually liked all the radio talk. "Let me know if you see anything, but try to stay out of sight."

They planned to observe the car in the late afternoon, just after sunset. They figured that the killer might actually be sleeping in the car, and evening would be a logical time to catch him there. Judi also had the whole evening off, and was dying to spend it with Kurt. Judi perched high above with binoculars, and Kurt squatted in the weeds down below. They'd snap the suspect's picture with Kurt's digital camera in infared night mode. Then they'd have something to go to the police with. Some hard evidence. Maybe if they turned in the killer, the cops would throw out Kurt's traffic tickets. Well, at least he'd be able to claim the seventy-five thousand and pay the tickets out of that.

Chapter 46

THE KILLER WALKED BACK to the park after venturing out to check the newspapers. No news of the Stalnaker murder yet. His stomach tingled with a perverse thrill, anticipating the news coverage. He planned to wait in the park for a few days until the news broke, then he'd relish the coverage, bask in the glory and the limelight before moving on to the next victim on his list. Besides, Austin in the spring, what better time to camp in a beautiful park and enjoy the great outdoors? He never got to spend this much time outside when he was working.

He got halfway down the path to the abandoned car before he spotted a chunky blonde woman sitting high on the cliff. What the hell? He stepped off the path behind some cedar trees. He saw her place binoculars to her eyes, and then raise her other hand next to her face. At the same time he heard a female radio voice crackling from a stand of trees up ahead. She was talking to someone on a walkie-talkie. A spaniel was sniffing around her, constantly moving, appearing and disappearing off into the weeds. He crept in closer and saw a man hiding in the trees down by the creekside. The man was looking at the car, then looking back at the path both ways, then mumbling into his radio. They were staking him out. What the hell? The murder hadn't made the news. Were these plainclothes cops? Maybe they'd tracked him somehow and withheld the news of the murder from the media. But how could they have tracked him? He hadn't left a trace.

Wait, something was wrong with this picture. Cops didn't use trained attack-spaniels. Cop dogs were always German shepherds. Who the fuck were these people? And why were they looking for him? He needed to find out.

The killer hid in the trees, motionless. After dark, he crept back up toward the parking lot. He found a game path leading up to the cliff the long way around. He stole up onto the cliff behind

Judi. Before he could get to her, he was greeted by the bark of her spaniel. He bent down to quiet the dog. As he stroked the dog's neck, something clinked. He slipped the collar off Nipper's neck and worked the rabies tag off its metal ring. He put the collar back on the dog and slinked back down the path. He didn't want to confront these people in case they were cops, but he needed to find out who the hell they were and why they were tracking him.

Judi called off the stakeout at fifteen to midnight. The killer hadn't shown up, and they didn't know why. She had to get up at six the next morning and couldn't spend all night hunkered down in the weeds looking for someone who might never show. And she hadn't gotten to spend the evening close to Kurt.

The killer slept on the floor in the men's room.

Chapter 47

March 9

"SPICEWOODVETERINARYSERVICES, howmayidirectyourcall?" The receptionist bolted her line out so rapidly that the killer at first wasn't sure if he dialed the correct number. In the background he heard echoes of a beagle puppy's shrill and constant barking. Yeah, this was the right number. The receptionist cracked her gum, waiting for a response. She was getting paid by the hour. She had all day.

"Yeah, uh, I found a lost dog in the park and it uh, had a rabies tag with this number on it. I need to like, uh, find its owner," said the killer.

"Oh that's wonderful! What's the tag number?" said the receptionist, slower now.

"Ninety-two oh-three," he said, looking over his shoulder to see if a passing SUV was going to pull into the parking lot. He was calling from the pay phone outside the restroom building in his park. Yeah, he'd come to think of it as *his* park.

"Hold on a sec," said the receptionist. In the background the beagle had stilled and in its place he could hear the receptionist clicking on her computer keyboard. She was at the same time processing a credit card transaction for another customer. He could hear the phone dialing out on another line for the automatic card verification. The receptionist was hired for her multi-tasking skills, but this morning she had it easy.

"Sir, I have the owner's number," she said, "have you got something to write with?"

Chapter 48

THE KILLER BATHED AND trimmed his beard in the men's room at his park. His hair was pulled back into a ponytail. He'd washed and dried his clothes in the laundromat in the Jester strip mall, and then stopped in at Java Judi's. He knew most of the local coffee shops had some level of free wireless computer access. He needed to look up the dog owner's address.

He looked and smelled the part of the business casual yuppie latte drinker, intent on career advancement and top-line profitability. He blended right in.

The killer ordered a sugar-free extra-tall latte, forked over four bucks plus a buck tip. Five bucks for a cup of coffee. That was the real crime here.

He grabbed a table that had one of the free laptops on it. The laptops were the latest design out of Cupertino, translucent plastic cases, neon effects, big color screen, a midrange multi-core processor chip suited for casual web surfing and multimedia, all connected to the internet through a high speed radio link. Each was tethered to the table with a cheap locking cable. The cable ended in a short locking tab that loosely fit into a plastic slot on the side of the machine. These were not a serious security feature; they were to keep honest people honest. He sipped his latte and called up a popular internet search engine. He typed the spaniel owner's phone number into the search engine, area code first. The search engine immediately returned:

```
Judi McBride
12876 Spicedale Springs Blvd
Apt #8403,
Austin, TX 78759
```

jMcBride@javaJudis.com

www.javaJudis.com

Bingo. It even showed her picture from her website. That was her. Fucking Java Judi herself. The chubby blonde from the cliff. He looked around, didn't see her. He wrote her name and address down on the back of a napkin.

The morning crowd filtered in, and Java Judi's jumped. A line of nervous caffeine addicts formed a jagged line to the door, George Benson's jazzy Pittsburgh guitar ringing over the speakers in a futile attempt to soothe them. The staff behind the counter blurred as they took orders, made change, poured scalding hot cups of coffee, steamed milk, pulled espresso shots four and six at a time. Equipment beeped, lights flashed, coffee makers buzzed and gurgled. The place smelled of deep roasted organic Arabica beans. Employees oblivious to the wonderful smells jumped and shuffled to service the beeps, buzzes and flashes. They were a model of efficiency, speed, and stress.

The killer drank the rest of his latte while searching news sources for any reports of his murder spree. Had anyone put it together yet? He needed to know. The urge to tell someone about his spree was becoming unbearable. His genius needed to be broadcast to the world. He must fight that urge. Someday it might come out but he needed to cross a few more names off his list first. He couldn't find any video coverage online of his murders, but a few had made the local papers. That was good. So far the police hadn't connected them. That was also good. They might never put it together. He could expand his list.

He pulled up his work history from his personal file storage on the internet and printed off a copy. This had most, but not all of the names of his victims and future victims on it.

Java Judi's corporate policy supplied a networked laser printer for their customers. It wasn't exactly a full-blown business center;

they intentionally supplied a slow printer, but you could print off a handful of pages while you drank your coffee. At five bucks a cup, the extra paper and toner expense to keep customers in the shop longer was one of their best investments.

The yellow light on the printer flashed on-on, skip, on. On-on, skip, on. Then it went blank and emitted a high-pitched squeal, and it wouldn't shut up.

Damn. Rachel pivoted from the steaming espresso machine, and then wiped her hands on a towel laying on the counter. She instinctively popped the latches on the front, dropped the roller mechanism, and carefully teased out the jammed printout. It was some customer's resume or work history. She set the printout next to the espresso machine, then slapped the mechanism back up into place and pressed the continue/feed button. You could tell she'd done this a hundred times before. Laser printers didn't like humidity, and they rebelled by jamming. When it detected the jam had been cleared, the printer automatically reprinted a new copy of the jammed page.

In the meantime, three more orders had come in and Rachel struggled to remember and build them. Small Mocha latte, half sweet, Carmel vanilla latte extra tall, and a sugar-free red-eye.

David, the new guy working the register this morning, hadn't learned the proper sequencing of the orders yet. Java Judi's prided themselves on getting every customer's order in their hand within ninety seconds of the order leaving their lips. One way they accomplished this was to standardize on the sequencing of the orders that were called out by the order taker. The standard sequencing for each order was size first, followed by drink type, then followed by flavors, then sugar free status. David hadn't quite gotten the hang of it yet, and would call the order out exactly as the customer said it, which was almost never in the right sequence. The long-time regular customers picked up on the sequencing after a few visits and said it in the right order to speed things even further, but most who just walked in off the street were likely to ramble. Rambling wasn't good for efficiency. David was rambling.

Meanwhile the espresso machine buzzed. The temperature had gotten too high while Rachel serviced the laser printer. The shots would have to be dumped out and remade. Java Judi's would rather dump ten bad shots than serve one bad shot to a customer, and at five bucks a cup, they could afford to dump a lot of espresso.

As Rachel struggled to mentally re-sequence the trio of orders and begin making each drink, she forgot about the jammed sheet she'd pulled from the printer. She left it sitting on the counter next to the espresso machine, where it was soon swished to the back and buried under damp towels, half-full paper cups of steamed milk, drops and spray of espresso from the espresso maker, and other random debris from the morning rush.

The killer picked up his printout from the out-tray on the printer by the espresso machine, and tossed his empty latte cup in the trash. He'd be adding more names to his list. Most of the names he needed were right there on the page.

Back at his table, he bit the tip of a cheap ballpoint pen until the tip and ink tube assembly slid out, and he pocketed it. He jammed the open end of the pen housing into the circular keyhole of the security cable and gave it a wiggle and twist. The lock unlocked, the locking tab popped free and released the laptop.

The line by now snaked out the door. Every chair was filled with a latte-sipping customer, and more were standing around, cradling their warm cups and hoping that another chair would free up soon. Cool morning air breezed in through the door, and the killer breezed out, carrying the laptop bundled in a newspaper under his arm. The staff, still a blur, didn't even notice the theft. Rachel, eyes fixed on the espresso machine's temperature dial, called out an automatic "Thank you," as the killer left.

Chapter 49

THE KILLER HIKED BACK down to the abandoned car.

What had those two meddlers found? Had he left anything incriminating behind? When he looked in through the passenger window, he saw a metal box camouflaged with fake plastic leaves glued to it. What the hell was that? He hadn't seen that there before. He turned it over and saw the block printing on the underside:

OFFICIAL GEOCACHE

GAME PIECE

DO NOT DISTURB

What the fuck? What was a Geocache? Game piece? What kind of Game was this? He opened the box, then dumped it out on the seat. Out spilled a random collection of cheap toys and useless trinkets. Key chains, coins, plastic animals, a fairly decent compass, die-cast cars, a couple dollar bills, a pack of Sweet-Tarts, some other useless shit.

He ripped open the Sweet-Tarts, crunched and ate them, winced at the cloying taste, then pocketed the dollar bills. He found a notebook, sealed in a plastic baggie. He flipped through it; he read a few of the pages. People had been coming here to find this box over the last several years, using their GPS receivers, then writing about it in this little notebook. Fucking geeks. He found a printout inside the front cover of the notebook:

`You found the cache!`

This is a game piece in a Global Positioning System (GPS) treasure hunting game called Geocaching. Players use GPS units to stash and find little containers like this one all over the globe.

Go ahead, exchange trinkets and sign the logbook if you like. Be sure to hide the container back just the way you found it. Come visit the website to learn more or to post an online note about your discovery:

www.cache-finders.com

He ripped that sheet out of the notebook and stuffed it in his back pocket. He tossed the ammo container in the creek, along with handfuls of the trinkets. The can bobbed, then sank. The trinkets floated downstream. He pocketed the compass.

The killer reviewed what he knew about the two stalkers. They weren't cops, that was certain. They drove away in an ordinary sport utility vehicle. One of them he discovered later was Java Judi, a coffee shop owner, not a cop or a private investigator, and that fat bitch had an old Brittany spaniel, not a young police dog. If they weren't cops, how did they know about him? Since these two were amateurs and not police, they must not have enough info to convince the police of anything, whatever they knew or think they knew. Still, they were staking him out. They must know something. They must have been playing this geo-finding game, maybe that's what brought them to this car. But how did they know he was there?

He'd have to take some time off from his plan to find out what they knew.

Chapter 50

JAMIE UNFASTENED HER BIKINI top and lay face down on her SpongeBob beach towel on the deck of the Sea Ray. The warmth of the spring sun tingled over her back and shoulders. The gentle rocking of the boat on the waves, the lapping of the waves against the hull of the boat, the cool breeze in her hair, and the forbidden taste of Mexican beer soon made her languid. She shifted, resettled, wiggled her toes, then rolled her arms slightly to turn the white undersides up for a more even tan.

Frank was below deck in the cabin, fetching another couple of Corona Lites and fantasizing about Jamie, mentally going over his plan, his lines, his moves. Jamie was thin, blonde, young, popular, and by all locker room accounts, wild in the sack. She'd been coming on to him all week ever since the weather turned, trying to get him alone out on his dad's boat. He was certain he'd be joining the Lake Club this evening. *Lake Club* was a term his buddies at Balcones High School coined to refer to those lucky bastards who'd gotten some pussy out on a boat on Lake Austin. Frank, only seventeen, wasn't a member of any club that required you to get naked with a girl, whether on land or sea. What a score if he could have Jamie as his first. He'd have bragging rights for years. He'd be a king.

His dad's brand new Sea Ray 215 Weekender was perfect for his induction into the club. It had enough power to get them out to the remote parts of the lake, and it had an ice box and private berth down in the cabin. His dad had purchased the twenty-one-foot craft to help entertain clients in his commercial real estate practice. It was a forty-one-thousand-dollar babe magnet. A floating bachelor pad.

What Frank didn't know is that Jamie had no intention of having sex with him, not now, not ever. She just wanted a free ride on a luxurious power boat, some free beer, and a chance to work on her tan lines. The word around the locker room was bullshit; she was actually a crummy lay. She was more interested in using guys to get whatever she wanted. The ones who'd been used had simply been too proud to admit it, so her reputation grew.

The Lower Colorado River Authority, commonly known by its acronym LCRA, was responsible for everything in, on, and under the lakes and rivers of Austin, Texas. They'd drained Lake Austin a month earlier to kill off a choking infestation of hydrilla. Yesterday they'd opened the gates on the Mansfield Dam and flooded Lake Austin with fresh cold water from the bottom of Lake Travis. The Lake Club could resume operations immediately.

Jamie jerked her head up. Something metal had struck the stainless steel deck railing, bounced off the deck, and splashed into the lake. She propped up on her elbows and looked over the edge. She could see sunlight glinting off a set of keys pulling a thick leather fob under the water. The brown leather fob twisted the keys as they sank, and the sunlight glinted off the keys and the shiny BMW logo on the fob, becoming greener and finally disappearing. *What the hell?* She rolled off SpongeBob onto the smooth warm fiberglass deck, cupped a hand above her eyes, and looked up. "Oh my God!--Frank!"

"Hah?" Frank popped his head up out of the companionway. His eyes immediately locked onto Jamie's perky young breasts, cream white, with pink nipples pointing up toward the afternoon sun. He'd never seen anything like these outside of the glossy pages of his older brother's magazines. He could not look away. "Mwhah," he exhaled, barely audible. His jaw slackened, drool forming at one corner of his mouth. Maybe he didn't need to work on his moves after all. She was just going to give it to him. Here. Now. Damn, this boat was awesome.

"Look up *there* you shithead!" she said, covering her breasts and pointing to the torn and bloody figure dangling from the underside of the highway 360 bridge. "Call the fucking police!"

Chapter 51

March 9

BREAKING INTO JAVA BITCH'S place had been difficult. He'd had to shunt the alarm and break a window. He had to move fast.

He couldn't find anything in her place that showed what they knew. He looked through her desk, rooted through her computer, even paged through her email to see if there was anything. Nothing. Nothing except a post-it note on the monitor with a local phone number, red hearts doodled around it. That would be the other meddler then.

He pulled up a search engine on her computer, punched in the phone number, then wrote down Kurt's address. *Who the fuck are these people?* he thought.

Chapter 52

GETTING INTO KURT'S PLACE was easy. The guy lived in an older neighborhood with lots of tree cover, and he'd left his back door unlocked. The killer didn't waste any time finding the office bedroom and the computer desk. He shuffled through a stack of papers sitting on top of a pile of trinkets and dirty dishes. The guy was a fucking slob, but what's this? His eye was drawn to a name on a computer printout half buried under a pile of bills, assorted jewelers screwdrivers, and a Rubik's cube:

DATE	PLACE	P	DOG	VICTIM	REWARD
12-15	MT. TAMALPAIS	Y	Y	NELSON	–
12-26	HARRISON VALLEY	N	Y	MCCHASNEY	$75K
01-15	SCHAUMBURG	Y	Y	CHORZEMPA	$5K
02-27	AUSTIN / ST EDS	N	Y	–NONE–	–
02-17	SUNSPOT NM	Y	N	LEXTON	accident?
02-17	AUSTIN / CITY PARK	N	Y	–NONE–	–

Shit. Somehow this slob had tracked him. But how? What was ST. EDS? It was obvious this guy was some kind of bounty hunter, since he'd carefully tallied up the reward amounts.

Just then he heard a key turn in the front door lock.

Chapter 53

JUDI ROLLED ON TOP of Kurt, straddled his hips, and pinned his shoulders to his bed. She clawed at his shirt, hiked it up around his neck, got it stuck on his arms, and then fumbled at the buttons on his shorts. Kurt wriggled the rest of the way out of his shirt, and let it fall to the floor by the bed.

Nipper had seen this type of activity before and knew that it never involved him getting to lick knees or rest his head in anyone's lap, so he'd gone off in search of Pokey, who was going to be getting some canine company whether she wanted it or not.

Kurt interrupted Judi's unbuttoning long enough to pull her polo top off over her head. He flung it across the room toward the dresser.

"Hold on a sec..." she said. She rotated away from Kurt, then slipped her holster out of the waistband of her shorts and carefully set the gun on the nightstand.

Kurt reached up behind her and pulled her toward him, simultaneously ticking off the three metal fasteners behind her bra. She pushed up and away, freeing her breasts. She slipped her bra down her arms, growled lightly through clenched teeth, then dug her nails of both hands into the skin on his chest.

"Ouch, whoa there, that hurts," he said, levering her arms away. They wrestled and kissed. Kurt unbuttoned her shorts. She rose to allow him to slip them off over her hips and she kicked them off the rest of the way, then lay on top of him, gazing into his eyes, stroking his hair.

Peering through the crack between the closet doors, the killer held his breath. His luck had changed. At first he'd been surprised and trapped. He tried to hide in the computer office but the closet was jammed with books and computer boxes. He'd slipped down the hall to the next bedroom and found room in that closet. The two meddlers hadn't wasted any time getting to the bedroom. He'd pressed himself deep into the closet when he heard them enter the room, but soon he realized that they were vulnerable. He had found a baseball bat stacked in the back corner of the closet, along with a catcher's mitt and some other dusty sports equipment. The bat was sweet, a nice old-fashioned vintage wooden Louisville Slugger. Heavy, solid, smooth. Not like the newer lightweight aluminum bats. He choked up on the grip a bit and waited for his chance. He wanted to take out the bounty hunter first. He could deal with the Java woman later, slowly. Had to wait for his chance.

Chapter 54

"WE DON'T HAVE TO do this, you know," she whispered, pulling back.

"What?" he asked, unbelieving.

"We don't have to do it if you don't want to. I'm not forcing you or anything."

"Uh, yes we do," he said, pulling her close and then rolling over on top.

The killer burst out swinging, a great overhead swing like a rail worker driving a sledgehammer down on a spike. Kurt heard the door and was already moving sideways and turning to face it; the swing only half-connected, the blow glanced off his head and struck mostly shoulder. Stunned, unconscious, Kurt collapsed onto Judi. From the other bedroom, Nipper woofed out an alarmed bark and came running.

Judi had spotted the swinging of the closet door out of her peripheral vision and instinctively reached back for the nightstand just as the Slugger was glancing the side of Kurt's head. As Kurt collapsed on top of her, she extended the weapon toward the attacker, wrapped her finger around the trigger and squeezed. She had no time to line up the sights. As it rolled away, Kurt's body interfered with her arm, so the shot went past the killer's head, high into the wall above the closet door.

The killer felt the copper-jacketed hollowpoint slug flick his ear as he was raising the bat for another swing. He didn't hear anything. No one in the room heard anything. The sound of the gun was a cannon shot. The killer didn't wait for the second shot. He leapt out the bedroom door, dropped the bat and ran outside. Nipper gave chase to the threshold, then trotted back to the bedroom.

It had taken Judi five minutes to locate the phone before she could call 911. She couldn't find a phone anywhere. She checked the bedroom, the kitchen, the office. Nothing, not even a cordless handset. Kurt didn't have a fixed phone line. There was only an empty phone jack in the kitchen where a normal person would have hung a telephone. She had to find his mobile. She'd left her own mobile back in her apartment, not wanting to be interrupted by business while out spending time with Kurt. First she tried Kurt's pockets, but it wasn't in there. She rolled him over, checked his face. He was still breathing. He had a little trickle of blood from his ear. She was shaking, still gripping the PM9 in her right hand, her trigger finger properly and safely extended along the barrel. Then she remembered that he'd dumped out his keys, wallet, and other pocket stuff on the counter as he came in the front door. She found the mobile there, flipped it open and punched 911, all the while looking around to see if the attacker was gone.

"Sprint PCS, what city please?" said the mobile operator.

"What city? --Austin!" she yelled. *Why don't they know this?*

"One moment please," said the operator.

"Nine-One-One, what is your address please?" asked the 911 operator.

"I'm --we've been attacked, my boyfriend is unconscious, please someone help!" said Judi.

"What is your address?" asked the operator.

"Address?" asked Judi. *Why don't they know this?* "I don't know the address! I'm at my boyfriend's house, um, on --by the dam, Lake Travis, uh, shit, wait, I think he's got a bill here or something, please hurry, he's been hit." Judi had no idea what Kurt's address was. She had to sort through the papers on his desk to find an envelope with his address on it. She read the address to the operator.

It only took the sheriff seven minutes to send a car to the house, since they only had to come up from the station on Hudson Bend, a few miles away.

Deputy teddy bear pulled his notebook out of his back pocket, scratched the back of his flat-top, and began writing. His mirrored shades poked out from his front shirt pocket. The paramedics had loaded Kurt onto a gurney and wheeled him out the front door and into the ambulance. He had a concussion, some cosmetic damage to the ear, bruise on the shoulder, nothing major, but he was unconscious and that was a concern. He was lucky the bat hadn't connected squarely with the back of his head or it could have been much worse.

Judi gave the sheriff a description of the attacker, as best as she could remember. The description wasn't enough for a composite sketch but at least they had a general description. Her ears were still ringing from the gunshot; she was still shaking.

The sheriffs deputies took the bat, they took Kurt's list of murder victims, they put Judi's PM9 in a plastic baggie and took that too. A sheriff's office technician traced the exit path of the bullet through the wall and found it embedded in a joist up in the attic. He dug the slug out of the wood and bagged that as well. Evidence.

Judi was driven to the Travis County sheriff's office in the back of their squad car. Officer teddy bear wasn't sure what the charge was, but a gun had been fired. *Someone* was going to the station, dammit.

Judi called her corporate attorney, who knew a good criminal attorney, and with some legal crank-turning, the sheriff let her go a few hours later. The sheriff confiscated the gun though, and her lawyer couldn't convince, threaten, or bribe them to let it go.

Visiting hours at the hospital were over by the time she got out of jail, so even though she really wanted to see Kurt, she went home. She discovered the broken window and the evidence that her place had been ransacked. *Shit*. The last thing she wanted to do right now was to call the cops again, and she couldn't stay here. She drove to her Jester store instead and spent the night on the couch in her office. Nipper spent the night at Kurt's.

Chapter 55

IN THE MORNING, JUDI called the sheriff and told them they'd probably find more evidence in her apartment. She suspected that the attacker had ransacked her place. How he found her, she had no idea, and she was getting tired of this.

Visiting hours weren't until after lunchtime, so on the way to the hospital, Judi stopped at the gun shop up in Round Rock and bought a new pistol. She considered getting another PM9, but she figured she'd probably get the Kahr back once the cops were done with it, and she didn't want to end up owning two identical pistols. So she bought a Glock 30, a forty-five caliber compact semiautomatic pistol with a polymer frame, similar in operation to the PM9 only larger and quite a bit thicker. She was still shaken from last night's attack and wanted a round with a bit more stopping power than the nine millimeter she'd fired last night. The Glock also held eleven rounds, compared to the PM9 which could hold seven, or at most eight with an extended magazine. The Glock was only slightly harder to conceal, but with the help of the shop owner, they found a decent leather inside-the-waistband holster custom-fitted to the Glock, and when she lowered her polo shirt over it, it disappeared. Perfect.

She filled out the yellow legal questionnaire and handed over her concealed carry permit, which would let the dealer skip the FBI background check. She also purchased two boxes of Federal Hydrashok hollow point cartridges, and some tritium night sights, which the dealer was happy to install on the spot. The dealer also demonstrated an auxiliary high-precision sight that fitted neatly inside the recoil spring, and she was sold.

She handed over her Visa card. It came back over a thousand bucks lighter. The store owner suggested she pop into the range, which was empty, and fire off a magazine or two to test the weapon, and he'd throw in a bag of range ammo for no extra charge. She accepted the offer. She wanted to get to the hospital to see Kurt but she didn't feel safe carrying an untested weapon. Besides, the nurses wouldn't let her in for another hour anyway.

She was happy to see that she could still hit the ten-ring from fifteen yards. When she switched on the auxiliary sight, she put a tight group on the bullseye from twenty-five yards. She loaded up the two ten round mags with the Hydrashoks, racked the slide, popped the magazine back out, thumbed in the eleventh round, then holstered the Glock.

She washed her hands, waved good-bye to the clerk, then walked out of the store, a reassuring weight hanging on her right hip.

Chapter 56

JAMIE AND FRANK MET the park rangers on the lake under the Pennybacker bridge. The rangers had been citing a young ski boat driver for creating a wake in a residential cove. When they got the emergency call from dispatch, they let the lucky driver go and blasted a one-eighty turn out of the cove at full speed, spraying the driver with frigid lake water and creating an even bigger wake that rocked the boats in their moorings and swamped the shore. They pulled their official Park Ranger speedboat alongside Frank and Jamie in the Sea Ray in less than five minutes. They radioed directions to the paramedics before pulling their boat up to the edge of the cliff under the bridge. One of the rangers jumped over to the rocky shore and scaled the ironwork.

What he saw when he climbed up the beam would star in his nightmares for the rest of his life.

Stalnaker had survived almost a week of expansion and contraction under the 360 bridge. He was broken, bloody, dehydrated, starved, and near death. A skeleton. Turkey buzzards had smelled death on him a few days ago and had taken turns casually pecking bloody beak-holes in his face, legs, arms, and chest. His left eye was gone, in its place a crusted red hole. The buzzards had pulled a thick painful strip of flesh off his calf muscle, which hung down and twisted in the breeze, trapping biting flies on the sticky surface of its bloody coagulation like some ghastly pest strip. The bridge hadn't crushed him. It had restricted his breathing, but that hadn't been enough to do him in.

Count Rodchenko would have wagged his long vampiric finger in a gesture of disapproval. The student hadn't done his homework. The 360 bridge, a suspension bridge, had a smaller coefficient of expansion than the other highway bridges and the expansion was not sufficient to crush a man. Add to that Stalnaker's state of dehydration at the time of his abduction, and subsequent loss of blood. He literally shriveled so that he didn't fill the gap any more. He'd slipped out of the gap and hung suspended from the ropes for a day.

Stalnaker was too weak to scream, and after the water came rushing into the lake, he heard the boats and jet skis buzzing underneath. He'd put his hand in his pants pocket, closed them around his keys, and waited, semi-comatose. He knew that young boaters often congregated under the bridge, drinking beer and partying in the shade of the bridge by the boat ramp. Many times he'd stood in the conference room at Digital Fabrication Systems and watched the boaters zipping by on the lake far below, as he intimidated his subordinates and ruled over endless meetings. He planned to drop his keys on the first boat that would get near. Then he'd be rescued. If he missed with his keys, he'd have another chance later with his wallet.

The plan worked, but it had taken two days before someone got close enough.

Chapter 57

March 10

THE HOSPITAL HAD TYPED the sign on a three-by-five index card and taped it to the glass inside the front door:

> PURSUANT TO SECTION 30.06, PENAL CODE (TRESPASS BY HOLDER OF A LICENSE TO CARRY A CONCEALED HANDGUN) A PERSON LICENSED UNDER SUBCHAPTER H, CHAPTER 411, GOVERNMENT CODE (CONCEALED HANDGUN LAW), MAY NOT ENTER THIS PROPERTY WITH A CONCEALED HANDGUN.

She stopped.

Shit.

The sign wasn't *strictly* legal. The wording looked correct (it had to *exactly* match the wording given in section 30.06 by law) but it had to be in letters at least an inch high and also, she was pretty sure, in Spanish. But she couldn't remember if hospitals were a special case or not. Let's see, schools?--No. Churches?--No. Courthouses?--No. Racetracks?--No. Hospitals?--Can't remember. *Stupid gun control laws.* The handbook that she had to memorize was fifty pages of legalese describing places and conditions where it was okay and where it was not okay to carry a concealed handgun, and the penalties and affirmative defenses and defenses to prosecution and Class A misdemeanors and felony this and felony that, until she was more confused after reading than before she started. And the simple fact remained that no matter where she carried the gun, whether to racetrack, church, school, airport, or hospital, she wasn't going to use it to commit a crime. No criminal was going to respect that sign, no criminal memorized that booklet, why did she have to?

She turned and walked back to her car, then thought, *this is silly. I'm not a criminal, but I know for sure there is a crazy bastard out there who just tried to kill me and/or my boyfriend. Fuck it. It's concealed. I'm going in.* She knew the penalty was severe and that she could very likely do time and lose her concealed handgun license. But this was life and death. She would go in.

She passed by the registration desk to find Kurt's room number. There were a couple Austin cops standing around, filling out paperwork. She tried not to look nervous. She glanced down at her watch, then sneaked a look past it to her hip to see if the gun was poking out of her shirt. It suddenly felt like a concrete brick jutting out from her waist. She was sure it was completely obvious to everyone including the cops, but no one saw it, and the cops would certainly have arrested her if they did.

The nurse looked up the room number and pointed the way. The cops just stood and talked to themselves, occasionally laughing. One of them gave her the quick once-over while talking; she recognized it as a man-look rather than a cop-look, and then went back to looking at his partner. Most men wouldn't give her a second look, having been conditioned by the popular media to believe that only emaciated women were attractive, but there were a few who appreciated her build.

She found the room down the hall on the second floor. The hospital was the most modern facility in Austin. Kurt must be on some kind of health insurance extension from his old job to afford this place.

"Hey, pal, how are you?" Judi asked, pulling up a metal chair next to Kurt's bed.

"I feel okay, got a hell of a headache though," said Kurt, his head bandaged on one side. Transparent air hoses clipped to his nostrils ran along the sheets to a small oxygen port in the wall behind the bed. A color computer monitor on a rack above the bed displayed his vital signs. Some kind of plastic machine on a wheeled rack fed a slow stream of clear liquid from a hanging bag into a tube on his arm.

"Yeah, you look terrible," said Judi, stroking his arm.

"Thanks," he said, squeezing her hand. His eyes teared and he wiped them with his free hand. "I'm happy to see you too." He was wearing a flower-print hospital gown. Tiny blue and yellow flowers from neck to knees. Who designed this stuff anyway?

"I sent you some flowers," she said, looking around.

"Yeah, that's them over there," he said, pointing to a vase full of assorted flowers on the night stand by the television. "Thanks, no one ever lavished me with flowers before," he said, "except whoever designed this fashionable gown, that is."

"They gonna let you outta here anytime soon?" she asked.

"Doc says maybe tomorrow if the swelling goes down," he said, "They're watching for any sign of internal bleeding."

"Well you're going to be fine. You've got to get out of here because we have a little unfinished business, sweetie," she whispered, cupping the side of his face in her right hand.

"I'm glad you're okay," he said, "The nurses told me that you weren't hurt. They said you got off a shot?"

"Yeah, but it went wild. Scared the shit out of the guy though. He didn't hang around for the second shot. You got a nice little hole in your wall though where they dug out the slug," she said.

"Did they find out who he is?" asked Kurt.

"Not yet, but the sheriff is on the case. I'm sure they'll catch him soon. They took your baseball bat," she said.

"Hmm. That was a classic slugger from when I was in the eighth grade. How about my house?" asked Kurt.

"I locked it up after they hauled you off in the ambulance; it's okay. The guy didn't break in or anything, they said he must have walked in through an unlocked door. Did you know you don't have a phone?" she asked.

"Yeah, I just have the mobile. I must have left the back door unlocked. Sorry," he said. "How's Pokey?"

"She's okay, I made sure she had a couple days' worth of food and water set out, and Nipper's keeping her company. The important thing is that you're all right," she said.

"Yeah I'll be fine," he said. "They got me on some good drugs. If I have any left over, I could make a fortune selling this stuff on the streets."

They sat quietly for a few minutes as Judi continued to stroke his arm and they held hands while listening to the beeping and whirring of the various monitors. A compressor kicked in as the automated blood pressure cuff began to inflate and take its measurement.

"That thing go off all by itself?" she asked.

"Yep, every couple hours or so, day or night. I don't get much sleep here," he said.

"You can sleep at my place when you get out," she teased.

"We don't have to do it you know," he said, "If you don't want to."

"Do what?" she asked.

"The 'Nasty,'" he teased.

"Uh, yes we do," she said, squeezing his leg just above the knee.

The blood pressure cuff inflated, held, took its measurement, then deflated with a long hissing.

After awhile, Kurt said, "Can you take me to the range with you, once I get out of here? --I want to get a gun."

Chapter 58

March 11

"SHIT, WILL YOU LOOK at this?" said Rachel, tossing the newspaper on the table in front of Judi. Judi had been helping Rachel close the store. After they'd wiped the kitchen area clean, they were gathering up the day's scattered newspapers and discarded cups. David had quit halfway through his shift that morning, leaving them shorthanded. If this had been a huge corporate coffee chain like Starbucks, she could have just called on one of the other stores to help pick up the slack. But the owner of a small business was responsible for everything. If that meant you mopped the floor, that's what you did. It was hard to find reliable help.

Austin American Statesman, March 11 Page D-4

CEO FOUND NEAR DEATH ON PENNYBACKER

AUSTIN (AP) - In one of the most gruesome crime scenes on record in Austin history, a local man was found near death Wednesday evening under the Highway 360 bridge. Police report that the victim, Trenton J. Stalnaker III, 38, of Lakeway, was found hanging from the structure of the bridge, placed there by an unknown assailant. Stalnaker is the president and CEO of Digital Fabrication Systems Inc., a local high-tech firm with headquarters just up the hill from the 360 bridge.

Sources close to the investigation say that Stalnaker was working in his office late Tuesday night, finishing up some loose ends on a recent merger with an un-named San Jose firm. His badly crushed body was found tied to the understructure, bound with rope.

Police have no leads in the case. Anyone with information about the attack is requested to please contact the Austin Police Department. Mr. Stalnaker's firm has posted a $250,000 reward for information leading to the arrest and/or conviction of the perpetrator.

According to the police report, the victim had been wedged into an expansion joint under the bridge, and was crushed slowly as the heat of the day expanded the bridge to fill the gap. "The body had been hanging there for at least twenty-four hours, suspended by the feet and chest," the report stated.

Stalnaker, formerly of Motorola Semiconductor, assumed the CEO role at DFS last November. His company employs 50 people in the Austin office.

"That's terrible," said Judi. "Didn't this guy used to come in here for latte?" She pointed to the file photo head shot of Stalnaker printed next to the story.

"Yeah, the face looks familiar," said Rachel. "He was one of the regulars, let's see: Extra large lowfat caramel latte, vanilla hazelnut syrup, and a pineapple scone. Some days he'd get a garlic bagel instead of the scone, but he never wanted it sliced or toasted. Guy was a real asshole, always hitting on me and the other girls, hard."

"Stalnaker... Stalnaker. That name's familiar. Seems like I just saw that name recently," said Judi.

"Well I don't know how that could be, you've been here all day" said Rachel.

"I remember now, it was on that scrap of printout I pulled from behind the espresso machine," she said. "Did you take out the trash?"

"Nope," said Rachel. "It's after dark." The staff weren't permitted to open the back service door after dark. There had been cases of rapists hiding out in the alley behind strip malls, preying on retail clerks and kitchen staff just doing their jobs. The service door was to remain bolted after dusk. Company policy.

"I'm going to see if his name's on that paper," said Judi. "Help me find it."

Gary Maxwell Navarre

12823 Bomber Road

Fort Worth Texas 76116

(817) 555-2315

Education

University of Texas at Austin

Bachelor of Science, Computer Engineering 1990, GPA 3.95

Employment History:

1984-1985 Harrison Valley Country Club, Harrison Valley PA.

Grounds Crew Worker. Manual labor on staff of 36 hole Championship Country Club.

Supervisor: James McChasney

Final Wage: $5.50/hr.

1989-1990 Motorola Corp. Schaumburg IL

Engineering Summer Intern. Computer Programming.

Supervisor: Chuck Andrews.

Salary: $28,000/yr.

1990-1994 Lockheed Martin, Fort Worth TX

Computer Specialist, Flight Simulation Engineering section.

Supervisor: Ramona Lexton.

Final Salary: $45,000/yr.

1994-2000 Motorola Semiconductor, Austin TX

Wafer Fab Computer Engineer.

Supervisor: Trenton Stalnaker.

Final Salary: $79,000/yr.

2001-Present Locklin Defense Aerospace, Fort Worth TX

"Oh my god Rachel, this is the guy, this is his resume or work history or something," said Judi, spreading the crumpled paper out on the table.

"Which guy?" asked Rachel. "The asshole?"

"Oh never mind. I'll explain later. Listen, can you finish up the closing? I've got to run this over to a friend," said Judi.

Chapter 59

"HEY MISTER, HOW YOU doing?" she asked. She'd snuck in just before visiting hours were over. She only had a few minutes.

"Doc says tomorrow for sure. The swelling has started to go down," Kurt said, "and there's no internal bleeding."

"That's great. How's the headache?" she asked.

"Like a sledgehammer," he said, "but it's drugged down pretty good. Makes me sleepy."

"Listen Kurt, I don't have much time before they boot me out of here but I wanted to show you this. You up to talking about the stuff we found on the net?" she asked.

"Yeah, anything to catch the asshole who clubbed me," he said.

"This was in the paper today," she said, handing him the page from the Statesman about Stalnaker. He held it up with his free arm, quickly scanned through it, then handed it back to her. "So?"

"And this was printed off on the laser in our Jester store a few days ago," she said, handing him the coffee-stained printout.

"What did you do, wipe the counters with it?" he asked.

"We found it jammed behind the espresso machine. Rachel cleared this page out of a paper jam and then forgot to throw it out, and it got messed up on the counter," she said. "It was back there a couple days at least. Read the names, Kurt."

"Holy shit. Look at these. This is the guy. Gary Navarre."

"He was in our Jester store a couple days ago. I bet he tried to kill this Stalnaker guy too. It looks like he's killing off some of his old bosses," said Judi.

"Shit. Judi, you've got to stay away from there. He knows who you are, and he knows what we know. This has to be the guy who attacked me. Take this information to the police right now; take the chart we compiled too. Now they have to listen," he said.

"I will. Call me tomorrow when you know you're getting out, I'll come drive you home."

Judi stopped at her Jester store on the way to the police station. She called her computer guy, had him pull the network logs from the previous few days, and had her security service pull the store security video tapes for the last few days out of the rotation. She wanted to see if they could correlate the time the guy printed this file with the video record to try to get the police a picture of the guy.

Part IV
Not Found

Chapter 60

March 12.

DETECTIVE JAY GARNER OF the Fort Worth P.D. was a twenty-year veteran of the force. He thought he'd seen it all. Race riots, murders, rapes, mutilation, gang shootings, auto accidents, addicts, psychos, child molesters, the works. He was no wimp. Still, he was not prepared for what he encountered this morning.

The house on Bomber Road was a small single-story cottage crouched back in the woods off the south shore of Lake Worth. It was built--literally--in the shadow of the old Consolidated Aircraft Company plant in west Fort Worth as part of a cheap tract of aircraft worker housing in the mid-1940's. It had weathered both the passage of the decades and the passing of the mammoth facility next door from corporation to corporation. It had seen Consolidated pass to Convair, General Dynamics, Lockheed Martin, and then finally to Locklin Defense Aerospace. This plant and its Fort Worth machinists and engineers had built everything from the legendary B-24 Liberator, the Vietnam-era F-111 swept wing fighter-bomber, the cold war F-16 Falcon, the stealthy F-22 Raptor, and now no one knew what space-age weaponry was being built behind those barbed wire fences and elevated guard towers for the dawn of battles yet to come.

Every so often the still spring air would be ripped apart by the thunder and roar of multiple jet engines lighting up with full afterburners on a test stand or flight line somewhere. Then just as suddenly the noise would stop. The air would be still again and the birds would resume their chirping as if nothing had happened at all.

Through it all the house sat, patiently, waiting while the oaks and maples planted by the children of Convair machinists grew up thick and tall around it. Many of the old homes were torn down after years of decay. The workers had an eight-lane interstate loop to carry them away from the plant at the end of the day now. They had fast Japanese cars and nice big brick homes outside the loop. A few old-timers, long since retired, remained in the original tract housing. Many of the lots reverted to trees and fields, stands of rusted automobile parts, and abandoned and gutted appliances. Where once Rosie the riveter's children played on swings and pools, now engines and hoods, tires, dryers, refrigerators, stoves, and washers rotted. From the direction of the plant wafted the acrid smell of burning oil and JP4 jet fuel and a hundred other chemicals and solvents that no one without a security clearance could ever name.

Gary Maxwell Navarre kept his old house in good repair. The exterior paint was good, the shingles were sound, and the siding replaced when it showed even the first sign of rot. He'd bought the house for a pittance back when he started work at the Bomber Plant. The former owners had been pried from their home; dumped into a retirement center across town. Their empty house was hastily put on the market by their impatient yuppie offspring. They were anxious to warehouse their doddering old parents, and to get on with the important and hasty business of life, stress, kids, career, money, and pissing blood.

The outside of the house was immaculate, but the inside of the house had been ripped screaming from the pages of a Stephen King novel.

Detective Garner was trained not to contaminate a possible crime scene. He wheeled back out of the doorway, spun around, grabbed his knees, ducked his face over a hedge, and heaved his breakfast into the mulch. The stench that bullied its way out of the front door was unbearable. He hadn't smelled anything that bad since the seventies, when he was a rookie and had to fish a hastily disposed baggie of dope out of a porta-potty on a drug bust at a crowded downtown summer music festival.

Garner sent in a rookie detective from his team who bragged that he couldn't smell. The guy claimed he was anosmic. Garner was pretty sure that was a religious term, not a disease, though he'd known long-time smokers who couldn't smell a skunk fart. This kid was still wet behind the ears, and a non-smoker. What the fuck, send him in if he thought he could stand it. He sent him in wearing latex gloves, clutching a plastic bag to puke in, just in case, and cautioned him not to touch anything. They had to get a window open and get some ventilation in there or no one was going to be investigating anything.

Once inside, the kid held his breath. He was truly anosmic, couldn't smell wet dog shit, but he could taste the air. It had a salty ammonia taste, a wet taste. Outside the air was dry as a bone. West Fort Worth in spring, when it wasn't pitching a tornado or hailstorm, was so dry your skin would crack. Inside this house was wet, steamy, stale, sickly. The metallic ammonia taste clawed its way up the sides and jabbed at the back of his tongue, but he gritted his teeth and held back his gorge. He made his way carefully to the back door behind the kitchen. He unlocked and opened the back door, leapt out, blew out a breath, spit a big wet mouthful of saliva in the grass, drew in a big breath of fresh dry air, then carefully propped the door open with a rock. He flashed a thumbs up sign to Detective Garner in the doorway.

The light from the back door merged in the middle with the light from the front. The curtains were drawn but there was enough light now to see where the humidity and stench were coming from.

The kitchen: On the table, they were stacked on the yellowed and cracked linoleum floor under the table. In every cabinet, some of which stood open, they were packed full. They were on the counters, on every square inch of counter space, stacked two high, and as deep as the counter. They were lined up on top of the darkened refrigerator, which stood open, unplugged. They were *in* the refrigerator, on every shelf and in every drawer and compartment. They were *in* the freezer, in the sink, in the pantry. Most of them were sealed, many were not. One had toppled over on the floor next to the refrigerator, busted glass glinting, the pieces and fragments stuck to a dried puddle on the floor.

The living room: They were stacked on the coffee table on a scattering of old yellowed newsprint. They were piled next to the couch. There were three on top of the television, and five more sitting on the stand beneath it. They were lined up in rows three, four, and five deep, stacked as many as five high along the wall under the big window. They were sitting like grisly bookends on the bookshelves lining the wall by the door.

The dining room: The dining room was almost completely filled by an antique Steinway grand which had been meticulously restored. Nothing was stacked on the piano itself, but the baseboards of the room were covered and stacked three and four deep.

The hallway: There was another row stacked three deep. There was room only to walk through the hall if you were careful. And you wanted to be careful; you wanted to be very careful. Because in the hall, not one of them had any lids.

The bathroom: The bathroom was a different story. It was empty. Spotless. No half-melted bar of soap, not a dollop of shampoo, not an errant drop of toothpaste stuck to the counter, not so much as a single fleck of beard stubble on the sink, or a hair in the tub drain. The floor tiles were polished white and the grout scrubbed and sealed. The cabinets were bare inside and scrubbed clean. Not even so much as a spider could be found hiding in the corner. A thick layer of dust covered everything, but the bathroom was otherwise as clean and as empty as the summer day in 1941 when it was built.

With the exception of the bathroom, the house was filled with an assortment of jars, bottles, coffee cans, and glassware, each and every one of them covered in thick dust and each one filled with urine.

Chapter 61

ONCE THE FBI LEARNED that there was an interstate spree-murderer on the loose, and especially when the killer might be a urine-hoarding wacko, they were only too happy to take over the case. The Defense Investigative Service turned over all the records they had on Gary Maxwell Navarre from his security clearance application, and the FBI located his fingerprints that had been filed years ago when his clearance was approved.

Detective Garner was happy to be shut of the case. He never got over that house. He took early retirement from the force the following year.

The anosmic rookie eventually went back to college and became a software engineer for a small telecom company in Rowlett, Texas. He left his stint with the Fort Worth police off his resume. He didn't *ever* want to have answer the question, "So why did you leave the force?"

Chapter 62

GARY MAXWELL "MAX" NAVARRE became a shadow.

In the parking lot of the old Home Depot off loop 360 he found a faded 'seventy-three Yamaha RD-350 two-stroke street bike parked in a line of old cars and motorcycles with for sale signs on them. He called the number and waited for the owner. When the owner showed up, Max test-drove the small bike. It idled rough but still had plenty of acceleration. He was looking for reliable transportation, not a project. It was too small for his frame, but the price was right. He didn't ask any questions. After the negotiations were over, he paid a hundred twenty, cash, then both buyer and seller disappeared. The bike was worth four, maybe five hundred. It had to be hot. That night he drove through the parking lot of an all-bills-paid apartment complex off Koenig Lane and swapped plates with a Honda Gold Wing that he found parked under a very weathered canvas tarp in the back of the parking lot near an equipment storage building.

He rented a room in a cheap hotel in a run-down section of town a couple streets off Lamar. He paid cash by the week in advance. The proprietor was not one to ask questions of a cash customer. Max shaved his head close and grew out his beard, changed out his wardrobe at the local Goodwill store, picked up a nice leather jacket for twenty bucks and a blue bandanna for fifty cents. He sprayed on a new darker skin tone from a bottle of instant tan from Walgreens and purchased some cheap brown contact lenses to disguise his eye color. He looked like an old Mexican biker. He watched the news and he waited.

From the sidewalk in front of a university hangout coffee shop, Max logged on to the cache-finders.com website, and established a free account. All they needed to know was a name and an email address, and the name didn't even have to be real; it could be faked and the site owners had no way to check. He quickly discovered that there was no means for the system to verify that you actually found a cache before you posted a comment about your find online. They were on the honor system.

He spent a few hours reading the website, reading the comments and the cache descriptions. He learned about the culture and jargon of geocaching well enough to pass for a cacher online.

He clicked over to the pages of the most obscure caches in Central Texas and posted a couple dozen of them with bogus *found* comments, back-dating them to give his player the appearance of a yearlong history. He chose caches where the owner had gotten tired of playing the game and hadn't logged in to the site for a while.

After building his player's fake geocaching history, he spent about fifteen minutes more on the Lower Colorado River Authority Parks website, browsing through descriptions of parks out west of Mansfield Dam, west of Denzer's place.

Chapter 63

A FEW WEEKS LATER, Navarre rode up to the Tiny's Electronics superstore up on the Mo-Pac loop. The store, one of two dozen in a national chain, packed a hundred thousand square feet with everything electronic: batteries, cables, electronic parts, test equipment, phones, hard drives, software, calculators, radios, DVDs, appliances, stereos, and everything else you could possibly apply electrical power to. He wondered why it was called Tiny's. It was bigger than a Wal-Mart supercenter inside. The place was staffed with hordes of teenaged clerks in shirts and ties, supposedly trained and expert on all things electronic.

He needed to buy a GPS receiver. He made his way to the correct area of the store and faced a wall of product boxes. There was a display area with plastic mockups on security tethers, so that you could get a feel for the size and heft of the item without opening the box. Max looked over the lineup and selected the cheapest one. When he found the shelf where the boxes were, there was only one left in this model and it looked as if it had spent a couple hours in a chimp cage. It was shrink wrapped and there were some thick plastic straps wrapped around the box to keep it from being opened in the store.

"Can this model be used for Geocaching?" asked Max.

"Geocaching? I'm not sure what that is. I'm new here; I don't know much about these units," stammered the clerk. If you spent more than a minute looking at items in any given department, a clerk would swoop down on you to aid in your purchasing experience. Because there were so many of them, they usually didn't have far to swoop, and because they were sent out onto the floor with little training, they usually couldn't offer much aid.

"Why's this box all mangled?" Max asked.

"It's been returned," said the clerk, a caffeinated high school kid who was only working here because he needed the money to add neon ground effects to his lowrider pickup truck.

"You guys sell returned shit?" asked Max.

"Our technicians check it out in our service lab and if it is still good, we repackage it and it goes back on the shelf." said the clerk, crossing his arms defensively.

"Is that legal?" asked Max.

"Yes," said the clerk, "and the items carry the full manufacturer's warranty."

"Why should I pay full price for something if it's been returned?" asked Max.

"That's store policy. Would you like to speak with a manager?" asked the clerk, pointing toward the front of the store. Getting a little nervous now.

Over the gasped protests of the clerk, Max whipped out a six-inch hunting blade and sliced off the plastic band, ripped through the shrink-wrap, and opened the box. The unit had some finger smudges on the display but the clerk swore it still worked. Another clerk came over to help the first one. They wouldn't let Max actually power it up though, until after he'd bought it. The second clerk carried the opened package up to the counter and waited with Max in line until a cashier was available. The store had a bank of no less than thirty numbered checkout stations all arranged in a line fronting an expansive office area containing the store managers, filing cabinets, and a mammoth metal vault. Max threw a pack of AA batteries on the counter next to the GPS and pushed a few bills toward the clerk.

He screamed out highway 620 on the bike with his purchase tucked in his backpack. Even with the rough idle, the RD-350 was still a jet fighter on wheels. If you were too quick with the throttle, it was a jet fighter on one wheel.

Just southwest of Lakeway, he spotted a sign for the new nature park. He slowed the bike, parked it in a handicapped spot on the brand-new asphalt parking lot, and then hiked in to check the place out. The park was so new that it had been posted off-limits to visitors until funding could be secured from the state legislature to staff it. Hiking was allowed by appointment only, but as there was no one there to staff it, they couldn't really enforce that.

Twenty percent of Texas is classified as Karst area. Karst is a geological formation created when bedrock partially dissolves in water. Sinkholes, caves, and other features form from the voids in the rock. Some of the caves are huge, measuring hundreds of feet long, and up to a hundred feet deep. The walls are razor sharp and jagged, made of dolomitic limestone, otherwise known as Texas holey rock.

Navarre wandered around a quarter mile or so into the park and found what he needed, just as described on the park website. He powered up the GPS unit, then quickly marked the coordinates.

Chapter 64

www.cache-finders.com Geocache Listing

Karst Area - Normal Cache Type
by RD350_Rider [email this user]
Texas, USA

[click to download geographic coordinates and hints]

It's a beautiful new park, just waiting for someone to come discover it! Who will be first?

The cache is a 50-caliber ammo box located within the boundaries of the new state park out southwest of Lakeway. Initial contents include some beanie babies, a few die-cast metal toy cars, a mystery novel, three sets of marble knick-knacks, and the FTF prize -- Get This -- A genuine $100 value quarter-ounce 22 carat gold Krugerrand coin! I've gotten so much out of Geocaching over the last year, that it's time for payback. Enjoy the hunt!

Cache Visitor Comments:

(0 comments total - This cache hasn't been found yet!)

Did you Find the Cache? Add your own comment! [click here]

Chapter 65

KURT SIPPED HIS COFFEE and clicked through on the new email message. He was drinking Java Judi's brand now, out of a Java Judi's brand French press. Seems everything in his life now was Java Judi's brand. Judi had gotten him a new four-cup French press and a couple pounds of organic coffee as a homecoming present after he got out of the hospital.

Judi was sleeping at Kurt's place almost every night now, not exactly moved in, but they both knew it wasn't far off. She just couldn't drink the store brand coffee, so she'd moved in her own coffee service. One morning she'd shown Kurt how to operate the French press and he'd gotten pretty good at it. It wasn't difficult, and he couldn't believe the difference in the taste. He wasn't sure if it was the beans or the metal screen filter in the French press itself, but something was wonderfully different. His old coffee tasted like just a pencil sketch outline of what coffee could really taste like, if only prepared right. After two cups of French press coffee, he'd tossed his Mr. Coffee on the Goodwill donation pile.

Judi wasn't officially moved in yet, but her dog Nipper was living here now. His arthritis had gotten so bad that he couldn't make the three-story climb up to her apartment anymore. Kurt liked the dog despite his knee-licking fetish, and happily offered the old guy room and board. Pokey was pissed, but then it was a cat's job to be pissed sometimes.

The new email message was a new cache posting. There'd been quite a few new cachers joining the sport lately, and many were just getting around to posting their first caches. The system could be set up to send you an email message any time a new cache appeared within a certain distance of your home coordinates. Kurt had a thirty-mile radius set up in his preferences, so he got quite a few of these messages.

As he read the message he slapped out a rhythm on the sides of his legs. Must have been an extra nervous system boost from the organically grown caffeine, or maybe it was the joy of surviving the attack last month and living to fall in love with Judi, or the promise of getting a big fat reward check the minute they caught that Navarre bastard, or maybe it was something else. He didn't even realize he was doing it. Pokey took the rhythm to be a sign that Kurt wanted to pet her and she came over and rubbed up against his ankles. He reached down and picked up the cat and put her in his lap. She climbed up on the desktop instead, and walked back and forth in front of his keyboard and screen. Nipper was sacked out in the livingroom.

The message was about a new cache, 'Karst Area.' It was nearby. There were few caches out in Lakeway, and Kurt liked it when someone posted a new one, especially if it was in a park he didn't already know about. This new park was a complete surprise to him. The cache even had a hundred dollar gold piece in it for the FTF prize. He wasn't usually interested in being the first to find, but in the case of a hundred bucks in gold, he'd have to make an exception.

He saddled up the Expedition, tossed a couple spare AA batteries in his fanny pack, checked to be sure that all the doors were locked, armed his home alarm system, and hit the highway. He'd become cautious since the attack.

The coordinates pointed him only four miles away down highway 620, but those were miles as the crow flies, what some geocachers were calling 'crowms' (pronounced like "chromes"). Kurt thought that word was stupid and refused to use it. Figuring in the curves around the south side of the lake, it could be as far as ten miles on the ground. He'd be cashing in that Krugerrand in no time, assuming no one else got there first. He'd have the rest of the day to locate a reputable coin dealer and shop the coin around for the best deal.

When Kurt pulled up to the park entrance, he was disappointed but not surprised to see another SUV parked there with geocaching bumper stickers on the back. Halfway out the gravel trail to the cache site, he met Nicholas, the older of the Krager twins.

"I looked for a good half hour, but man those coordinates suck. I didn't see a thing out there but cactus and rock. But I've got to be at work by ten thirty, so I can't hang out to help you anymore. Fuckin newbies," said Nicholas, kicking a small chunk of holey rock off the trail. Nicholas, who refused to let anyone call him Nick, was twenty-three. He was deeply tanned with long black hair pulled into a ponytail, rippling with muscles underneath his tie-dye T-shirt. He could have probably been a soap opera star if he hadn't been so good at programming embedded sixteen-bit microcontrollers in assembly language.

"Yeah, that's probably one good reason why I don't try so hard to be first to find," said Kurt. "I like to let the others work the bugs out of a new cache placement, then I'm sure to waste less time on bad coordinates or whatever."

"Yeah, me too, but there's that Krugerrand this time," said Nicholas, "I wanted that quarter ounce Krugerrand for my coin collection. I think it may be uncirculated."

"Yeah, that's why I'm here," laughed Kurt. "But I'm not a coin collector, I just need the money. I'll be happy to sell it to you if I find it."

Nicholas agreed to the deal, and then instructed Kurt not to touch the coin because it would be worth more if left in its plastic sleeve. Kurt got a few tips from Nicholas on places where he'd already searched, so he didn't waste any time looking there. The descriptions were all pretty vague though, since the area was all the same, just rocks, stinging nettles, and prickly pears.

He'd be out here awhile.

After forty-five minutes of beating the prickly pears, Kurt was about ready to give up. His fingertips smarted from being pricked by cactus spikes, his socks were full of sticker burrs, he had a bloody gash on one shin from when he slipped on a moss-covered rock, and he was starting to sweat. He had left his water bottle back in the truck. He thought about retrieving it a couple times during the search, but he knew that if he went back to the parking lot he'd probably just give up and lose his shot at the hundred bucks in gold. How it would hack him off later to learn that Maari or Jason or one of the Krager twins or someone else with a job had found the hundred-dollar Krugerrand when he so desperately needed it and had all day to find it.

How the coordinates could be so far off was not a mystery. Many players, especially those new to the sport, didn't take enough care when marking coordinates with their GPS receivers. Kurt pulled out the printout on this one and looked at the guy's user name. He didn't recognize it, but he thought he might've seen this guy's finds posted on some other caches in the area. The guy wasn't a total newbie, maybe had a year of caching in. Still, there wasn't a lot of tree cover or any nearby obstructions to mess with the signal. He couldn't figure it out. His own unit was reporting eight feet accuracy, the best he'd ever seen. The guy had to have a crappy GPS unit, probably one of the cheap knock-offs out of China that Tiny's was selling.

After another half-hour of searching, Kurt found the cache. It was over one hundred twenty feet away from the posted coordinates. Damn, those numbers were seriously fucked up; he'd have to take a new averaged reading and post better coordinates with his online comment. The cache was in a deep hole in the ground, but it was the grate that caught his eye first. The hole was surrounded by prickly pears on three sides that formed a thick natural screen. There was a six-foot wide shelf of uneven holey rock surrounding the hole, between the edge of the hole and the prickly pear screen. The hole itself was irregularly shaped, ten feet around, and maybe thirty feet deep. The walls were jagged, lined with razor sharp honeycomb limestone. The occasional piece of honeycomb jutted out from the walls, which could provide a foothold or handhold, if one were careful. There was a heavy black welded steel grate cemented over the top to keep animals and visitors out. Kurt had seen that done before, in other parks. These grates always had a man-sized grate trapdoor in the center that was kept padlocked shut. Kurt had never seen one like this where the trapdoor was unlocked and propped open.

The Lower Colorado River Authority parks department was concerned about preserving the Karst features in this and other

Karst preserves, and cave explorers could only go in to explore if they had an LCRA park ranger to guide them in. This was a new park, and not even officially opened yet. He guessed that they must not have deployed all the locks.

Down at the bottom of the cave, he spotted a flash of yellow. This guy had to be a newbie. Most veteran cachers would spray paint their ammo cans to help camouflage them. Certainly they'd at least paint over the yellow-stenciled military markings on them so that if non-players found them, they wouldn't trigger a terrorism alert. This had happened a couple months ago in South Austin. Someone hid an ammo can cache in a neighborhood park. The military markings freaked out one of the residents, and the Austin police had come in with the bomb squad and blown up the cache, ammo can, logbook, trinkets, pen, and all. The Department of Homeland Security wasn't taking any chances these days, and if that meant a few dozen hot wheels and beanie babies had to pay the ultimate price, so be it.

Kurt clipped his GPS to the inside of his pants pocket and sat on the grate, dangling his feet into the hole. Damn, it was a long way down. How the hell was he going to get back out? He inspected the walls carefully. The walls were jagged, with holey rock step-stones jutting out on all sides, and they'd likely hold his weight. So he could climb down, then climb back out on these rocks. The hard part would be transitioning from the grate to the rock wall without falling. He thought about calling Maari to see if she wanted to come out and help. That sounded like a good idea, so he climbed off the grate, stood up, pulled out his cellphone and punched up her number.

He held the phone to his ear. There was a short ringing sound and then nothing. He pulled the phone away and looked at the display. The little bar graph next to the antenna symbol showed only one short bar, then that disappeared. Not enough signal strength to get out a call.

Well, if phone service weren't available, he'd have to go it alone. Certainly if he waited until after the day was over, he'd lose the hundred bucks to one of the other cachers. He looked around. No other cachers coming, no one in this park for miles in any direction. Nothing but holey rock, prickly pears, and fire ants.

He sat on the edge of the grate again and dangled his feet into the penetrating damp chill of the hole. He checked his pockets to make sure his GPS, phone, keys and wallet were secure, then lowered himself through the trapdoor. He scraped his shoulder against the hasp on the way down, ripped his t-shirt and watched as the scratch filled with a thin line of blood. *Shit.* Well, he often said it wasn't really geocaching until someone drew blood.

He wasn't as fit as when he was twenty, and it took a bit of kicking and monkey-bar work to get from the trapdoor over to the stone walls. He clung to the cold stone walls, caught his breath, and began his descent. From here on down it should be easy, if the rocks weren't too slimy and he didn't slip. His arms and shoulders threatened to cramp from the unusual exertion. Ten years of desk work had left him soft. About this time he began to wonder if all this was worth a hundred bucks. If he fell he'd be either killed on knocked unconscious, and no one except Nicholas Krager knew he was out here.

Kurt was clinging to the walls three feet from the bottom of the cave, trying to decide between two likely candidate rocks for his last foothold, when he heard the trapdoor slam shut.

Chapter 66

NAVARRE HAD BEEN CAMPED about four hundred feet away, in a stand of ash juniper trees surrounded by a turbulent sea of prickly pear. Footsteps on the gravel early that morning had woken him up. It was some musclebound geek, clutching a fancy GPS receiver. That was bad news. He hadn't considered that anyone else would arrive before Kurt. He wasn't sure what he'd do if muscle boy got to the cache first. That would ruin the trap. For some reason the guy was looking all over the wrong place. Maybe he just wasn't too bright? Max couldn't be sure. Max had no gun and no way to sneak up and club the guy, as the whole place was blanketed in crunchy limestone gravel. He'd have to let him crawl into the trap, then figure out what to do with him.

To Max's relief, after a half hour of searching, the guy gave up and left.

Kurt had arrived a few minutes later.

Kurt jumped to the bottom of the hole, landed on all fours on the spongy black earth, rolled over, saw a silhouette squatting over the trap door, clicking a padlock into place.

"Hey!" Kurt cried, "What the fuck!"

He scrambled up the cold rock walls as fast as he could. He only got as far as a few feet up the sides before the figure leapt off the grate and disappeared. A few pea-size bits of honeycomb bounced down along the walls; Kurt ducked these. White rock dust drifted down through the shaft of light coming from the hole above. Then nothing. All Kurt could see was sky and clouds, behind thick black bars. Off in the distance, he could hear a red-tailed hawk cry. It sounded a million miles away.

"Hey!" he shouted again, louder this time.

Nothing.

His voice felt puny, powerless inside the cave. The walls closed in on him and absorbed the sound. He knew his voice wasn't heard outside the cave at all. That and there was no one around for miles.

He didn't have to think for more than a minute to know who the silhouette was.

Gary Maxwell Navarre.

Chapter 67

www.cache-finders.com Geocache Listing

Karst Area - Normal Cache Type
by RD350_Rider [email this user]
Texas, USA

Cache Visitor Comments:
(1 comment total - This cache hasn't been found yet!)

[1] April 17 by TeamKrager [125 caches found]
I hate to write a 'Not Found' comment, but these coordinates are way, WAY off. I spent a half hour out there and couldn't find anything but cactus and scorpions. I recommend you steer clear of this one until the owner goes back out to mark those coords again. Nice Karst area though. Just wish I could have bagged that Krugerrand!
[email this user]

Kurt climbed back up and tried to force the lock on the grate, but he couldn't get it open. He had no tools other than his keys, wallet, GPS and cellphone. He had nothing to pry with. There wasn't even a stick on the cave bottom, and he was not surprised to find the ammo can was empty. His footing up here was solid but it wouldn't last all day. He couldn't see out beyond the edge of the hole, and the prickly pears blocked the rest of the view. There was no sign of Max.

Kurt pulled out his GPS and powered it up. A desert horse fly ducked in under the bars and buzzed his head; he swatted at it, lost his balance, then quickly snatched an overhead bar. His heart drummed in his ears from the adrenaline. The fly continued to pester him, hovering around his ears, taking a bite here, a sting there. In the desert, everything was either pissed off or sharp; desert horse flies were both. Kurt swatted at it with his GPS hand when it was near his head and kicked at it when it went for his ankles. After a few minutes, Kurt got a tenuous satellite lock, and the fly flew out of the hole to bother someone else.

Kurt reached up and set the GPS on the rock outside the bars. He pulled out his cellphone and held it as high as he could. Earlier, the tiny display had displayed a single bar next to the antenna symbol. Now it showed none. The display flashed an antenna and question-mark symbol, indicating that it was searching for service. *Shit*. He had to find some way to get a call out.

Chapter 68

THE SUN TOUCHED THE western horizon, and a band of red and pink clouds slipped across the sky over Lake Travis, moving south over the new park. What was taking her so long? Max waited in the shade of the ash junipers for Judi to come rescue Kurt.

She didn't show. If she didn't come by this time tomorrow, he'd go after her himself. Kurt? That asshole could stay locked in the hole forever. Die down there with the scorpions and snakes.

He spent the night under the stars, camped next to his motorcycle. The park didn't have any shelter, not even a restroom building in which to hide. He needed to be where he could see the trap at all times.

He didn't want to miss Java Judi.

Chapter 69

IN THE HOLE IT was already black. The sky overhead was baby blue with patches of pink, but that feeble light didn't help illuminate the bottom. Kurt was determined to wait patiently for rescue. He'd tried everything he could think of.

During the first hour back in the hole after getting the coordinates, he'd tried a panic attack. The walls had closed in on him and threatened to suffocate, but that feeling had lasted only about three minutes, then burned itself out.

He'd tried the phone up by the grate again two more times that day, but gave up on the second attempt after he slipped halfway down on a mossy rock and nearly tumbled back into the hole. There just wasn't any signal.

He briefly thought about opening the GPS to see if there was any wire in it he could use to make a better antenna for his cellphone, but he didn't want to ruin the GPS, and he was pretty sure there weren't coils of wire in electronic equipment anymore, just printed boards and chips.

He hadn't seen his captor since morning.

The cut on his arm was crusted over and it throbbed. It might get infected if he stayed here much longer. Where were all the other geocachers looking for the Krugerrand? Surely someone must be out here looking for it? He couldn't understand why Krager didn't come back after work to resume the search.

He had all day to investigate the hole. The hole narrowed to a small point at the bottom, maybe three feet on a side. There wasn't room for Kurt to lie down. He had to sit against the uncomfortable holey rock wall. There weren't any cracks in the wall or any side passages out. The walls were solid layers of holey rock. The floor was spongy black dirt. It was cold, and getting colder. He had no food or water. Judi had better come find him, but he had to find some way to warn her about Max.

Chapter 70

JUDI DROVE HER CONVERTIBLE into Kurt's driveway, switched off the engine and killed the headlights. She grabbed her purse and organizer off the passenger seat and slid out of the Sebring. It was eleven thirty. She'd had to help close the Jester store again. Her shift supervisor had quit that morning, defected to Starbucks, leaving her short handed. This shit had to stop. She needed an experienced general manager who could keep the operation running, which included keeping it properly staffed. She was frazzled, tired, and her feet hurt.

As she approached the door, she sensed something was wrong with Kurt's place. The lights were out. It wasn't like Kurt to go to bed without greeting her first, and he almost never went out at night for any reason.

She cautiously unlocked and let herself in the front door. The alarm beeped its thirty-second warning. She keyed in the disarm code on the alarm panel, flipped on the lights, and looked around. Nipper stirred from his nap at the foot of the couch and trotted out to greet her, licking her knees.

The Glock was a reassuring bulge on her hip, but if Nipper wasn't upset about anything, she didn't feel the need to draw it. She checked the livingroom. It was neat, uncluttered. She checked the kitchen. It looked like someone had eaten a hasty breakfast here. The French press still had grounds in the bottom, and there were a couple of granola bar wrappers on the counter next to the press. Pokey and Nipper both had food. There was no sign of the cat, but that wasn't unusual, she'd been miffed ever since Nipper moved in, and was rarely seen unless Kurt was there to protect her. The back door was locked.

Judi moved down the hall and checked the bedroom. Nipper trotted ahead and circled at the foot of the bed. The bed wasn't made, but the comforter had been pulled over the rumpled sheets.

Typical Kurt. Nipper confirmed there was no one hiding in the closet. She checked Kurt's office. His computer was still on, in sleep mode, its monitor light and power light glowing, slowly brightening and dimming in synch, like some mechanical animal breathing slowly, deep in electronic dreams.

She called Kurt's cellphone on the house phone she'd made him install after the attack. He didn't answer. It sent her to voicemail. She called Maari to see if those two were hanging out together. Maari was awake. She hadn't seen him all day. Judi punched up Jason's number off the speed-dial, woke him up, and apologized for the late call. Neither Jason nor Bonnie had seen Kurt either.

Judi went back into the computer room looking for some more clues. She wiggled the mouse. The screen flicked on. It wanted a password before it would let her view anything. After the attack Kurt had gone overboard with security. She clicked the sleep button and put the machine back into hibernation.

She re-armed Kurt's alarm system, then dialed the police on 311. Ten minutes and five handoffs later she was forwarded to a clerk who told her that a person wasn't considered legally missing until after they'd been gone twenty-four hours, at a minimum.

Judi walked back into the livingroom. She hated to even contemplate this next thought: Could Kurt be having an affair? They weren't officially living together, but could he be sneaking someone else in on the side, while she was busy at work? *Fuck and run*, she thought. Even the good ones; they were only men. She wouldn't believe it, not after what they'd been through together.

She pulled the Glock off her hip and set it on the coffee table next to the overstuffed chair. She sank into the chair, felt it surround her, cradle her. She wouldn't believe it, no. Still, he wasn't here. She hugged her knees while staring at the local news, on mute. Nipper pushed into the chair from the side to get closer, she petted his head and then he curled up on the floor beside the matching ottoman.

After an hour of nervously watching silent heads mouth the news onscreen, exhaustion overcame worry. She slept.

Chapter 71

JUDI CALLED RACHEL IN the morning, asked her to take over running the Jester store. Rachel was good. She had no management experience but she seemed to have a knack for it.

Judi called Jason at work.

"Kurt's still missing, and I need to find out where he's gone. I'd like to look at his Mac, see if there's anything on there that can help me find out where he went, but the screen's locked and I need help getting in. You're a computer guy, can you help?" she asked.

"Well, I'm a PC guy, I don't do Macs," he said, "and we don't have any Mac people here."

"I think if I could see what he was doing last, at this point I'll try anything," she said.

"Wait a sec, those new Macs use Unix, and we do have a Unix guy here," said Jason. He put down the phone and pulled his Unix guy out of a network game.

Eric had been working with Unix since the late seventies, and looked like he hadn't been outside in all that time, either to get some sun or a haircut --or a date.

Judi typed the commands exactly as Eric spelled them out. When she rebooted she was able to log right on to the machine as if she owned it.

"Browser history?" she asked.

"Yeah that's right, there should be some menu on the browser that lets you see the last pages that he viewed," said Jason, who'd taken the phone back from Eric and sent him back to his game.

"Oh, yeah, okay, yeah here it is," she said. "Oh shit, there's a lot here," she said, then after a few more clicks, "Job postings mostly, CNN, and, oh here's a cache page. It's the last thing he looked at. I bet this is it."

"What?" asked Jason.

"Karst Area," she said, "it's a new cache, uh let's see, a few miles from here. It's got a gold piece. Kurt's not interested in first-to-find but he'd go for that gold. He's broke."

"Okay, I see it. Looks like one of the Krager twins tried it yesterday. I'll call him. I'm headed that way, I'll meet you at the park," said Jason. "Oh and be careful, those Karst areas can be treacherous."

Chapter 72

JUDI PULLED UP TO the entrance to the park. Nipper sat in the passenger seat, riding shotgun. Technically he wasn't allowed to ride up front due to the airbag danger, but he was very old and each year he got away with breaking a few more rules than the year before.

A small sign on the fence by the entrance declared that the park was on LCRA land. Judi stopped the car at the side of the park road, just short of entering. She switched off the convertible, removed her Glock from its holster, popped the magazine, ejected the round from the chamber, and locked the whole mess in the center console box. It wasn't strictly legal to store it there, but she didn't want to get caught carrying in the park and have a class C misdemeanor on her record. Despite repeated attempts by the legislature to repeal it, in some buried statute in the parks and wildlife code, all LCRA land was declared off-limits to licensed concealed carry, and they didn't have to post.

She restarted the car and pulled it a hundred feet past the entry gate into the parking lot, parking it next to Kurt's truck. She got out of the convertible. Nipper bounded out behind her and sought out the nearest plant to pee on. She locked her car, then checked the Expedition. It was locked, and a fine film of dust coated the windshield. It'd been here since yesterday.

"Kurt!" she yelled.

Nothing. A few hundred feet to her left, a turkey buzzard squawked in protest as it soared down from its perch on a high-tension tower and flew away.

She grabbed a park map from a dispenser on the wooden signboard, rousting a small green skink lizard, which peeked out from under the map holder, stopped for a second, cocked its head at her, puffed out its neck, then skittered down off the signboard and across the gravel into a stand of cactus. Nipper was still busy marking the new park and didn't even give chase.

The signboard displayed a larger, color version of the park map and some more information and photos of the Karst caves, plus a laser-printed sign saying that the park wasn't yet open to the public.

Judi didn't have a GPS receiver, but there was a topographic map on the cache page she'd printed, with a little red X marking the place where the cache was supposed to be located. The X was located a few hundred feet from the largest Karst cave in the preserve.

According to the comment he posted on the cache page, Krager'd had trouble finding the cache, maybe it was in the cave. He wouldn't have found it if he blindly followed his GPS and didn't look at the park map. Typical computer geek.

Chapter 73

FROM THE COVER OF a stand of cedar trees, Max watched. He waited until Judi and her dog walked away from the car onto the trail to the cave, then he circled around behind her car. In the back of his mind he could still hear her nine-millimeter hollowpoint slug whistling past his ear. He had to avoid a direct confrontation and a chance for her to draw and fire on him again. He tried the door. It was locked. He pulled out his knife and sliced through the soft-top on the passenger side and slipped a hand in to unlock the passenger door. Once inside, he put a hand on the console box to steady himself as he reached across and under the steering column to pop the hood release. He looked around under the hood briefly, then pulled the distributor cap and plug wires and tossed them away, behind a cluster of agave plants. He lowered the hood gently, then pushed down on it until it clicked closed. He relocked the passenger door. From the driver's side, the slice in the soft-top wasn't visible.

Chapter 74

USING THE MAP, JUDI found her way along the trail to the Karst cave. Nipper found it first. He stood near the entrance and looked down, confused. He wasn't used to seeing people below him.

"Kurt!" Judi yelled.

"Down here!" he yelled back. The sound was faint, and Judi could tell that he was a long way down in the hole.

"Are you okay?" she asked, pushing Nipper aside and looking over the edge.

"The killer's up there, watch out!" he yelled.

Judi looked around, saw no one. She heard nothing, save the wind in a stand of cedars, and the whine of the occasional horse fly.

"I don't think he's here anymore. I don't see anyone," she said.

"He's up there, alright. You gotta get me out of here and fast," he said.

"I could shoot off the lock but I'm afraid it might ricochet into the cave. I have a tire iron in my trunk," she said.

"Be careful!" he yelled.

Judi ran back down the trail to the car to get her gun and a tire iron. Gun first. She unlocked and opened the driver's door. Nipper, thinking they were going for another ride, jumped into the passenger seat. Judi slipped in after him, then reached for the console box.

Max ran up from behind the wooden signboard, with a six-inch knife in his fist, teeth bared. Nipper heard his footsteps and barked in surprise.

Judi heard the running footsteps on the gravel parking lot, then twisted her head to see a crazed figure coming at her. There wasn't enough time to get her gun. She slammed the door, fumbled the key into the ignition with one hand as she pushed the lock down with the other. The car wouldn't start. *Shit.* She pulled the key out and jammed it into the lock on the console box. She yanked the empty pistol out of the box, pulled it from its holster, then fumbled for the magazine. Max banged on the glass, then slashed at the roof. The knife plunged within inches of Judi's head, one swipe actually touching her hair, then the blade lodged in the soft aluminum of the ragtop framework. Max struggled with both hands to lever the blade out of the frame.

Judi ducked, slammed the magazine into the pistol. It jammed halfway in. She'd inserted it backward. She yanked it out, rotated it, then slammed it back in again. She released the slide while rolling flat onto the seat across the center console box. The shifter knob poked rudely into her lower back.

The ragtop was in tatters. She raised the Glock with both hands and fired one shot blindly into the jagged hole in the top, then fired a double-tap at the crazed figure through the driver's side window, shattering it.

Max saw the gun come out, darker, bigger, and louder than the last gun he'd faced. In slow motion he saw the gaping black well in the barrel looking big enough to crawl into. At the bottom of that well he thought he saw a glint of the copper teeth on the hollow face of death.

The first shot exploded over his head, the second one slammed him on the upper arm, a hard burning punch. The third shot whistled past his right ear, he felt the wind, and he was gone. He abandoned the stuck knife and ran.

Judi jumped out of the car screaming. She followed Max a few yards; she aimed at his back, but held her fire. He was fast into the cedars, jumping side to side as he ran to avoid the cactus patches and Judi's aim. Nipper stayed by her side and barked at Max's retreat. He was too old to give chase and he knew it.

Judi ran back to the car to get the tire iron out of the trunk, being careful to see that Max didn't come back. Tire iron in one hand, gun in the other, she ran back along the path to free Kurt.

Chapter 75

MAX RETURNED TO THE car to retrieve his knife, then stole back to his hiding place in the cedars. He sat on his motorcycle. He checked his wound. It hurt like hell but it wasn't serious, just bleeding like a motherfucker. The slug punched clean through, taking a small chunk of his left triceps muscle with it. He wrapped a red bandana around it to staunch the flow. Through the trees, Max saw Judi working to free Kurt from the hole, but he didn't dare get close to her again, since he had no weapon equal to hers. He couldn't sneak up either because the gravel would betray his footsteps.

He straddled the motorcycle, flicked out the kick-start lever, and just as he was about to kick it, he saw the ancient bottle of Old Grand-Dad that he'd been storing his urine in, looked at the gas tank of his bike, and came up with a better idea.

Chapter 76

"IT WON'T BUDGE, THE lever's not long enough," she screamed.

"Try kicking it," he yelled, standing in the bottom of the hole, looking up at her.

"No that won't work, there's nothing to kick," she said.

"Go ahead and shoot it then," he yelled.

"I'm afraid it will hit you," she said.

"You gotta get me out of here before he comes back," he said, "Shoot the lock!"

"I know I hit him; he's bleeding," she said.

"Yeah but you're not sure he's dead," he said, "Shoot the lock!"

"Okay, try to get up against the wall on this side," she said, pointing to the side where she was standing. She stood up and looked around to make sure Max wasn't coming. She didn't see him. Propping the lock up and away from the grate with the tire iron, she fired across the top of the grate into the lock mechanism. The lock bounced but despite a smoking hole in the center of its mangled body, did not open. The tire iron clattered to the bottom of the hole, nearly hitting Kurt.

Kurt climbed to the top of the hole and handed Judi the tire iron through the bars. She tried wedging the lock again with the tire iron, and this time was able to pry it open. She flipped the grate up and reached in a hand to pull Kurt out.

Just as Kurt placed a foot out on the ground outside the hole, the prickly pear nearest the hole exploded in a bright orange searing ball of fire.

Chapter 77

KURT AND JUDI WERE showered with flaming gasoline, shards of burning broken glass and chunks of singed cactus. The back of Judi's shirt caught fire. She rolled on the gravel to put out the flames, driving cactus needles into her skin. She screamed, and Kurt patted the flames out with his bare hands, driving burning cactus needles into his palms.

In her haste to put out the fire, Judi dropped her Glock.

Kurt scooped handfuls of sandy dirt and gravel and threw them on her shirt until it smoldered and the fire was out.

While Kurt smothered the flames, Max ran up from behind a wall of cactus and jumped up on Kurt from behind, like a child playing piggy-back, then held his blade under Kurt's chin. Kurt dropped to his knees under the sudden weight, grabbed Max's knife arm with both hands and pulled the knife away.

Nipper stopped his barking and lunged at Max, biting him savagely on his knife wrist. Max held on to the blade as Nipper began a vicious tug-of-war with the punctured and bleeding wrist, growling deeply through clenched red teeth, his lips drawn back in an angry snarl. He might have been too old to chase, but an old dog was never too old to bite.

Kurt rolled over on top of Max and punched him in the face, breaking his nose with a wet snap like the sound of a branch breaking. Max howled in pain but did not waver in his attack.

Judi crawled away and retrieved her gun. She followed the ball of rolling and fighting arms, legs, and paws with her sights, but held her fire, knowing that there was a good chance the bullet could go through Max and kill or injure Kurt.

Max rolled on top of Kurt. Nipper gave a hard tug, ripping a strip of flesh off Max's arm, and he dropped the knife.

The two men struggled on the ground, first Max on top, then Kurt, then Max. They rolled into the cactus patch, reversed direction across the smoking ground, then onto the grate, across the trapdoor, and back onto the ground.

Nipper leapt into the fight again and snapped his jaws down on Max's ear, then gave a vigorous shake. Max shrieked, sat up, straddled Kurt, then threw his arms up to fight off the dog.

Judi saw her shot.

She held her breath. She lined up her sights on Max's head. Her hands were shaking. Her sights bounced, first covering Max's head, then Kurt's. She was about to drop the gun and give up when she remembered the auxiliary laser sight. Without lowering the muzzle, she flicked her trigger finger forward.

A brilliant red spot played across Max's eyes. He saw the blinding starburst and in that instant he knew he was dead, unless he moved--and fast.

Judi's trigger finger pressed against the trigger face. The Glock's trigger safety disengaged and the trigger started its deadly rearward travel.

The laser spot pooled, frozen inside a bead of sweat on Max's forehead. His mouth open, his tongue pressed the back of his front teeth, to form the N sound in the word "No" The laser reflected in Max's pupils, dilated, looking off to one side planning for escape.

He wasn't going to get away this time.

Chapter 78

THE STILL MORNING AIR was shattered by a woody *CRACK* that echoed off the cedars, through the prickly pears, and rolled out over the hill country southwest of Lake Travis before dying out. The flies startled, stopped their buzzing, then resumed.

Max saw a white starburst, then his vision closed down until he could only see as if through a tunnel. He fell limp onto Kurt's chest and wheezed out a spray of blood.

Standing over Max was Jason Heckmann, who'd burst through the cactus at the last minute, following through on a swing with his custom carved hickory hiking stick.

Kurt rolled hard and pitched Max's stunned body into the sinkhole. Max mustered up enough consciousness to grab the grate on the way in. He dangled by his fingertips over the cave. Nipper charged the hole and snapped at Max's fingers. The killer dropped into the pit.

Kurt slammed the grate, and jammed the tire iron through the hasp. Jason pulled on the iron until the hasp bent and couldn't be opened.

Judi flicked her index finger out of the trigger guard and lifted the Glock up and away with both hands.

She breathed again.

Chapter 79

Later that Summer

KURT PUSHED THE THROTTLE lever forward. The Bayliner dug into the dark green water and the motor kicked up a cool white spray out from behind the stern as the bow rose. The passengers held on to anything they could grab to avoid being tossed off into the wake.

"Hey, take it easy there Captain, you don't want to wreck her," said Ratkus, being careful not to spill his beer.

When they had motored out to the cliffs on the edge of the lake, Kurt killed the engine and Jason dropped the anchor. The guests plopped off the side and treaded water in the cool green, then swam off a dozen feet toward the rocky shore.

"Did you hear anything more about the killer?" asked Maari, when they'd climbed out onto the rocks and found a flat place to sit. Ratkus and Jason tossed a nerf football back and forth in the shallows at the base of the rocks. Judi climbed up and sat next to Kurt, propped up on her elbows, soaking in the sun. The day was cloudless and even though it wasn't yet noon, it was already pushing ninety degrees.

"Yeah," said Kurt. "I just got back from the first trial, out in San Francisco. Let's just say the rest of his old bosses won't have anything to worry about for a very long time."

"Was it just old bosses? I thought there was one guy that didn't fit in with that pattern?" said Maari.

"Yeah, Navarre made a long list of anyone who'd ever done him wrong at work. The first guy, that park ranger he gassed, he was a co-worker from back when Navarre was sixteen," said Kurt, "and you wouldn't believe how petty the beef was with that guy, I mean it was really trivial shit, some juvenile taunting, you or I wouldn't give it a second thought, and it was from twenty years ago, when they worked together on a golf course back in PA. But Navarre, he'd remembered and stewed about it all that time. It was like it was always fresh in his mind. I'm guessing it will be pretty much the same for the rest of his victims, if any of those cases make it to trial."

"Man, that's creepy. Makes you stop and think. So what was the deal with the dogs and the jars of urine? Did you ever find out about that?" asked Ratkus, heaving the sopping-wet nerf ball toward Jason, landing it two feet in front of him and spraying him with cool lake water.

"Yeah, they had a shrink come in for the defense and try to paint this guy as an abused child, like that would excuse what he did or something. Turns out he'd been attacked by a pack of dogs as a kid, then from the trauma or being catheterized in the hospital, when he came home he was a bedwetter. His mother couldn't stop it with beatings, so after awhile she forced him to drink his own urine whenever he wet the bed."

"No way," said Maari, "that's criminal."

"Yeah, it was some pretty sick shit. Eventually even that didn't work so she resorted to keeping him locked up every night in a furnace closet in the garage. The shrink said he suffered from panic attacks. Apparently over the years he came to believe that the only way to stop the attacks was to drink his own urine. And it worked too, but only because he believed it would. He had a handful of other mental problems I can't remember, but the jury decided it just wasn't enough to declare him legally insane. He knew what he was doing, the printed list was the damning piece of evidence to prove that."

"What'd he get?" asked Jason, firing the soggy nerf ball toward Bonnie, who ducked underwater just in time to avoid being hit in the face.

"He got life, no parole, but it'll be years before all the other trials are finished in all the other states, if they even get that far. When they bring him down to Texas he'll probably get the chair," said Kurt.

"Well, actually we use lethal injection here. So he was an engineer, right? How did he get that job? You can't be crazy and get through engineering school, can you?" asked Ratkus.

"He wasn't crazy, I mean he had mental problems but not severe enough to keep him from functioning. Eventually when he got into his late teens, he ran away from home and--he's a smart guy, make no mistake, maybe not a genius, but close--he put himself through college," said Kurt.

"So what set him off?" asked Maari.

"He got fired from his last job at the defense plant. He spent about six months stewing over it. When he couldn't get another job, that's when he decided to get revenge instead," said Kurt.

"That's twisted," said Bonnie, dunking Jason under the water and holding him there.

"So have you decided what you're going to do with your share of the reward money?" asked Maari.

"Well, I'm not going back to work for awhile, that's for sure. I actually have been kicking around the idea of starting up my own management consulting firm, and I've started writing a book on how managers can improve productivity by rooting out the slackers in their organization. I've always been amazed at how many companies are infested with slackers," he said.

"Just whatever you do, don't root out my slackers," said Jason, who'd come up for air and was forcing Bonnie's head under the water. "I need those guys to help me win the Onslaught Deathmatch tournament next month."

"Actually, I'm still trying to get most of the reward money out of that last victim's company," said Kurt. "Digital Fabrication Systems. They promised $250,000, but now the victim himself, this Stalnaker guy, he's urging them to renege on the deal, claiming that their acting CEO didn't have the authority to offer any reward. So I'm taking them to court."

"Wow that's pretty low," said Jason, "what an asshole."

"Yeah, that could take a while to straighten out. Luckily I've got a good lawyer," said Kurt.

"My lawyer," said Judi, throwing her arm around Kurt.

"The best in the coffee biz," said Kurt, giving her a squeeze.

Chapter 80

Early Fall

"WHAT'S THAT SMELL?" KURT asked, wrinkling his nose, "Smells like battery acid, and--"

"--rotten eggs! Ugh! Like something died in there," said Judi, pinching her nose shut and fanning the air in front of her face. The two had hiked a half mile into Barton Creek Park, in search of one of the older, more difficult caches that neither of them had found yet. Judi decided not to renew the lease on her apartment and Kurt had helped her move into his place. She was spending every night there anyway, and they were ready to live together.

Judi had become a geocaching machine, with over three hundred finds in the last several months, and no one could beat her to be the first to find on a new cache. Once she'd put Rachel in charge as general manager, she had a lot more free time and much less stress. Judi handled the big picture now, and left the details to Rachel. It worked, though it was tough for Judi to let go at first. They were opening two more stores and Judi was kicking around the idea of expanding the operation to Dallas first, and then maybe Houston.

"There's the cache, I think," said Kurt, "Wait, isn't it supposed to be an ammo can?"

"Yeah, says here it's a 50 caliber ammo can, but that looks like a glass jar, that can't be it," she said, folding up the cache printout and putting it in her back pocket.

"Let me see that," he said, picking up the glass jar. "Oh shit, that burns!" he cried, tossing the glass jar away and wiping his hand on his shorts. The glass jar burst into fragments on a rock, and the contents coated the rock in a smoking wet film. "It *is* battery acid. Aw fuck, that burns."

"Here, hold still, let me wash that off," she offered, unscrewing the lid from her waterbottle and pouring some water over his hand.

"That's better, thanks," he said, wiping the water off on his shirt. "Man what the hell is that doing out here?"

"I don't know but look at all this other junk under here," she said, lifting a rotted sheet of plywood. "Looks like a fire extinguisher or maybe a scuba tank, more of those jars, a turkey baster, and a propane tank.

"Huh, that's weird, look at the valve on that tank," he said.

"Looks like corrosion," she said, "like what you get on your car battery right before it dies.

"Oh shit, Judi we gotta get out of here--and fast," he said, taking her arm.

"Why?" she asked.

"This is a meth lab," he said, pointing to the mess in front of them.

"A what?" she asked.

"C'mon, just back away slowly, and watch your step," he said. When they were safely back a few dozen feet, he said, "I read about this online a few months ago. These labs are set up out here in the woods by drug dealers to make crystal meth."

"A lab?" she asked, "Out here in the woods?"

"Yeah, the smell's so bad they can't set it up in a house or the neighbors will complain and call the cops. Besides, this stuff explodes easily, and *boom*, there goes the neighborhood. These labs are really hazardous too. Jeez that still burns. Give me some more of that water, there's no telling what got on my hand," he said, pouring more water over his burned palm and fingers. "Help me get a photo of this stuff," he said, reaching into her pack for the digital camera, "I read a posting on the cache-finders site last month where they found a lab just like this up in Cincinnati." He took a couple steps toward the lab and said, "Were there any rubber hoses in there? That's a dead giveaway..."

Judi reached forward and grabbed Kurt by the arm. She pulled him back out onto the trail and grabbed her camera back from him. "Oh no you don't, Buster." She pulled out her cellphone and punched up 9-1-1. "This time we're just going to call the police."

ACKNOWLEDGEMENTS

A number of individuals helped me with this book. I'd like to thank:

Jim Gessner, for carefully reading through the whole manuscript and asking lots of thoughtful questions.

Scott Gessner (aka Daddycacher), Psychologist and geocacher who proofread the manuscript and helped me understand and formulate the psychological motivations behind the twisted mind of Gary Maxwell Navarre.

Brad Belk (aka bbelk), for his boundless nautical knowledge and plenty of free boat rides on his huge collection of boats, including one that really was unsinkable.

Officer Michael Blevin, of the Austin Police Department, for his help with some of the forensics.

Bill Schroder, for his help with police procedures and proofreading the entire manuscript.

Eric Smith, for help in proofreading the entire manuscript and offering up lots of good suggestions.

Julie Perrine, Shelly Pain, Ralph & Eileen Gessner, and my wife Allie Gessner for careful proofreading.

The geocachers of Austin Texas, for some truly inspiring and creative cache hides. A few are mentioned in this book.

My Brittany spaniel "Nipper" (1989-2006) and my grey tabby cat "Pokey" (1990-2006), for just being great pets for all those years. I miss you guys.

About the Author

Mark Gessner lives in North Texas with his wife Allie and their young son Skyler. To date, he's found almost a thousand geocaches, which isn't really considered a whole lot anymore, considering that he's been at it for seven years. He's hidden more than 100 caches in a half dozen states, some of which have won local awards.

He seldom tries to be First To Find.

Made in the USA
San Bernardino, CA
29 November 2013